Mark Halloran gritted his teeth. One of Dolan's men had grabbed Tessa and carried her off to Wortley's Hotel, which had been turned into a fort by Dolan's gunmen. The town of Lincoln had become a battleground, with McSween's sharpshooters forted up on this side of the street, ready to shoot at anything that moved.

"Wait, Halloran, you'll get killed for sure," someone shouted, but by that time he was out the door and zig-zagging across the dusty street.

A rifled cracked and then another. Something stung his arm. Then he was inside the hotel.

"Where is she?" he shouted at one of the men inside.

"Old Hank carried her upstairs a while ago. Reckon he's having a bang-up time."

There was laughter, but by that time, Mark was halfway up the stairs.

He found the right door, heard a woman's low cry. He hurled himself at the door, but it wouldn't give . . .

THE OUTLAWS

Lee Davis Willoughby

A DELL/JAMES A. BRYANS BOOK

Published by
Dell Publishing Co., Inc.
1 Dag Hammarskjold Plaza
New York, New York 10017

Dell TM 681510, Dell Publishing Co., Inc.

ISBN: 0-440-06742-1

Printed in the United States of America

First printing—April 1984

Chapter 1

Mark Halloran swung into the saddle and left the line camp behind. His sorrel snorted, the horse's breath misty in the chill morning air. To the east, across the river, the sun hadn't risen high enough to touch the ice-choked water of the Pecos. Thin, rosy-tinted clouds lay above the distant caprock of the Staked Plains.

There was something about dawn that took a man out of himself.

Two years ago Mark had seen an Apache standing on a faraway bluff with his arms raised to greet the rising sun. He'd felt a flash of kinship with him, though that hadn't kept Mark from making sure the same Indian wasn't trailing him with a night ambush in mind.

He hadn't ridden line since he'd begun as a cowhand five years ago, wouldn't be riding it now if Hank Hendricks hadn't gotten himself knifed in a San Patricio cantina in a fight over some *señorita de la noche*.

Mark didn't mind line-riding, checking for stray Dolan calves and turning them back before they strayed onto Chisum land. This was a welcome break from riding herd on that new bunch of drifters his boss, Jim Dolan, had hired. They were a lot handier with Colts than with cows. Dolan sure must be expecting trouble.

He headed west, away from the Pecos and its straggle of leafless cottonwoods. Across the rolling brown plains to the north, Capitan Peak's snowy dome glowed red. It was going to be a fine day—cold but sunny, with no snow except in the mountains. Maybe he'd scare up a turkey; he was getting a mite tired of chewing jerky.

The faint notes of a bird drifted on the dawn breeze. Mark listened, then reined in the sorrel. Not a bird. A man, whistling. One of Chisum's hands? The sound came from somewhere beyond a clump of cottonwoods to his right, on Dolan land.

The whistler could be anyone as Dolan and Chisum land abutted along here. A year ago he might have hailed the cowboy, no matter who he worked for, and talked a few minutes, but Chisum, like Dolan, had been hiring gunmen lately. Mark wasn't looking for trouble.

He started to urge the sorrel on when he smelled wood smoke. His eyes narrowed. Could be a breakfast campfire, or could be another kind of fire altogether. His fingers touched the stock of the Winchester in its saddle scabbard. The whistling continued, clear and plaintive, and triggered a memory from last summer's round-up.

Riding with a teen-aged hand named Billy Bonney, flushing cows from the salt-cedar tangles, he'd listened to the same damn melody. "Silver Threads Among the Gold."

"My ma's favorite song," Bonney had told him. "She died young."

If Bonney was his name. Dolan had said Billy's last

name might be Antrim or maybe McCarty, but in the New Mexico Territory you called a man by whatever name he chose to give you.

Which was one reason Mark was here.

Billy had quit Dolan to ride for John Tunstall, a newcomer from England who was a friend of Chisum's. Mark turned the sorrel and headed north, keeping to the cover of an outcropping of rock near the trees. If Billy was boiling coffee, he'd join him for a cup. If he'd lit the fire for a different reason, Mark's visit wouldn't be so friendly.

He dismounted and tied the sorrel to a cottonwood sapling. Carrying his Winchester, he eased his way among the rocks, snaked his way through until he could see beyond them but still remain concealed.

A slight young man crouched beside a tiny fire with his back to Mark. A branding iron heated in the flames. A gray horse stood some yards away with a rifle still in the scabbard. A yearling lay beside the fire, its legs roped together and topside rump carrying the Dolan brand. It looked like Billy was aiming to change that.

Mark had never caught a brand-blotter in the act before. He raised the Winchester and sighted through the rocks. Shoot now; ask questions later. He lined up Billy's head, shifted down to his back.

Mark lowered the rifle. Damn it, he'd never shot a man; he sure as hell wasn't going to start by shooting one in the back. He climbed through the rocks into the open and swung the Winchester up again.

"Hey, Kid," he shouted.

The man whirled around, reaching for his Colt. Still Mark held his fire. For a moment neither of them moved; then Billy flashed his bucktoothed grin, took his hand from the Colt and waved.

"Hey, Mark," he called. "Ain't seen you for quite a spell. Come and jaw a bit."

Just as though he wasn't caught with a hot iron and another man's calf, Mark thought in amazement. Just as though I didn't have the drop on him. He sighted on Billy's chest.

He couldn't pull the trigger.

Hell. How was a man going to throw down on a buck-toothed youngster he'd ridden the trail with? The Kid had been a fine *compañero*, whose cheerfulness and good spirits more than made up for his youth.

What in God's name was he going to do now? He plain didn't trust the Kid, for he remembered damn well what Billy had once told him.

"Did you ever shoot a man?" Billy had asked one evening by the campfire. Mark shook his head and Billy's blue eyes had narrowed.

"You never forget the first one," he'd said, "but if I had to, I'd do it again. Billy Bonney don't take insults from any man alive."

Mark said nothing. He'd heard Billy had shot a man in Arizona and maybe a couple more in Mexico before coming to work for Dolan, but that was his business. It wasn't wise to ask many questions in the Territory.

"I was in Arizona working for this blacksmith named Cahill," Billy had gone on. "Big man. Hardly ever see a smith that ain't. Anyway, he made fun of me right along, and one day he called me a pimp and I had enough, so I jumped him. I didn't have much of a chance after he got me down—he must have weighed two-fifty. He was bound and determined to beat the hell out of me, so I just up and grabbed his Colt from his holster and shot him."

Mark stared through the sights of his Winchester at Billy. Would the Kid trail him if he made Billy free the calf and let him go? All Billy had to do was pick the right moment and Mark Halloran would be as dead as the blacksmith.

He lifted his head. Billy had stopped smiling. Make up your mind, Mark told himself.

As he began to lower the gun, hair-raising shrieks froze him in position. A rifle cracked off to the south.

"Apaches!" Billy yelled.

Mark had no need to be told. A man never forgot an Apache war cry.

Billy ran to the tied calf; his knife flashed and the freed animal struggled to its feet as Billy leaped onto his horse. Mark raced back around the rocks to where his sorrel was tied.

Mark kicked his horse into a gallop, heading south toward a flat-topped hill. Before he reached its base, Billy's gray tore out of the cottonwoods and headed in the same direction. Mark checked Billy's guns. Holstered. He slowed, letting the gray catch up.

More shots from behind the hill. Rifles. A pistol—a Colt .45, by the sound.

Billy grinned at Mark as they galloped up the slope. "Knew you wouldn't shoot me,'" he said.

They reined in and dismounted below the crest. Mark hesitated only a moment before handing Billy the reins of his horse. It could be a trick; Billy might throw down on him as he climbed to the top. Mark shrugged off the notion.

He thought if the brand-blotting had been reversed, Billy wouldn't have pulled the trigger either. Not that he'd ever throw a big loop over another man's dogie. The Judge had knocked that kind of nonsense out of him when he was a boy back in St. Louis.

Mark dropped to his knees near the summit, crawled the

last few feet on his elbows, then lay flat and wriggled across the level top of the hill until he could see below. He swore under his breath.

One wagon, canvas-topped. Four mules in harness, one down. Six mounted Mescalero Apaches circling mules and wagon, whooping and hollering. Snapping off a shot now and then. One brave used arrows. Looked to be a body slumped on the wagon seat. A puff of smoke ballooned behind the body as a Colt roared. Someone was still alive in there anyway.

Mark slid back down to Billy. "Wagon. Six Apaches." As he swung onto the sorrel, he reached for his Winchester.

"Whooee," Billy cried, mounting his horse. "Let's go turn those Mescaleros into good Indians."

Tessa Nesbitt pushed back a strand of her blonde hair and, raising her father's big Colt .45, did her best to aim at the galloping Indian before she pulled the trigger.

Damn. Missed again.

She heard the crack of Ezra's rifle from the back of the wagon. An Apache jerked backward, then slammed to the ground. The others yelled louder.

"Damn you! Damn you!" she screamed at them.

Seven-year-old Jules clutched at her dress, whimpering, trying to bury his head in her lap. She thrust him away and aimed over the body slumped across the wagon seat. Her father's body. A bullet zinged past her, hit a metal pot with a clang.

Tessa fired. Aimed. Fired. Behind her Ezra had stopped shooting. She glanced back. No, Ezra wasn't wounded, just taking his time aiming. He fired.

An Indian pony stumbled, pitched forward to its knees. His rider leaped off. She fired and the Apache faltered. Recovered. Jumped onto a pony behind another Apache.

"You winged, him," Ezra called. "Jolly good, Tess."

Tessa wished she could shoot as well as her fourteen-year-old brother—something that hadn't seemed important before.

She winced as a bullet jerked her father's body. Bullets couldn't hurt him. He was dead; she was certain of it. Yet she couldn't believe it.

"Tess!" Jules' voice quavered in terror, but she had no time to comfort her little brother.

If Jules wasn't killed by a bullet before the end, the Indians might let him live. She'd heard the Apaches sometimes spared little children, carried them to their camps and raised them as Indians. As for herself, she'd die fighting. Make them kill her as if she were a man. No Apache was going to turn her into his squaw!

She aimed at the two braves on the one horse as they returned on the other side of the wagon. Fired. They swept past unharmed. Ezra's rifle cracked. A pony staggered but recovered to gallop on. Amid the stink of powder she smelled the acrid scent of burning wool, glanced around, saw a thin tendril of smoke rising from the blankets on the wagon bed.

Tessa bit her lip as she eased her father's canteen from under his body, unfastened it from his belt. She darted back and dumped the water onto the smoldering hole. Hurrying back to the front of the wagon, she checked the Colt, reached for the cartridges she'd taken from her father's belt. Her heart sank. Only three left.

She'd been shooting too fast, too wildly. There were still five Indians. All of the bullets would have to count.

A spurt of dust to her right caught Tessa's eye. Two horsemen were plunging down a hill.

"Ezra!" she cried. "More coming. Look!"

"Change places with me," he called.

Tessa stumbled to the back of the wagon, pulling Jules with her, his hands clenched onto her skirts. Ezra passed her as he headed for the front.

"Only got two more bullets," he mumbled.

Tessa stared at an Apache galloping toward the tailboard of the wagon, knelt and snapped off a quick shot. Missed. He veered away, firing as he went. His bullet thudded into the wooden chest next to her.

"They're not Indians!" Ezra shouted.

For a moment Tessa didn't know what he meant.

"They're white men!" Ezra cried jubilantly.

An Apache tumbled from his horse to sprawl unmoving in the dirt. Tessa stared, then realized one of the oncoming men had shot him and the roar of the Colt had temporarily deafened her so she hadn't heard the rifle crack.

The remaining Apaches bunched together, facing the riders pounding toward them. Ezra squeezed off a shot and one of the Indian ponies stumbled.

"Damn," Ezra mumbled. "Missed."

Tessa held her breath, afraid to hope. She eased toward the front of the wagon. Ezra had one shot left. She had two.

The hat of the rider on the gray flew off. He crouched lower on the horse but kept coming. The man on the sorrel aimed his rifle. Smoke puffed. An Apache veered off to the left. His horse galloped on without wheeling. Wounded? Or fleeing? Either way he was out of the fight.

Ezra fired his last bullet. She felt Jules trembling against her side, put her left arm around him, drew him to her breast and held him close. His thin body shook with tearless sobbing.

The three Apaches left suddenly turned their ponies sharply to the right and galloped south. The two men stared after them, then reined in and dismounted. She saw smoke puff from their rifles.

"Licked 'em!" Ezra cried.

The Colt in Tessa's right hand felt too heavy to hold and she laid it aside. "There now," she murmured to Jules. "We're all right."

Her eyes rested on the limp body of her father, shot through the head by an Apache before he'd had time to draw his pistol. Tears burned in her eyes.

"Papa's dead," Ezra said, his hazel eyes no longer sparkling with the excitement of battle.

Tessa reached for his hand and gripped it hard as they watched the two white men remount and lope toward the wagon. The one on the gray had fair hair and looked to be scarcely older than Ezra. The rider on the sorrel was older, taller and very dark, with a highcheekboned face. He was better looking than any man she'd met in Texas—or in England, for that matter.

"Hello the wagon," he called as he neared.

Tessa handed Jules to Ezra. She couldn't bring herself to climb over her father's body, so she went to the back and slid off the tailboard, then walked around to meet the riders.

"I'm Tessa Nesbitt," she said. "Thank God you came."

Mark couldn't find any words as he stared at the young woman standing in front of him. He dismounted, his eyes fixed on her pretty, dirt-smudged face. Her blonde hair glinted like gold in the sunlight and tears brightened her gray-blue eyes. He was transfixed by her beauty.

"The Apaches killed my father," she said, her voice quivering.

Mark's urge was to take her in his arms and comfort her as he would a child, but he held himself back, knowing he must not. The pleasing curves outlined by her brown dress showed she was no child.

He took off his hat. "I'm sorry," he managed to say. "My name's Mark Halloran." He glanced behind him. The Kid jumped off his gray and sauntered toward them.

"This is Billy Bonney," Mark said.

"Too bad about your father, miss," Billy said.

A boy about Billy's size came around the wagon carrying a younger boy.

"These are my brothers," Tessa said. "Ezra and Jules."

"How about your mother, Miss Nesbitt?" Mark asked.

Tessa bit her lip. "She died when Jules was born."

"You hit that Apache square through the heart, Mr. Bonney," Ezra said, staring wide-eyed at Billy. "Awfully good shooting from a horse."

Billy grinned. "Some call me Kid and some call me Billy, but no one calls me mister. If I can say Ezra, I reckon you can say Billy. You don't sound like you're from these parts."

"We were on our way from Texas to the town of Lincoln," Tessa told him.

"Don't sound much like Texans either," Billy commented.

"We came from England eight years ago," Ezra said.

Mark strode to the mules. The three survivors looked to be in good shape. He took out his knife and cut the harness off the dead mule.

Billy hastened to help him. As they dragged the mule's body to one side, Billy muttered, "What about him?" He nodded his head toward the dead man on the wagon seat.

"Do you have a blanket we can use, Miss Nesbitt?" Mark asked.

Tessa disappeared into the wagon; she returned a few moments later with a tattered brown blanket that Mark spread on the ground. He and Billy eased Nesbitt's body from the seat onto the blanket and wrapped it around him, then lifted him over the tail into the bed of the wagon.

Tessa, meanwhile, had spread another blanket, equally worn, over the bloodstained wagon seat. Ezra handed Jules to her and climbed up to the seat himself. Tessa took the reins.

"Why not let your brother drive the mules?" Mark asked, alarmed at how pale she looked.

Tessa shook her head. "I've been told the Indians always come back for their dead. Ezra will hold the Colt. He's a better shot than I am."

A bright girl. Practical and plucky as well as pretty. He'd never met one quite like Tessa Nesbitt.

"You have a point," he told her. "We'd all best get moving." He glanced at Billy and raised his eyebrows.

"Be a privilege for me and my *amigo* Mark to escort you into town," Billy said to Tessa, giving her his bucktoothed grin.

Tessa managed a ghost of a smile that touched Mark's heart. "We were heading for John Tunstall's place. Do you know him?"

"He's my boss," Billy answered.

Mark's mouth tightened. "We'll see you safely there," he said.

"Reckon they knew Tunstall back in England?" Billy asked once they were riding alongside the wagon. "That's where he's from."

"I haven't met Tunstall," Mark said shortly.

Billy jerked his head toward the wagon. "Pretty girl. And that Ezra's a good shot. Picked off one of those Mescaleros before we got there. Not much in the wagon. If that's all they own, they ain't got shucks." He shook his head. "The little boy was scared silly. I'd like to wipe those red devils off the face of the earth."

"They're savages all right," Mark agreed. "The reservation was supposed to civilize them, but it sure as hell hasn't."

Billy snorted. "Only way to civilize any Apache is with this." He patted the stock of his Winchester.

"That reminds me." Mark's voice hardened. "Steer clear of Dolan calves, Billy."

Billy shrugged. "Hell, if I'd known you were out line-riding, *amigo*, I'd have kept my rope hung on the saddle."

Mark opened his mouth to tell Billy they were no longer friends, but the words stayed put. He was glad he hadn't shot the Kid. Dolan hated Chisum and Tunstall, but that didn't mean Mark had to dislike Billy.

As for brand-blotting, it was common practice. That didn't make it right, but law in the New Mexico Territory was a lot looser than back home in St. Louis where the Judge's strict ideas of right and wrong had been passed on to Mark for all time.

Here, stray calves wound up belonging to the first man who found and branded them. Or rebranded them. It wasn't worth killing a man over.

"I'll pick you for riding with against the Apaches anytime," Mark said, giving Billy a reluctant smile.

Glancing up at the sky, Mark saw the thin clouds of morning were gone and the sun's warmth cut the chill of the December day. Tessa's eyes weren't as bright a blue as the winter sky. They were a softer color—like the gray-blue of early evening.

Tunstall wasn't married. A wealthy man, Mark had heard. How well did she know him? Was it possible they had an understanding?

Mark's hand tightened on the reins. He forced himself to relax. What was the matter with him? "Too much imagination," the Judge had always said. "Painting mind pictures of what's going to happen when you don't know beans is what makes a man out to be a damn fool.''

It would be easy to be a damn fool over Tessa Nesbitt.

"What'll happen to us if Mr. Tunstall won't let us stay?" Ezra asked Tessa.

"I'm certain he will," she assured him.

She was anything but sure. Papa had rambled on about going to school with John Tunstall's cousin, about how Englishmen should stick together in a strange land. He'd urged her to make herself a new dress, blind to the fact she'd used up all of her mother's old gowns and there was no money for new cloth.

"He comes of fine stock, Tessa, this John Henry Tunstall," Papa had told her. ''A monied family. I have to think of your future, child.''

That's when she realized Papa planned to marry her off to this Englishman none of them had ever met. She'd protested, unhappy with the idea, but there was nothing for it but to go along with the trip to New Mexico Territory. There was nothing else to do.

Their money was gone, their cattle sold or stolen. Even her small stock of canned vegetables had been eaten. Foggy London seemed like Eden compared to Texas.

She glanced right and left at the countryside. This New Mexico valley along the Pecos River was brown with winter, but she could see the bare branches of cottonwoods and willows. A mountain peak to the north was white with snow and the hills in the distance were green with pines. Perhaps everything didn't turn brown and dusty here as spring gave way to summer, the way it did in Texas.

Where else did she have to go? It was humiliating to ask help from a stranger, but there was no choice but to swallow her pride and do it. She dreaded the moment she'd have to face John Tunstall and beg him to take her and her brothers in.

Tessa didn't blame Papa for any of it. She blinked back tears, thinking of him lying dead behind her on the wagon bed, wrapped in one of their old blankets. She couldn't cry now; it would upset Ezra and frighten Jules all over again.

Poor Papa. He'd tried hard, but he wasn't fit for the life of a Texas rancher. Grandfather Nesbitt had been a minister and Papa ought to have followed in his footsteps. He'd have been happy in some country parish in England.

Even then, though, they'd have made it through another year and maybe things would have gotten better, if it hadn't been for the range war. Papa didn't want to be on either side, but when the shooting started, he had to choose and he chose wrong. There wasn't much left when the smoke cleared.

Tessa heard Billy laugh and looked over at him, then at Mark Halloran. How handsome Mark was. Was he married? Her face flushed as she realized where her thoughts were leading. If John Tunstall were Mark, she wouldn't mind a bit going to live in his house.

"Do you think Billy was joking when he said people called him Kid?" Ezra asked. "I don't like being called that, even if I am only fourteen. But he's old enough to be a cowboy. Why would anyone call him Kid?"

"He looks young," Tessa said absently, her mind still on Mark.

"Billy's a keen shot. Do you think he'd mind if I asked him to show me how he does it? Papa tried to teach me but . . ." Ezra's words trailed away. She saw him clench his jaw as he remembered Papa.

Papa hadn't been a very good marksman, but what did that matter—he'd always done his best, had always been there to depend on. Now he lay dead, killed by an Apache bullet. They were alone.

Tessa swallowed. She mustn't let Ezra know how frightened she was. "Billy seems friendly," she said. "I think he'll be glad to help you. But, Ezra, there's more to being a man than shooting. You know Papa wanted you to have schooling and . . ."

"I know how to read and write and do sums. What more do I need?" Ezra shifted the Colt so it rested on one knee. He gazed steadily at the two men riding alongside the wagon.

"*I* won't ever call him Kid," Ezra said.

Chapter 2

Tessa stood on the river bank in back of John Tunstall's store. Behind and below her the Rio Bonito was crusted with ice. She wore a black silk gown and a black wool coat borrowed from Susie McSween. The minister's words swept over her father's rough-planked coffin and blew past her on the keen north wind. Tessa closed her eyes momentarily as they lowered the coffin.

"Ezra said Papa was inside that box," Jules cried accusingly. "Don't let them put Papa in a hole."

Tessa crouched and put an arm around her brother. "Papa's dead,", she told him. "His soul is in heaven."

Jules began to cry with his face turned against her breast. Around her she heard sympathetic murmurs from the small group that had gathered to watch this stranger's burial.

Poor Papa. Laid to rest in a town he'd never seen. So far from the green countryside of his native Kent.

Tessa felt John Tunstall's hand pat her shoulder and glanced gratefully up at him. He'd taken charge from the moment Mark and Billy had brought her and her brothers into Tunstall's store and bank.

John's English speech was like an echo of their dead father and both boys had taken to him right away. Tessa liked him immensely. Though he was slight and fair with a boyish face, his air of authority gave her confidence

John had immediately taken the Nesbitts to the McSween house next door to his store, for he feared Tessa's reputation would suffer if she came to live at his ranch with no other woman there except his Mexican cook. Alex and Susie McSween seemed delighted to have Tessa and the boys to stay with them, although the Shield family—father, mother and five children—already lived in the east wing of their large adobe house. Elizabeth Shield was Susie's sister.

Susie was young and attractive with curly red hair. Her nose might be considered a trifle large for true beauty, but her sparkle and vivaciousnes made her irresistible.

"I can't tell you how wonderful it is to talk to an educated woman," Susie enthused. "It's true I have Elizabeth, but she's so busy with the children. There are so few women in the Territory, and almost none of them have had schooling."

Her lawyer husband, Alex, was somewhat older than she, with dark hair and a drooping black mustache. He was as friendly as Susie. Their expensively furnished house seemed like a dream come true. There was even a piano. Tessa hadn't seen one since she'd left England.

The McSweens were at the graveside, standing next to John Tunstall. Susie had introduced Tessa to the other men who made up the little group, but she couldn't remember who they all were—a Southerner named Calvin Rutledge and several men who worked for John. Billy Bonney was the only one she knew.

Clouds slid over the sun and Tessa shivered. Did the howling, bone-freezing blue northers sweep down from the Arctic to New Mexico as they had to Texas?

The day was nothing like the hot and dusty afternoon seven-and-a-half years ago when they buried her mother. She'd scarcely cried then, her thoughts on the tiny infant temporarily left in the care of the minister's wife. Tessa, at twelve, would have to be responsible for her baby brother from now on. She'd been terrified.

Tessa took a deep breath, wiped Jules' face with her handkerchief, and stood up, holding him against her side. She'd managed somehow with Jules. Now Papa was gone and she was responsible for both boys. At least they had temporary shelter, thanks to the McSweens. When she could think straight, she'd find a way to manage again.

Beside her Ezra shook with sobs. Her own eyes were dry, her crying done. Last night, after she'd climbed into the almost forgotten luxury of a featherbed, she'd heard Susie at the piano playing "Home Sweet Home," and she'd wept for her father and the loss of all that had meant home to her.

"Dolan's man," someone whispered behind her.

Tessa looked up and her breath caught. Mark Halloran was walking toward her. I knew he'd come, she told herself. He stopped near the minister and looked across the grave, his compassionate gaze warming her.

She liked and trusted John, but the sight of Mark triggered a quite different emotion. Tingling all over, Tessa lowered her eyes. It was like nothing she'd ever felt before and it frightened her.

*　　*　　*

Mark wished he could take John Tunstall's place beside Tessa. She looked so pale and fragile in her black coat that he longed to put his arm about her, to comfort her.

The minister concluded the prayer and walked around the grave to Tessa and her brothers. Mark hesitated, then finally followed him, ignoring the mutters of Tunstall's men. He wasn't looking for trouble, but, damn it, nobody was going to stop him from attending a funeral if he chose.

Mark caught Billy's eye and they nodded to each other, Billy smiling. His companions glowered, especially a a tall man in a black frockcoat and black silk cravat. His trim goatee and mustache made him look like a affluent riverboat gambler. He was new to town and Mark didn't know him.

Mark passed the men and stopped beside the minister, where he waited for him to finish consoling Tessa.

"Mr. Halloran."

Mark turned to face John Tunstall.

"Mr. Halloran," Tunstall said once again. "I didn't have a chance yesterday to tell you I think you're a hell of a brave man, rescuing the Nesbitts from those Apaches."

Mark smiled wryly. "A brave man rode beside me. That always helps."

"Billy Bonney. Yes, Billy's a good hand. Loyal." Tunstall smiled. "As a matter of fact, I could use another like him."

"I have a job," Mark said.

Tunstall nodded. "Keep my offer in mind."

"Oh, John, is this the man who saved poor Tessa?" Susie McSween advanced on them, holding out her hand to Mark.

Tunstall introduced Mark and Susie clasped Mark's hand between both of hers, holding it tightly. Looking over her black bonnet, Mark saw the minister move on. Tessa glanced toward him.

Mark tried to withdraw his hand, but Susie held him and continued chattering away.

"Maybe I shouldn't be talking to a member of the opposition," she said with a roguish toss of her head.

"I'm not in opposition to you, ma'am," Mark replied, finally able to ease his hand from hers.

"But you work for that awful Mr. Dolan!" Susie cried.

Alex McSween was talking to Tessa now. The tall man in the black frockcoat had left the other men and was striding toward Mark with an angry frown.

Mark tensed. Except for McSween, who was well known to be a Bible-thumper who never toted iron, every man here was armed.

"I'm sure I don't know why anyone would want to be associated in any way with Mr. Dolan," Susie went on. "Do you know he's been accusing poor Alex of simply unspeakable . . . ?"

"Excuse me, ma'am," Mark interrupted. "I'd like to pay my respects to Miss Nesbitt before I head back to camp."

Mark took three steps toward Tessa when the goateed man cut across his path and blocked it. When Mark attempted to veer around him, the man shifted to intercept him.

"You're not welcome here," he drawled. "I suggest you leave. Now."

"Get out of my way," Mark growled. Who the hell did this Southern bastard think he was, ordering him around?

"You heard what I said." The Southerner didn't move.

"I'm not telling you again. Get out of my way!"

The Southerner sneered.

Mark walked straight at him. The Southerner grabbed at

his shirt-front. Mark seized his arm, crouched, and with a quick twist flipped the man into a somersault. He thudded onto his back on the ground.

Mark eyed him. Would the bastard draw? Instead, the Southerner's hand slid along the side of his boot.

"What have you done to Mr. Rutledge?"

Mark spun around at the sound of Tessa's voice. She hurried past him to offer a helping hand to Rutledge.

"Are you all right?" she asked Rutledge as he scrambled to his feet.

Mark caught a glimpse of a boot with a specially designed pocket. He knew those pockets could hold either knives or derringers. Sneaky bastard.

Rutledge nodded to Tessa. "Don't worry your pretty little head over me, Miss Nesbitt. I'm fine." He dusted off his coat.

Tessa turned to Mark. "I'm surprised, Mr. Halloran," she said.

The hurt in her gray-blue eyes fueled his anger at Rutledge who'd managed to put Mark in the wrong.

"I'm sorry," he said to Tessa. How could he explain why he'd become involved in a fight at her father's funeral?

"You ought to aplogize to Mr. Rutledge, not to me," she said.

"No," Mark said.

Tessa's eyes widened.

Before Mark could explain, Alex McSween and Tunstall hurried up to flank Tessa.

"What's happened here?" Tunstall demanded.

Rutledge shrugged. "I'm afraid the *gentleman* misunderstood me and took offense. Dolan's hands aren't noted for courtesy."

Mark clenched his fists.

McSween raised his hands, palms up. "Now, lads. If

we all obeyed the law of God rather than the law of the jungle, life on earth would be a prelude to heaven instead of a preview of hell. Don't you agree, Mr. Halloran?''

"I'm sure you're right,'' Mark said as evenly as he could.

"If I could persuade every man in Lincoln County to do as I do,'' McSween went on, ''to put aside their weapons and not bear arms, we'd soon have no need for Sheriff Brady. Nor for the hangman either.''

"I'm afraid that would take some tall persuading, Mr. McSween,'' Mark said. "Most men in the Territory are pretty attached to their Colts. But I do regret upsetting Miss Nesbitt.''

Tunstall offered Tessa his arm. Without another look at Mark, she took it, giving Tunstall a little smile. Mark gritted his teeth. A glance at Rutledge gave him the dubious satisfaction of knowing the Southerner didn't like to see Tessa walking off with Tunstall any better than Mark did.

I can't let her leave this way, he told himself.

"Miss Nesbitt!'' he called.

Tessa looked back at him.

"I'll come by and see you in a week or so,'' he said. "If you don't mind.''

"If you like,'' she said coolly, turning away and continuing on with Tunstall and McSween.

"I suggest you keep away from the young lady,'' Rutledge said softly.

"You can go to hell,'' Mark told him.

"You've been warned,'' Rutledge said.

The two men eyed one another. Mark wanted to walk away, but he didn't trust the Southerner enough to turn his back on him.

"There you are, Calvin," Susie McSween called. She waved.

Without another word, Rutledge stalked off to join Susie. As Mark watched her take his arm and smile flirtatiously up into his face, he thought fleetingly that McSween seemed oblivious to his wife's coquettishness. Maybe not being jealous went along with his peace-on-earth preaching.

Not that Mark wouldn't like to see Lincoln County a tad more peaceable. But the way he saw it, laying aside weapons would just get the decent men shot first.

Two weeks before Christmas, Mark rode into town from Dolan's ranch. A Yule tree stood in the center of the plaza, a pinon pine from the hills. Red ribbons tied to its branches fluttered in the wind and reminded him of festive St. Louis Christmases of years past.

The Judge wouldn't have allowed a skinny pinon pine into his house.

If the Judge was still alive, he probably wouldn't allow me inside either, Mark thought ruefully.

That wasn't today's problem. What troubled him was whether McSween would let him in his house so that Mark could see Tessa.

When he reached the U-shaped McSween adobe, Mark tied his sorrel to the post and squared his shoulders before walking up the steps to thump the iron knocker against the front door.

He waited for someone to answer the door. He knocked again. At last it opened. Little Jules peered up at him.

"Hello, Jules," Mark said. "Is your sister at home?"

The boy nodded. Behind him Mark saw the brown face of McSween's cook.

"*Quien es*?" the woman asked. "Who is it?"

"Mark Halloran. To see *Señorita* Nesbitt."

"*Entrez, señor.*" She pointed to the left and turned to

hurry away. Mark stepped around Jules, who tagged after him into the parlor.

Mark perched uneasily on the leather seat of a wooden chair. Jules sat on the piano stool and stared at him. He couldn't think of a thing to say to the boy.

"Where's your big brother?" he asked finally.

"He went off to Mr. Tunstall's with Billy." Jules' lower lip pushed out. "Ezra *never* takes me. Says I'm too little. I'm not." Jules swiveled the stool until his back was to Mark. He hit middle C on the keyboard.

"Can you play the piano?" Mark asked.

In answer Jules ran the fingers of his right hand up and down the scale.

"That's very good."

"Mrs. McSween's teaching me. But Ezra says I ought to be learning to shoot. He says men don't play the piano." Jules spoke with his back to Mark.

Mark walked over to him and spun the stool so Jules faced him. "Every man needs to know how to shoot. There's no reason a man can't learn to play the piano, too."

"Ezra says only girls play."

"Do I look like a girl?"

Jules shook his head.

"Well, I know how."

Jules slid off the stool. "Show me."

Mark glanced over his shoulder. Now I've done it, he told himself. Reluctantly he sat on the stool and poised his hands over the keys.

He couldn't think of a thing to play. He didn't want to play. Not only because he was at the McSween's piano without their permission, but because he didn't want to be reminded of the past.

Mark saw Jules' mouth tighten, saw doubt gather in his

eyes, eyes that were grayer than Tessa's but black-lashed the same as hers. Behind Jules he noticed a fat red candle flickering in a silver holder on the mantel.

It was the Christmas season.

Mark brought his fingers down on the keys for the first chords of "God Rest You Merry, Gentlemen." As he played, he felt Jules lean against him. When the last notes died away, the boy sighed.

"I know that song," he said. "Papa used to sing it at Christmas. Will you teach me how to play it?"

Soon Jules was picking out the melody with one hand.

"You've got a good ear for music," Mark told him.

"I heard you playing," Tessa said from behind them.

Mark turned from the piano. "I'm sorry," he said. "I didn't hear you come in. I hope my playing won't upset Mrs. McSween."

Tessa smiled. "If I know Jules, he wheedled you into it."

His heart leaped to see her smile at him. Tessa looked especially lovely in a high-necked, cream-colored wool dress with the hint of a bustle. He was about to tell her so, when Susie swept into the room.

Her gown was of bright green, pointing up the red of her hair. It had an elaborate train over the bustle. The neckline dipped to show the tops of her breasts. There was no doubt Susie was a stunning woman.

"Why, Mr. Halloran," she exclaimed, taking his hand. "You're a man of hidden talents, aren't you?" Still holding Mark's hand, she turned to Tessa. "Be a dear and ask Rosalita to bring in some wine and cake."

As Tessa left the room, Susie said to Jules. "Run along now, Jules; you've practiced enough for today. Rosalita will give you your cake in the kitchen."

"He's a dear boy," she said, "but children can be

tiring. My sister has five and I swear I don't know how she manages.'' She drew Mark toward a settee, seated herself and patted the place beside her.

"Right here. We can have a cozy little chat.''

Mark sat down but protested, "I came to see Tessa—that is, Miss Nesbitt.''

"Of course. But Tessa simply insists on helping Rosalita—she's so concerned about paying her way—so we might as well talk until she returns." Susie leaned toward Mark, her bodice gaping slightly so that he could almost see her nipples.

The scent of jasmine surrounded him. Susie looked up at him through her lashes. "It's a shame we didn't meet before now," she murmured as her hand brushed along his thigh, as if by accident.

Mark swallowed. He'd been a long time without a woman; Susie might be obvious, but she was tempting. He wondered how much was teasing and how much she meant.

"I only hope you'll stop by to see *me* after we return from St. Louis," she said. "We're going there for Christmas. You and I have music in common already.'' She ran her tongue along her lips. "I wonder what else we might find to share an interest in?''

Damn it, her nearness was having its effect.

He smiled at her. "I'll keep your invitation in mind.''

"See that you do." Her voice was husky.

I've got to move away from her, he told himself. He looked up. Tessa stood in the archway to the foyer with a tray in her hands, staring at Susie and him.

A knot tightened in Tessa's stomach as she carried the loaded tray to the table at the far end of the room. She knew Susie liked to flirt, and if Alex didn't mind, it was certainly none of Tessa's business.

But Mark didn't have to sit so close to Susie with such a silly smile on his face. What was the matter with him? He knew perfectly well Susie was a married woman.

Maybe he'd really come to see Susie instead of her. The knot inside Tessa twisted.

"May I help you?" Mark's voice asked, close to her.

"No, thank you. I wouldn't think of troubling you." He stood beside her, but she didn't look at him.

"You're angry." He spoke softly, almost in her ear.

Susie began to play "Joy To The World," with frills and flourishes.

Tessa turned toward Mark. "I am not angry." She spit the words through her teeth.

"I haven't had a chance to talk to you since the first time we met," he said.

"That's hardly my fault."

"This was my first chance to get into town. I've thought of you all the time. Worried about you."

Tessa looked into his eyes, eyes as deep and rich a brown as an English chestnut. The knot in her stomach dissolved as a tingling warmth shot though her. She wished he would touch her and yet at the same time feared he would, for she didn't know what would happen if he did. Nothing in her entire life had prepared her for the way Mark affected her.

"Tessa," he said. "Tessa."

She felt as though she couldn't breathe.

Susie finished the carol with a thundering chord and turned on the stool. All the gaiety had drained from her face.

"Isn't there something you can do to persuade Mr. Dolan to stop persecuting Alex?" she asked Mark.

"Persecuting him, ma'am?"

"Oh, don't call me that. I'm Susie. But, yes, it's obvi-

ous his intention is to force poor Alex to leave Lincoln.
Alex is so kind. A God-fearing man. He wouldn't harm
anyone. Yet the man you work for makes him out to be a
criminal and threatens to have him put in jail. I'm quite
beside myself.''

"Susie and Alex are making a trip to St. Louis in a few
days," Tessa put in.

"Alex insists. He knows how nervous all this makes
me." Susie raised her chin. "But I'll be back. My duty is
to remain at Alex's side.''

"I'm afraid I'm not in Mr. Dolan's confidence when it
comes to his personal affairs," Mark said. "I'm just the
ranch foreman.''

"Your employer is a devious man.''

"That's as may be, ma'am.''

"Don't call me that!" Susie's voice rose almost to a
scream as she got up abruptly from the piano stool.

Susie *was* upset, Tessa thought. When she'd seen her
flirting with Mark, she'd thought Susie had quite forgotten
all the problems Alex shared with her, problems Tessa
didn't exactly understand, except that it seemed Mr. Dolan
claimed Alex had kept insurance money he should have
paid out to Mr. Dolan's partner, Mr. Murphy. It was
rather confusing.

"I'm sorry," Mark said. "Susie.''

"That's better." She smiled at him, but it was plain to
see her heart wasn't in it. "I find I'm more tired than I
thought, so if you'll excuse . . .''

The front door opened. Alex strode in, followed by John
Tunstall. Alex went directly into the room he used as an
office and Susie trailed after him. John advanced on Tessa.

"I've come to persuade you to go east with Alex and
Susie," he said. "Until this affair with Dolan blows over.''

He caught sight of Mark and stopped abruptly.

"Oh, no, I couldn't do that," Tessa said. "I'm staying here with my brothers."

John eyed Mark, frowning, before turning again to Tessa.

"You could bring Jules with you. Ezra can stay on my ranch. He and Billy Bonney get along famously."

Tessa shook her head. "That's kind of you but no."

She felt panicky at the notion of separating the family. Besides, she was already obligated to the McSweens and wouldn't dream of having them pay her fare from the railhead at Trinidad, Colorado, to St. Louis.

"I'm certain Mr. Dolan isn't going to harm me," Tessa added.

"Not directly perhaps," John said. He looked at Mark. "It's hard to understand why a decent sort of chap, as you appear to be, would continue to work for such a conniving and unscrupulous man."

Mark scowled. "I don't think I need to explain myself to you or anyone else."

"No?" John took a step closer to him. "The way things stand, neither Alex nor myself can trust any man who works for Dolan."

"But, John," Tessa said, "he came here to see me."

"Did he? Or was he sent as a spy?"

Tessa saw Mark clench his fists. Not another fight! she thought in dismay.

"Maybe you'd better leave, Mark," she said hastily.

"And I suggest you don't return," John added.

Mark brushed past John, picked up his hat and jacket. At the door he turned to look at Tessa. "I'll come back if you want me to," he said.

She bit her lip, glancing from him to John. She was staying with the McSweens. She mustn't cause trouble for them. She wanted to see Mark again, but . . .

"It's obvious you're embarrassing the lady," John said.

Mark nodded his head in farewell and went out. Tessa took a quick step toward the door but stopped when John held up his hand.

"You're better off without that chap, my dear," he said.

She smiled uncertainly at him. Her head told her John was right, but her heart ached all the same.

Chapter 3

A norther swept in the second week in February, the icy winds piling the snow in drifts, and no one left their firesides unless they had to.

Alex McSween, who'd wound up spending Christmas in a Las Vegas jail, had been released on eight thousand dollars bail and was back home. He sat with Jules by the parlor fireplace, telling him stories from the Bible, while Tessa sewed.

Susie was still in St. Louis. Once he'd gotten out of jail, Alex had seen her safely there but came back to Lincoln early in January. He'd traveled to Mesilla, on the Rio Grande, the first of February for a court hearing and had just gotten back to Lincoln before the norther blew in.

Tessa rather enjoyed the coziness of being shut in; it reminded her of when Papa was alive, but Ezra, after the third day, grew restless.

"I could make it to Tunstall's ranch; I know I could," he told Tessa as she polished silver in the dining room.

"It's *Mr*. Tunstall."

"Aw, no one says mister when he's talking about a fellow."

"Your father tried hard to teach you good manners," she reminded him.

"English manners. I'm not English; I'm American." Ezra looked at her defiantly.

"Whatever you think you are, you're not to try riding to the ranch in this weather. You spend too much time there as it is. You mustn't presume on Mr. Tunstall's kindness."

"I do chores for him."

Tessa raised her eyebrows. "In the winter? With all the hands he employs, I can't believe even half of them keep busy this time of the year."

"Well, I did do chores before Christmas. Besides, Billy says when a man's practicing shooting, he ought not to miss a day. I have to get better so I can protect Tunstall, because Dolan threatened to get him soon."

Tessa frowned. "Did Billy tell you that?"

"Everybody knows about how Dolan and Jesse Evans and his gang threatened McSween and Tunstall on the way back from Mesilla last week."

"I didn't know it."

"Dolan threw down on Tunstall, but some deputy stopped him."

"How terrible!"

"So you see I have to practice with Billy. He's the best shot Tunstall's got."

"I realize he's an excellent shot. I've never forgotten he and Mark saved our lives. But, Ezra, I don't think it's good to tag after Billy all the time. You need to make friends your own age, too. What about Ira Fowler, here in town? He's fourteen and I thought he was a nice boy.''

"Yeah, he's okay.'' Ezra's tone lacked enthusiasm.

"Okay? What kind of word is that?''

"You know what it means. I'm going to talk like I want to.''

Tessa looked at her brother helplessly. He'd grown so these past couple of months. John had given Ezra some of his old clothes and already they were almost too small for him. He was going to be a big man, like their father. He'd be a good-looking man, too, she thought, surprised, for she'd never considered Ezra as a man.

She firmed her mouth. He was growing up, but he wasn't yet a man and it was her job to protect him from his own impulsiveness. She was sorry to hear John had been threatened, but it wouldn't help him to have Ezra involved.

"Ezra, you're not to ride to Mr. Tunstall's ranch for the rest of the month. When spring comes, you'll be of some use doing chores, but this time of the year you're not. As far as protecting John goes, you haven't been asked to. I'm certain he has many men capable of that, if it becomes necessary.''

"You just want to keep me away from Billy!'' Ezra burst out. "You'd rather I acted like Halloran, I suppose. Playing the piano. Keeping company with liars and thieves like Dolan hires.''

"Ezra!''

He spun away from her and flung out of the dining room, stomping off to the east wing where he shared a room with Jules.

What was she going to do with Ezra? So far he hadn't openly disobeyed her, but she sensed he soon would. Then what? He needed a man's influence. Not Billy, who was only three years older than Ezra and, according to what she'd heard, wild and wise beyond his years.

Ezra liked John. Maybe if she talked to John about him, John would be able to help.

There was Calvin Rutledge, too. Ezra didn't know him well, but she'd been seeing a great deal of Calvin since Christmas and he struck her as an upright man.

Alex quoted Bible verses to the boys in lieu of discipline. He'd asked both of them to call him Uncle Alex, and that's what he seemed to be—a benevolent uncle to them. Too easy-going.

Resolutely she kept her thoughts from Mark. She hadn't seen him since his December visit. Even though she'd asked him to leave that time, she'd thought he'd come again.

Tessa couldn't believe Mark was a liar; she wanted to believe he'd come to the house that day to see her and for no other reason. But she'd seen him flirting with Susie and it surely was a coincidence he'd picked the day before the McSweens left town.

And then Alex had been arrested, on Dolan's order, in Las Vegas on Christmas Eve. How could Mark have had anything to do with that?

If only she could prevent herself from dreaming about Mark—strange, unsettling dreams where he held her in his arms, his hands caressing her until her entire body throbbed with delicious pulsations. Shameful dreams.

For the next week Ezra obeyed her order to keep away from the Tunstall ranch, although he moped sullenly about the house until she longed to shake him. But on the eighteenth, when he didn't appear for breakfast and she went to his room to call him, he was gone.

Tessa ran back to the west wing and into the kitchen

where Jules sat at the scrubbed pine table eating one of Rosalita's tortillas. As soon as he saw her, he ducked his head.

"Where's Ezra?" she asked.

"He left," Jules mumbled.

"When?"

"I don't know. It was still kind of dark."

"Jules, why didn't you come and tell me?"

"Ezra said not to. Said I'd be a tattletale and no one likes tattletales."

Tessa sighed. "Did he tell you where he was going?"

Jules shook his head.

Tessa knew where Ezra had gone. To John's ranch.

I'll ride after him, she decided. And while I'm there, I'll see that John understands what the problem is. If I let Ezra get away with this, I'll never be able to control him again.

Mark swung on his heel and strode away from the men near the corral. Damn it, this stunk worse than a Pecos catfish three days dead. No sheriff in his right mind would deputize Jesse Evans or Buck Morton, even if they were the last men left in the Territory.

Months ago Mark had protested to Dolan when he hired Evans and Morton, but Dolan had insisted he needed a couple of tough gunslingers for protection. Protection was one thing. This was another.

I'm heading into town to talk to Sheriff Brady, he decided. Dolan, too, if I can locate him. Why isn't Brady leading this posse? And why so many? Why eighteen when four or five could do the job? Gunmen, every last one.

The real trouble had started on Christmas Eve when McSween was arrested in Las Vegas; Dolan had filed suit against him, saying McSween had embezzled money from an insurance claim. Then, in January, Brady had attached McSween's cows, and now that posse was heading out to drive in some of Tunstall's stock, claiming that the two men were partners and so Dolan had the right.

Gunslingers instead of cowboys.

Mark mounted his sorrel and urged him into a fast lope. The day was sunny and cool, the snow gone. A gray and white bird called from the bare branches of a cottonwood.

Just before noon he passed the abandoned adobe casita beside a frozen stream that was his mark for the halfway point between Dolan's spread and Lincoln. In warmer weather he often stopped there to eat and water the horse. The sorrel slowed, remembering, and Mark kneed him on. He topped a rise and quickly reined in. Below him, on the trail to Tunstall's ranch, a lone rider trotted.

Could be Tunstall. Since December, Mark had no desire to ever meet him again, but, damn it, if the rider was Tunstall, he was going to have to warn him. He had no real grudge against the Englishman, and he'd hate to see any man come up against that crowd Brady had deputized for his posse.

He rode down the hill to intercept the rider.

As he drew closer, Mark frowned. It wasn't Tunstall. In fact, it wasn't a man. The woman rode astride, wearing men's pants under her skirts, but that wasn't as unusual as the fact she was alone. And that was dangerous as hell in this country.

She turned her head and caught sight of him. Mark drew in his breath.

Tessa Nesbitt!

She slowed her gray horse, waiting for him. He pounded up to her and rode alongside.

"You shouldn't be out here alone," he growled at her, breaking into her greeting. "Where are you headed?"

Tessa blinked, then touched the Colt in the gunbelt buckled around her waist. "I'm armed. If it's any of your business what I do, Mr. Halloran, I'm headed for the Tunstall ranch."

"You didn't pull that pistol when you spotted me coming. A Colt's not much use holstered."

"For heaven's sake, I recognized you!"

"Another thing, you didn't spot me soon enough. I'd have had the drop on you before you had a chance."

Tessa put one hand on her hip and glared at Mark. "Stop lecturing me as though I were Jules' age."

"You ought to get your older brother to ride with you if none of the men has time. Ezra's a good shot."

"As far as I'm concerned, Ezra is in disgrace at the moment."

"One more thing. It's not a good idea to be heading for Tunstall's ranch today. You'd best turn around. I'm going into town and I'll be glad to escort you back."

"I don't know what you're talking about. I have no intention of returning to Lincoln."

Her eyes were like thunderclouds when she was angry, Mark thought, almost completely gray. Even in the man's hat she wore—one of her father's, he suspected—and the pants, Tessa looked so pretty he found it hard to breathe.

"There may be trouble at Tunstall's," he said. "I'm going in to talk to the sheriff about it. And you're coming with me."

"Trouble? What kind of trouble?"

"Some deputies are on their way to attach Tunstall's stock," He said reluctantly, certain she'd be even angrier.

"Dolan!" She spat the word out. "He's behind it; he's out to destroy John like he's tried to destroy Alex. How can you go on working for such a monstrous person?"

"You've got the wrong idea about Dolan. Besides, who I work for is my own business. Come on, we're heading back." He reached for the bridle of her horse.

Mark heard the slither of metal against leather, an ominous click. He dropped the bridle and twisted his head to stare at Tessa.

Her Colt was cocked and pointed straight at his chest.

"Turn your horse and ride for town," she ordered. "You go your way and I'll go mine."

"You're not going to shoot," he told her. "Put the damn gun away."

"If I can shoot an Apache, I can shoot you," she snapped. "Do as I say."

Mark shrugged, started to wheel his horse away from her, then suddenly jerked the sorrel's head back around, kicked free of his stirrups and leaped from his saddle at Tessa. His weight and momentum flung them both off the far side of her horse. The Colt barked as they slammed to the ground. Both horses bolted.

Mark scrambled to his feet. He knelt beside Tessa, sighing with relief when he saw she'd only had the breath knocked out of her.

"Sorry," he said. "Didn't mean to hurt you."

She raised herself on one elbow. Her hat was on the ground some distance away and her golden hair glinted in the sun. "You—you ruffian!" she gasped.

Mark rose and retrieved her gun, emptied the chambers and stuck it under his belt. He reached a hand to her and pulled her to her feet. When he looked around, neither horse was in sight.

"Thanks to your foolishness," he said, "we've got a long hike ahead of us."

Tessa stopped brushing dirt from her skirt. "*My* foolishness!"

"You pulled the gun, not me."

She put both hands on her hips, glaring up at him. "You come riding at me out of nowhere, order me to go back to town, try to force me to return when I refuse, then get upset because I tried to free myself by using my Colt. I hate you, Mark Halloran. I wish I *had* shot you."

She was so damn unreasonable. And so damn pretty. He wanted to wrap her in his arms and hold her safely there for the rest of time.

A flicker of motion on the hill to his right made him look up. He caught a glimpse of the sorrel disappearing over the top.

"Maybe we won't have to walk," he told her. "I sometimes stop at a place just over that hill and my horse is used to it. I think he's headed there now. Let's go see."

Tessa glanced at the hill, then looked at the trail heading south to Tunstall's ranch, north to Lincoln. There was no sign of her horse. She sighed. "I suppose I have no choice."

They walked in silence until they reached the hill. As they began to climb, Tessa said, "Jules asks about you all the time."

Mark smiled. "He's a fine boy. Looks a lot like you."

"He does?"

"Well, his eyes are lighter and his hair's darker, but his face is like yours. There's no doubting you're kin. I'm sorry things worked out so I couldn't come back to see Jules again. To see you again."

She said nothing.

"Seems as though I'm forever telling you I'm sorry," he said. "I wish . . ." He paused.

"What do you wish?"

He waved a hand. "Oh, that things were different.

You're a friend of the McSweens; I work for Dolan. We're on opposite sides and their feuding prevents us from being friends.''

"Yes, I suppose it does." Her voice was softer.

He caught her hand and helped her climb the last few feet to a shelf of rock at the crest of the hill where they stopped to rest.

"We could try to be friends anyway," he said.

Tessa pulled her hand from his and pointed down at the abandoned *casita*. "Is that the place you meant?" she asked. "I don't see your horse."

"That's it. Might as well go on down and wait around a bit. I have a hunch he'll show up there rather than travel all the way back to Dolan's ranch."

She glanced in the direction of Lincoln, maybe a four-hour walk to the north, then toward Tunstall's ranch, even farther to the south.

"We may as well, I suppose," she said, finally.

At the bottom of the hill Tessa examined the inside of the adobe. "Look, there's wood in the fireplace. Does someone actually live here? It seems so dilapidated."

"Never seen anyone. Could be that herders use it sometimes. I'll start a fire if you're cold."

"We won't be here very long, will we?" Mark heard a tinge of apprehension, and something else he couldn't identify, in her voice.

He shrugged and knelt to the hearth, struck a match and touched it to the pine kindling underneath the logs. They caught and soon flames licked up along the logs.

Mark went out the sagging open door and cut branches from one of the pinon pines behind the casita. Returning, he began to lay them near the fire. Tessa picked up one of them, using it as a broom to sweep away accumulated dirt and debris from the ground in front of the fire. She arranged the rest of the boughs over the cleaned space, sat down on them and held her hands out to the flames.

Mark smiled as he watched her busying herself like a wife at her own hearth. He sat beside her. "The heat feels good," he said.

"Yes."

He glanced at her, wondering if he'd imagined the quiver in her voice. She was gazing at him. She turned her face away quickly and color rose to her cheek. Her hat was off and her hair lay over her shoulders in glorious disarray. Desire stirred in him.

He leaned toward her, raised his hand to her face and, with gentle fingers on her chin, turned it back toward him.

"I can't stop looking at you," he said softly. "You're so beautiful. I've never seen a woman so beautiful."

"Not even Susie?" The words came out breathlessly.

He blinked. "Susie McSween?"

Tessa nodded.

"She doesn't compare to you!"

Her eyes dropped. "You seemed to like her."

He had to admit Susie's flirting had aroused him—she was a handsome woman. But Tessa stirred more than his body. What he felt for her was more complicated than simple desire.

"I like Susie," he said. "But you're different. I don't know how to tell you." He stroked her cheek, traced the curve of her lips with his forefinger, his heart beating faster and faster.

Her lips parted.

The blood roared in Mark's ears. He tried to warn himself he must stop this now, before he was out of control. Tessa wasn't the kind of woman a man took for his pleasure and then forgot.

She raised her eyes to his again. In their gray-blue depths he could see a glow that warmed him more than the flames of the fire. He bent his head and kissed her.

At first her mouth was soft under his, the innocent lips of a girl not used to kisses. But as he put his arms around her and drew her close, he felt the answering pressure of her mouth, felt her hands on his shoulders, holding him to her.

His need for her drove every other thought from his mind. He unbuttoned her coat, slid his hands along her breasts, soft under the cloth of her dress. Tessa drew in her breath and started to pull away.

He dropped his hands to her waist, holding her as he kissed her throat, feeling her relax against him. He undid one button of her high-necked gown, then another and another, his lips traveling along her flesh as he bared it.

"Mark," she murmured. "Please . . ."

He couldn't tell if the plea was to go on or to stop, but he was driven on and soon the dress was down about her waist. He removed her camisole and her pink-peaked breasts sprang free, the nipples taut with desire. As his fingers caressed first one breast, then the other, she made little moaning sounds.

His world narrowed to the woman in his arms. "Tessa," he whispered against her ear. "So lovely."

He bent his head to her breasts, his tongue circling the nipples. Tessa held him to her. Her fresh, sweet scent mingling with the fragrance of pine excited him so much that his hands trembled as he laid her back among the boughs and pushed her gown lower, then unbuckled the belt that held up the pants she wore. He drew off the pants and gown and then her undergarments.

He threw off his clothes as quickly as he could, then lay

on his side next to her. She gazed at him with eyes darkened by passion. Gently he drew her to him and kissed her.

The feel of her bare flesh against his made him groan, but he forced himself to wait, stroking the velvet-soft skin of her hip, her thigh. His fingers trailed between her thighs, exploring and caressing.

"Mark," she breathed. "Oh Mark, I don't know what's happening to me. I feel so . . ."

He stopped her words with his mouth, pressed her over onto her back and raised himself above her. Easing her legs apart, he lowered himself until his sex touched the welcoming warmth of her womanhood. He thrust into her as gently as he could, but after a moment she gave a cry of pain and tried to draw back.

Mark couldn't halt; he was beyond reason, she was his, he would make her his, he'd never wanted any woman so much, he had to have her. He thrust hard, once, twice, felt her tightness give and then he was deep inside her.

"I'm afraid," she cried. "Please . . ."

"It's all right, love," he said, his voice hoarse with passion. "It's all right."

He forced himself to slow, then to cease moving altogether, although he was on fire with need. He stayed within her as he kissed her lips, her breasts, tasting the sweetness of her skin.

His tongue probed her mouth and soon she was clinging to him, gasping. He began to thrust again, very slowly. Tessa started to writhe underneath him, arching up against him, moaning, calling his name.

Still he held back.

Tessa moved wildly, pushing her hips against him, her fingers digging into his back. He matched her rhythm as pulses of pleasure throbbed through him.

Tessa cried out, hugging him to her. The sound of her passionate release shot through him and he groaned, thrusting faster and faster, feeling her pulsating, and it flashed into his mind that it had never been like this before, never before; he was truly making love to Tessa, not only with his body but with all of him.

A flash of yellow and red shot across his eyelids; then all was sensation, and he seemed to rocket sky high before exploding into a thousand shards of pleasure.

He dressed quickly, once again noticing the chill of the February afternoon. Tessa was already clothed when he finished and was standing before the dying fire, her back to him. Mark walked over to her and turned her to face him. She met his eyes shyly.

"Tessa," he said. "Tessa." He wanted to tell her he loved her, but the words refused to leave his heart.

What did he have to offer her? Marriage? To ask her to be Mrs. Halloran would be the worst kind of lie.

A horse snorted outside the adobe and, relieved at the interruption, Mark turned toward the door.

"Looks like my horse is here," he said.

Once he had her in front of him on the sorrel, heading for Lincoln and holding her close, Mark felt desire rise in him again. His arms tightened until she made a sound of protest and twisted to look into his face.

Damn it, he thought, I'll have to tell her, even if she hates me afterward. I want things clear between us. He took a deep breath, trying to think how to start.

With what happened in St. Louis, of course, but where to begin?

With the Judge? Or with the sordid details of the triangle of hate and passion that had made him an outcast?

"Tessa," he began, "I grew up in St. Louis."

Before he could say another word, a rifle cracked to the south of them. Another gunshot echoed among the hills. Then a third.

Mark kicked the sorrel. All he could think of was that he had to get Tessa back to Lincoln before anything happened to her. He was very much afraid that a shooting war had broken out between the two sides and that they might be caught in the crossfire.

Chapter 4

Ezra's urging kept the pinto galloping south. Tessa might never forgive him, but she was a woman and they didn't understand men's business.

It'd be late afternoon by the time he reached Tunstall's ranch on the Feliz. He'd taken the trail over the hills around San Patricio. The main road was better but longer.

This part of Lincoln County was pretty with its hills and pines and canyons. A lot nicer than where they'd been in Texas.

Papa had always talked of how close together everything was in England, where a man might ride clear across the entire island in a day and a night if he'd a mind to. Ezra couldn't remember much at all about England or even crossing the Atlantic Ocean. His memory of his mother was only a faint recollection of someone holding and rocking him.

Tessa was who'd mothered him. And Texas was the

country he remembered. He hadn't wanted to leave, but now he liked the New Mexico Territory.

"Best place in the world," Billy said, and Ezra couldn't help but agree.

Tunstall needed Billy and right now he could use Ezra, too. Not for chores, but because Ezra was a pretty good shot and getting better all the time. Not that Tunstall wanted a shooting war.

"I won't sacrifice the life of a single man to keep my cattle," he'd insisted more than once since the trouble started.

Ezra scowled. It was a cinch Dolan didn't feel the same.

"I know some of those boys Dolan hired to tote iron for him," Billy had told Ezra the month before. "Jesse Evans would as soon kill a man as pass the time of day. And I heard that son-of-a-bitch Morton say he was sharpening his scalping knife. He doesn't mean to use it on Mescaleros."

"What do you aim to do about it, Billy?" Ezra asked.

Billy grinned. "Why, I mean to turn you into a crack shot, Ez. Then the two of us'll do for all the bastards."

Ezra's jaw dropped and Billy laughed outright. After a moment Ezra grinned sheepishly. Billy liked to joke and it seemed like Ezra could never catch on to when he was and when he wasn't.

"You can count me in when you go after them," he told Billy. "Even if it does turn out there's only the two of us."

Billy had nodded. "Keep practicing, Ez. Don't forget what I told you. You got to say to yourself, 'I'm pointing my finger,' before you aim the Colt. Never fails to send the bullet true."

Ezra slowed the pinto a little as he began to climb. The land over toward the Pecos was more like Texas with its grassy high plains and only a few cottonwoods and willows by the streams, maybe a tangle of salt cedar. Around Lincoln, though, there got to be real mountains with snow on the peaks and pines covering the sides. He'd heard there was desolate and arid country to the west, but he hadn't yet seen it.

This trail he rode to Tunstall's was over Pajarito Mountain, not so high as some of the others, but not a hill either. Today he wished the going was easier and quicker.

Lincoln itself was a little town of several hundred people with the usual Mexican plaza in the center. Most every building was of adobe bricks. When you entered from the east, you came on the jail and the courthouse and the little San Juan Church before you got to Tunstall's store and the bank. Then came McSween's house.

If you came in from the west, you passed Dolan's store, still called the "House of Murphy," and right across from it was the town's biggest hotel, Wortley's.

Lincoln was built along the south bank of the Rio Bonito right where the canyon opened up. There were lots of cottonwoods scattered between the buildings. Right now they didn't have any leaves, but Ezra thought it must be nice and shady in the hot summer.

He glanced back toward Lincoln. Tessa ought to be safe enough without him in the house. True, McSween didn't carry a gun, but Shield did and he lived right there in the east wing. Besides, with two women and six children in the McSween house, Dolan wouldn't have the nerve to start any trouble.

Or would he?

Ezra slowed the pinto. Maybe he ought to head back. He felt Tessa and Jules were his responsibility since Papa died. If only Tessa and Tunstall would get married. Next to Billy, Ezra admired Tunstall the most of any man in the Territory.

Tessa liked him, too, Ezra could tell. But she also seemed to like that smooth-talking Rutledge. And Halloran.

Billy said Halloran was okay, but Ezra didn't think any man who worked for Dolan could be trusted.

You couldn't even trust Sheriff Brady. When Dolan said jump, Brady only asked how high. Ezra sighed. He couldn't take any chances. He'd better go back.

As he started to wheel his horse, he saw a rider come into sight over the hill ahead of him. Ezra's hand rested near his Colt as he reined in.

The rider drew closer and Ezra relaxed. The man was a Negro ex-cavalryman named George Washington who worked part-time for McSween as well as playing the fiddle when anyone had a dance. He seemed to be everyone's friend. If you wanted to know what was going on just about anywhere in the county, Washington was the man to ask.

Ezra raised his hand, hailing the black man.

"Heard tell there's a sheriff's posse after Tunstall," Washington told him as he drew up. "Said they was gonna settle accounts once and forever."

Ezra tensed. "How many men?"

"I was told about two dozen, give or take a couple. They started off this morning from Dolan's. Bound to be trouble. 'Specially since Brady ain't even with them."

"Does Tunstall know?"

Washington shook his head. "Don't rightly think so. I'm heading in to let Mr. McSween know what's going on."

Ezra watched Washington trot on toward Lincoln, then turned to look down the road leading to Tunstall's ranch. The news killed any plan to return home. He had to get to Tunstall; he'd have to ride like hell, try to get to the ranch in time to warn him. He'd take the shortcut Billy once showed him.

As he turned off the trail and kicked the pinto into a gallop, excitement pounded through Ezra. Maybe there'd be shooting. He'd grab the chance to stand with Tunstall against Dolan's men.

The snow on the high peaks to the west glistened in the sunlight, the pines on the lower slopes green against the white. A crisp, chill day, good for riding. Ezra slowed his horse to pull his Colt, spinning the chamber. All full. When the pistol was back in its holster, he yanked Papa's old Winchester from the saddle scabbard and checked it. The rifle was loaded and ready.

Ezra Nesbitt was ready, too.

His fervor flagged as the day edged into afternoon. He'd finished the tortilla wrapped around the beef and beans he'd gotten from Rosalita and he was still hungry. Damn it, he should have taken more food. The pinto was tiring, besides, and needed to be paced, slowing Ezra.

All of a sudden three turkeys flew up from under the horse's hooves. The pinto shied violently to one side and stumbled. Ezra grabbed the saddle horn to stay mounted. He heard the turkeys scurrying into the underbrush of a canyon off to the right as he fought to steady the startled horse.

As the pinto quieted, Ezra swore. The horse limped. He dismounted to check the off foreleg. Nothing was broken, but when he remounted, the pinto continued to favor the leg and couldn't be urged faster than a walk.

He'd lost any chance of reaching Tunstall's before Dolan's posse. He'd be lucky to get there before dark as this rough trail would be hard on a lame horse.

Ezra sighed. On the one hand, he ought to offer to stand

with Tunstall against Dolan's men—except now he'd probably get there after it was all settled.

On the other hand, Sheriff Brady was still in town and might be fixing to arrest McSween again after sending the posse to get Tunstall. Maybe Shield would be arrested, too. Leaving the women and children without any man between them and whatever Dolan planned to do next. Tessa had the other Colt, but she wasn't much of a shot.

Ezra slammed his fist into his palm. He shouldn't have gone off and left Tessa and Jules like he'd done. Tunstall had a whole crew of men to help him, including Billy, the best shot in the Territory. Tessa didn't have anyone. Oh, Rutledge, maybe, but Ezra didn't think he'd be much help. A talker, not a doer.

He'd been too damn hasty, that's what.

"You've a good head on your shoulders, Ezra," Papa used to say. "I'd be happier if you remembered to use it oftener."

Ezra turned the pinto toward town. The horse's head drooped as he limped over the rocky trail. Ezra's shoulders slumped. Shadows lengthened, creeping out from the canyons to hint that the afternoon was growing old.

A rifle cracked. Both Ezra's and the pinto's heads came up. A fusillade of shots rattled from somewhere in the hills behind Ezra. He heard faint shouts, the rattle of hooves on stone.

Ezra quickly changed course, urging his horse into the brush of a canyon. He dismounted, led the pinto into a thicket where he was concealed from view, tied him to a sapling and grabbed the rifle. Darting out of the canyon and up the nearest hill, he dodged from boulder to boulder in case any horseman galloped into view.

Better off on foot than on a lame horse. Easier to hide.

Hide he must, until he saw who was doing the shooting and what they were shooting at.

Ezra eased in among a cluster of boulders near the crest of the hill and carefully worked himself onto a ledge to peer down at a trail winding through a canyon.

Seven horsemen galloped toward a lone rider who was trotting along the trail toward Lincoln. Ezra heard the hooves of many more horses coming up behind the seven, but they weren't in sight.

The seven horsemen slowed. Stopped. Motioned to the lone rider to come up to them. Ezra's eyes widened as the three men nearest the rider threw up their rifles so the butts rested on their knees. The oncoming man made no attempt to pull a gun.

By God, the lone rider was John Tunstall!

Before Ezra had time to decide what to do, one of the armed men lifted his rifle to his shoulder and fired.

Tunstall jerked backward and pitched off his horse. Ezra was frozen in place, unable to believe what he saw.

"Through the heart," he said under his breath. "Oh God."

Another rider dismounted and ran forward to bend over Tunstall, yanking Tunstall's pistol from its holster. He pointed the muzzle at Tunstall's head. Fired. Jammed the Colt back in place. Took the rifle he had tucked under one arm and battered Tunstall's head with the stock.

Ezra gagged.

Twenty or more riders pounded up and milled around the dead man. Ezra, the sour taste of bile in his throat, watched as two of the riders threw Tunstall's body over the back of his horse and one of them led the horse into the gloom of a pine grove. The other horsemen followed. A single shot cracked.

Tunstall's horse, Ezra told himself. Killed like his rider.

He thought he'd recognized some of the men, but the gathering dusk made it hard to tell one from another. Was it Morton who'd shot Tunstall first or had his killer been Evans?

Why hadn't he brought up his Winchester and killed the son-of-a-bitch, whoever he'd been? What was the matter with him? Was he a coward? Afraid of getting killed?

They'd have gotten him if he'd fired; that was as certain as snow in January. On foot, his horse lame. One of him and twenty-seven or eight of them.

He should have shot just the same.

Ezra waited to be certain they weren't coming back before sliding down the hill and cautiously making his way to the pines where they'd taken Tunstall.

There was barely enough light to see under the trees, but he made out the bulk of the dead horse on the ground. Tunstall's blanket-covered body was laid out beside his horse. Ezra lifted the blanket, caught sight of Tunstall's battered head and face and quickly covered him again. He turned away, retching, and spewed out vomit.

Still gagging, Ezra hurried back to his pinto. He mounted and headed for town. Dolan hadn't been with the posse, not that Ezra had seen. But he had no doubt Dolan was responsible for the murder. He'd gotten Tunstall, exactly as he'd threatened to.

Tunstall hadn't a chance, had been gunned down without even a Colt in his hand. Would McSween be next? Jesus, he didn't even own a gun!

And what about Tessa and Jules, in the house with him? Ezra cursed and tried to urge the lame pinto on faster.

He reached Lincoln by midnight, afoot and leading the hobbling horse. Lanterns bobbed in the plaza as men hurried back and forth in the street. Exhausted, Ezra stumbled among them. He started to blurt out his terrible news. Stopped.

Why were all these men in the plaza? Who was an enemy? Who a friend?

Ezra turned into an alley and took a roundabout route to the McSween house. The first person he saw as he opened the door was Billy. The house was crowded with men.

"Tunstall," Ezra said to Billy.

"The damn dirty cowards!" Billy cried before Ezra could go on. "Me and Middleton never had a chance to stop the bastards."

Ezra blinked, not understanding. "Tunstall is dead," he told Billy.

"Where you been, Ez? We brought word more than an hour ago about Dolan's men killing him." Billy's eyes narrowed. "Going to get me a couple of those boys before the month is over. I ain't going to watch them walk the plaza boasting how they shot Tunstall. He was a good man, Ez."

Tears glittered in Billy's eyes.

Ezra clenched his jaw, afraid that if he let himself go, he'd bawl like a baby. "How did you know about the killing?" he asked.

"Me and Middleton were riding behind him. Saw the posse. Told Tunstall to run for it like we meant to do. We did. He didn't. He never stood a chance."

"I didn't see you," Ezra said.

"Where were you?"

"Riding for Tunstall's ranch. To warn him. Horse went lame. I heard the shooting and hid."

"Lucky they didn't see you. Widenmann and Brewer were riding in front of Tunstall and the posse tried to bring them down first, but they got away. All we were doing was driving some of Tunstall's horses into town. Not looking for any trouble. Me and Middleton were a ways in back of Tunstall. Tried to yell at him to take cover, but he didn't do it. I'm going to get those bastards if it's the last thing I do.''

Ezra stared at him. "I want to go with you. Take me with you.''

"Ezra!'' Tessa pushed her way through the crowd of men and flung her arms around him. "Oh, Ezra, I've been so frightened that you'd been killed like John.'' She put her head on his shoulder and wept.

Ezra stood helplessly, feeling his throat tighten and tears sting his eyes. Up until now Tess had always been the one to comfort him. He forced himself to straighten his shoulders and began to pat her back.

He'd always thought of his sister as stronger than he, even though he'd grown taller and heavier than Tess in the past year. Now she felt small and fragile in his arms. He swallowed his own grief and began to murmur to her.

"I'm here, Tess. I'll take care of you.''

At noon the next day strangers from the east arrived at the McSween house—Presbyterian home missionaries who'd been recruited by McSween the year before: Dr. Ealy, his wife and three children and a young woman named Susan Gates.

When Tunstall's body was brought into Lincoln in the evening, Dr. Ealy, a medical doctor as well as a minister, examined the dead man before assisting Dr. Appel, the Fort Stanton surgeon, with the embalming.

The next morning Ezra trailed Billy and Fred Waite as they marched up to Dolan's store with Constable Martinez. Martinez meant to serve murder warrants issued by Justice of the Peace Wilson against twelve of the posse. With some surprise, Ezra saw that Negro soldiers from nearby

Fort Stanton, thirty miles over the mountains, stood in front of the store, blocking them from entering.

Sheriff Brady came out of the store and pushed past the soldiers. A dozen grim-faced men with their hands gripping Colt handles followed him. Ezra's fingers hovered over his holstered pistol.

"You can't serve those warrants," Brady told Martinez. "Every man in that posse was there by my order. You can't arrest men who ride in a sheriff's posse and you know it."

Martinez eyed him a moment, glanced at the soldiers, shrugged and started to turn away.

Billy grabbed his arm. "Don't let that bootlicker talk you out of it," he told Martinez.

Martinez jerked his head toward Brady, the armed men backing him up and the contingent of soldiers.

"I don't know if the sheriff is right or wrong about these warrants, but he's sure as hell making it impossible to serve them." Martinez eased his arm from Billy's grasp.

Ezra, some four feet behind, let his hand slide down so it almost touched his Colt.

"Peppin! Martin! Longwell!" Brady barked. "Arrest these men."

Brady's deputies surrounded Martinez, Waite and Billy before they had a chance to resist.

"What about the other one?" Peppin asked.

"I said men, not snot-nosed boys," Brady answered.

Several of the deputies laughed.

Ezra's fingers clutched at the Colt.

A hand clamped onto his wrist.

"Don't be a fool," Washington said in his soft drawl. "You won't help no one lying dead in the street." He pulled at Ezra. "We got to get away from here."

Ezra resisted, seeing cuffs being snapped on Martinez, Waite and Billy.

"Come on," Washington urged.

Ezra gave up and retreated with the Negro. There was nothing he could do to help Billy. Not at the moment.

"What's Brady going to do with them?" he asked Washington.

"Reckon he'll toss 'em in jail."

"Billy's not guilty of anything! It's Dolan's men who ought to be in jail. They killed Tunstall."

"One thing you learn in the army if you didn't already find out, life sure ain't fair. Looks like Dolan's got the sheriff and the army on his side now. Ain't no use to fuss and carry on."

Tunstall's funeral was two days later. A company of infantry from the fort watched as Dr. Ealy spoke over the open grave.

"If a man die, shall he live again," the minister intoned while Tunstall's friends, armed with Colts and Winchesters, stood by.

Despite all Ezra could do to dissuade her, Tessa stood beside him.

"What do you mean, danger?" she'd demanded. "At a funeral? I certainly intend to pay my last respects to poor John, no matter what."

Billy and Waite weren't there because, though Brady had let out Martinez, he still had the other two in jail.

There was no good reason for it, Ezra told himself. Maybe Brady was afraid of what Billy might do. How long would the sheriff keep him locked up?

Tessa began to cry softly as the coffin was lowered.

"John was a good man," she sobbed. "He would never have harmed anyone. Why did it have to happen?"

Only a few feet away, the earth mounding their father's grave was still raw and mounded. What would Papa have thought of Tunstall's murder?

"I expect you to know the right thing to do, Ezra," Papa had said so often. "Know what's right. Then do it."

Ezra took a deep breath. The right thing was to avenge Tunstall's death.

He stared at the unfinished pine coffin that hid Tunstall's remains. I won't forget who did this, he promised the dead man. I'll remember and I'll do my best to see those bastards don't get away with it.

Chapter 5

The day after Tunstall's funeral, Sheriff Brady released Waite and Billy from jail.

"Worst jail I was ever in," Billy said as he and Ezra walked toward Justice of the Peace Wilson's office. "A damn hole in the ground."

Ezra stared at him. "Were you in jail before?" he asked.

"Once, over in Silver City, when I was your age. Didn't last long. I climbed out the chimney and took off."

Ezra wanted to ask what Billy had been in for but decided maybe he'd better not.

Tunstall's foreman, Dick Brewer, was at Wilson's when Ezra and Billy arrived. He waved papers at them.

"Warrants for Tunstall's murderers," Brewer said. "Wilson's made me a special constable and I'm forming my own posse. You in, Kid?"

"You can bet on it."

"Okay, we'll get you deputized all legal like. I got ten now, counting me. You, Waite, Middleton, McNab, Skurlock, Bowdre, Brown, Smith and French. That ought to do the trick."

Ezra gazed wistfully at Brewer, but he didn't seem to notice.

"We're going to go by regulations," Brewer went on. "We got papers and we'll make arrests. Won't be no powdersmoke lynchings."

"I reckon you'll be calling us the Regulators then," Billy said, winking at Ezra as if to show he wasn't taking Brewer all that seriously.

But Ezra had trouble smiling back at Billy. He badly wanted to be chosen to go with the posse and he could see it wasn't going to happen.

Nobody can stop me from trailing after them when they ride out, he told himself. I'll help whether they want me or not.

Early in March, Brewer called the ten Regulators together in Tunstall's store.

"We got word that Buck Morton's in a Dolan cow camp down on the Pecos," he told them. "We're going after him. Remember, we ain't going to be like that posse who did for poor old John." Brewer paused to eye them. "We aim to see his killers hung by fair trial and any man who feels differently won't be riding with me."

Ezra, standing beside Billy, felt his heart pound. At last something was going to happen.

Jules came into the store, saw Ezra and ran over to him. "Tess wants you to come home right away," he said.

Ezra paid no attention. "I mean to go along with the Regulators," he said to Billy.

"Ain't no one stopping you," Billy told him, smiling.

"Tess says you got to hurry," Jules persisted. "She says I'm supposed to bring you back."

"I'm riding out," Ezra said. "You tell her that."

"Where?"

"To get the men who killed John Tunstall."

Jules stared up at him. His gray eyes filled with tears. "You'll get shot like Papa and John," Jules sobbed.

As Ezra started after Billy, who was leaving the store by the side door to the corral, Jules flung himself at Ezra, clutching him around one leg. "Don't go," he begged.

Ezra tried to pry him loose, conscious of amused smiles from several of the Regulators.

"You better take your brother home," Billy said. He swung onto his gray.

"I'll catch up," Ezra promised.

Tessa breathed a thankful sigh when she saw Ezra returning with Jules. She'd been terrified he'd go off with some of the men trying to avenge John's death. Go off with Billy.

"I told you he'd come back," Calvin Rutledge said, walking over to stand beside her. "I'll speak to the boy, if you like, about protecting you. Dolan's men are totally unscrupulous and since I can't be in Lincoln all the time, Ezra must understand it's necessary for him to be here with you."

"Thank you but no," she said hastily. Ezra didn't take to Calvin for some reason she couldn't understand and would resent anything Calvin told him.

Calvin reached for her hand. "You know I'm ready to take care of you permanently any time you wish, Tessa. More than ready." He pressed her fingers.

Tessa smiled at him but eased her hand from his. She'd been in a whirl of confusion and guilt ever since John's death. How could she have made love with Mark while others of Dolan's men were riding on their way to shoot John down in cold blood?

She felt as though she never wanted to see Mark again, no matter what had passed between them. The color crept into her face as she thought of her wanton behavior. How could she have taken leave of her senses as she had? And with John's enemy, as any Dolan hand must be.

"Ah, you're blushing," Calvin said. "I didn't mean to embarrass you, my dear." He stepped back and picked up his hat.

Ezra flung open the door, scowling. He barely returned Calvin's greeting as the man went out. Jules, tagging at Ezra's heels, was sniffling, his face dirt-streaked where he'd rubbed away tears. Tessa directed him into the kitchen.

"You shouldn't have sent Jules after me," Ezra said.

"He's afraid," Tessa said, "and so am I. You've got to promise me you won't do something reckless."

"I can't make promises like that."

Tessa put her hands on her hips. "Your first duty is to take care of your brother. I can't protect him with this— this war going on in Lincoln County. Who knows what will happen next? Every day there's a new threat. We both know Dolan's men are trying to drive Alex out of the Territory."

Ezra glowered at her.

Tessa held out her hands. "We Nesbitts must stick together. Oh, Ezra, you and Jules are all I have. If anything happened to either of you, I couldn't bear it!"

His face lost its sulky look and he sighed. "All right," he said. "I won't go off with the Regulators to the Pecos."

In the next few days Tessa became better acquainted with Susan Gates, the young teacher Dr. Ealy and his wife had brought with them to Lincoln, as she helped Susan move from the McSween house next door to rooms in Tunstall's store. The Ealys and their three children also moved into the store.

"There's a sore need in Lincoln for a Christian influence," Susan said to Tessa, who was helping carry her gowns, as they walked across the field to the store's side entrance. "I hope we'll be able to set up the church and school as planned." She shook her head. "It doesn't look promising. Folks seem to feel that since it was Mr. McSween who requested a minister be sent to Lincoln County, that we must be for him and against his enemies."

"*I'm* certainly against his enemies," Tessa replied.

"Jesus admonished us to love our enemies," Susan reminded her. "It's difficult, I know, when someone you love has been killed and you yourself might be in danger."

Tessa's mouth set into a straight line. "It's impossible!"

As they neared the side door, Tessa recognized the man approaching and stumbled. She regained her footing, breathless, her heart pounding.

"Tessa," Mark said.

She couldn't speak for a moment, staring at him, her emotions jumbled and chaotic. Susan stood looking from one to the other. With great effort, Tessa gathered her wits.

"Susan," she said, "I can't introduce you to this person since I intend to have no dealings at all with the enemy."

Tessa pushed at Susan, forcing her ahead toward the door. Susan opened it and went inside. Before Tessa could follow, Mark's hand on her arm stopped her.

"Tessa, you know better," he said. "I don't condone . . ."

She struck at his hand. "Don't speak to me!" she hissed.

"You've got to listen to me. I want to take you and the boys away from Lincoln. It's not safe for you to . . ."

"Leave me alone!" she cried.

"Is he annoying you, Tessa?"

She started. Calvin had come out of the store without her seeing him and now stood glaring at Mark.

"He certainly is!" she snapped.

"We don't need your sort here, Halloran," Calvin said, stepping in front of Tessa. "If I find you anywhere near these premises again, you'd better be ready to defend yourself."

Mark gazed past him to Tessa, who was peering around Calvin's shoulder. She saw muscles bunch in Mark's jaw.

"This is none of your business, Rutledge," he growled.

Tessa felt Calvin stiffen and caught her breath. She didn't want them to fight over her; there'd been too many killings already. She heard ominous muttering from men watching them from the store porch, men she knew were guarding the store. She suddenly realized that Mark was in danger, a lone Dolan man facing McSween supporters.

She didn't want anything to happen to him.

"Get out of here, Mark!" she cried.

Tessa pulled on Calvin's arm with all her might. Off guard, he stumbled with her as she headed for the store porch. She strode directly at the armed men, forcing them to make way for her. Stopped.

"Let him go," she said to them.

"You'd best stay out of this, miss; we're aiming to teach that Dolan bastard a lesson he won't forget," a sandy-haired man said, starting to push past her.

She held out her hand. "He wasn't with the posse—you know he wasn't."

"Don't make no difference. No Dolan hand's any damn good."

"Men!" Dr. Ealy's voice held a note of command. Everyone turned to look at him.

"Your friend and mine, Alexander McSween," Dr. Ealy went on, "has told us time and again he intends to deal with Mr. Dolan and his supporters by legal means. We must respect his wishes and not add to the violence that's already occurred. Defense, yes, but not attack."

For an instant Tessa thought the sandy-haired man would defy the minister, but finally he shrugged and turned away. Calvin gently urged Tessa toward the front door of the store and she realized she was still carrying Susan's gowns.

"I heard Mr. Halloran offer to take you out of Lincoln," he said as they went inside.

"I've no intention of going anywhere with him. Ever!"

"Of course not. But his point is sound enough. You shouldn't be in the midst of this violence. As you know, I have friends in Santa Fe. They would welcome . . ."

"I'm not leaving. The McSweens offered me help and friendship when I needed it desperately. I certainly won't desert Alex and Susie."

"You know Susie's in St. Louis," Calvin said.

"All the more reason for me to stay. If I leave, Elizabeth Shield will be the lone woman in the McSween house. Besides, I'm not certain Ezra would leave Lincoln under any circumstances. He's growing up, Calvin, but he's not yet a man. He needs me. I'd never leave him behind."

A week later, Alex came to Tessa about exactly the same matter.

"Dick Brewer brought me unsettling news last night," Alex told her. "The Regulators have gotten themselves into trouble—and me with them, I'm afraid. It would be prudent for me to stay with John Chisum at his Roswell ranch for awhile. You and your brothers must come with me.''

"But what about the Shields?'' she asked.

"They prefer to stay here. You must not. I feel responsible for you and I believe you'll be safer at Chisum's. Susie plans to join me there and I know she'll be much happier if you're with us at Chisum's.''

Tessa didn't argue further but hurried to tell the boys to pack.

"Billy and some of the other Regulators did for Morton and Baker,'' Ezra said. "That's why we're leaving town.''

"You mean they killed two men?'' she asked.

"Three. Someone named McCloskey, too. I never heard of him. But Morton and Baker were in that posse. They sure as hell needed killing.''

"Ezra!''

"Well, they did. Don't you want to see John avenged?''

"All these killings can't be right.''

"You just don't understand. Sheriff Brady's the law and he's on Dolan's side. Billy knew if they brought Morton and Baker into town like Brewer wanted to, Brady wouldn't so much as lock them up. So he and the others handed out a little gunpowder justice, that's all.''

"I don't like it.'' Tess put her hand on Ezra's arm and looked into his eyes. It seemed strange to her to be gazing up at this boy she'd raised from the time he was going on eight.

"You must promise me to stay away from Billy Bonney,'' she said.

"He's my friend!''

"I don't want you to ride with a man who sets himself up as judge and executioner. Billy has a wild streak—he's dangerous. Stay away from him.''

Ezra looked steadily back at her. "Billy's my friend," he repeated.

The trip to Roswell and their stay at Chisum's ranch was uneventful. Ezra, restless and eager to be where there was more going on, was delighted when, near the end of March, Billy and Fred Waite rode in to see McSween.

Ezra knew that Alex, Susie, Chisum and three of their friends from the East planned to head back to Lincoln in a day or two because Alex wanted to be in town for the April first court session. Tessa and Jules would be in their party and, with armed Chisum men as outriders, they'd be well protected. He wouldn't be needed.

When Billy and Waite rode out the day after they'd visited Alex, heading for Lincoln, Ezra left a note for Tessa and rode with them. Near San Patricio, south of Lincoln, some of the Regulators joined them. They rode into town the last day of March, going at once to Tunstall's store where they meant to spend the night.

After eating, the talk turned to Dolan.

"Them sons-of-bitches," Waite said. "They gun a man down and mash out his brains and Brady don't do nothing. Who did he throw in the *calabozo* after Tunstall got shot? Me and the Kid, that's who. And what for? Cause we tried to come after the murderers all legal like. Brady's no damn good except to empty Dolan's shit-pot."

There was a chorus of agreement.

"We got three of them anyway," Billy said.

"Damn good thing," Middleton told him. "Too bad Brady wasn't along with 'em."

The tension in the room made Ezra's scalp tingle. Something would happen, he was sure of it.

"I'd give ten bucks to see Brady eating dust," Waite said. "And that smart-ass deputy of his, Peppin."

"You're a piker; I'd give a hundred," Middleton told him.

"The day you see a hundred bucks, hell will freeze over and we'll all go ice-skating."

Everyone laughed and Ezra relaxed a little, feeling the tension ease. He was both relieved and disappointed when the men laid out their bedrolls. Nothing was going to happen tonight, after all.

Ezra crawled into his own blankets. Tessa was probably mad as the devil at him, but she had to realize he wasn't a little boy any more. Nothing in the world was going to keep him from being Billy's friend, and the sooner she knew it, the better.

He was awake at dawn. Billy was already standing by a front window, looking toward the plaza. Ezra hastened to join him.

"You going into court this morning?" Ezra asked in a low tone.

He knew Billy and the others were supposed to be present for the court session, either as witnesses or because they'd been accused of crimes. Wrongfully, as far as he was concerned.

"I was thinking about Brady," Billy said. "He put me down that hole once, but he ain't going to again."

That's all the jail was, a hole in the ground with a watch tower built over it. Ezra wonder how any man could stand being shut up there.

"He's aiming to get me," Billy went on, "and I don't fancy being got."

As the others began to roll out of their blankets, Washington burst in from the rear of the store.

"There's talk Brady's carrying handcuffs for McSween," he said. "He's been bragging that when McSween shows up for court, he's gonna put him in the hole and run enough water in to drown him.''

The Regulators cursed Brady as they pulled on boots and buckled on gun belts.

''What are we going to do about it?'' Ezra asked Billy.

''Why, it just ain't going to happen,'' Billy said.

They ate a quick breakfast; then Billy drew McNab, French, Waite, Brown and Middleton aside. Ezra trailed after them.

''Reckon we better spy out the land,'' Billy said. ''If we use the back way, we can get into the corral without anyone seeing us on account of the adobe wall. If we ease up quiet-like to that plank gate that faces on the road, we ought to be able to see what's going on. If we're careful, no one will spot us.''

Billy glanced from one to another of the men. Ezra's pulse quickened. Billy was the youngest of them all, except for him, and yet he was the leader. What a man!

''What're you aiming to do, Kid?'' Waite asked.

''We'll wait and see what Brady's up to. But better make damn sure there ain't nothing the matter with your rifles or your Colts.''

Ezra spun the chambers of his Colt, saw Billy was watching him.

''All loaded and ready,'' Ezra said, stammering in his excitement.

''I was thinking your sister's going to be down on me if I let you come with us,'' Billy said.

Ezra straightened his shoulders. ''I do what I want to. I don't have to ask Tess.''

Billy shrugged. ''Come, then.''

One by one, the seven of them slipped into the corral. The sun was up, the day promising to be mild. Doves cooed mournfully from the cottonwoods near the river in back of the corral.

The men took positions near the gate. The jut of the store hid the road from the west, but they could see along it to the east past the courthouse which was catercorner across the road. After what seemed like hours, Billy whispered, "Brady."

The men started to bring their rifles to their shoulders but Billy's raised hand stopped them. They waited, crouching to be out of sight, peering through the gaps in the planks of the gate.

Five men appeared on the road, walking toward the courthouse from the west. Brady. Hindman, Mathews, Long, Peppin, his deputies.

Ezra tensed, waiting for Billy's next order. Across the street near the courthouse, men had begun to gather. Jurors, Ezra decided.

The five men passed by, none even glancing at the gate, and approached the courthouse. They stopped to talk to the men waiting there. In a few moments the jurors dispersed.

"Ain't going to be holding a court session," Billy muttered. "Figured as much. They want blood, not law. Get ready, boys."

The five lawmen started back the way they'd come. Brady paused for a moment to call a greeting to a woman near the courthouse, then hurried to catch up to his deputies.

Six men leveled their rifles. Ezra tried to get his into position, but his hands were shaking so badly he could hardly hold the Winchester, much less aim.

Six rifles cracked.

Brady fell in his tracks. Didn't move.

Hindman staggered back toward the courthouse. Fell. Began to crawl. "Water!" he cried.

Long stumbled, recovered and ran with Mathews and Peppin to take cover.

A man rushed from the saloon next to the courthouse and knelt beside Hindman. A moment later he raced back to the saloon. Hindman lay motionless, a tin cup beside him.

Brady's and Hindman's Winchesters lay in the road.

"Damn, that looks like the one he took from me," Billy said.

Before Ezra realized what was happening, Billy pushed the gate open and dashed into the road, stooping to pick up one of the rifles. Bullets from the deputies hidden across the street kicked up dirt around Billy. Ezra held his breath.

Billy lurched to one side, dropping the rifle. He stumbled back inside the gate, blood oozing from a bullet hole in his left thigh. Ezra hurried to help him.

"Not into the store," Billy said. "That's the first place they'll look."

With Ezra supporting him, Billy limped through the west gate of the corral and across the field to the opening in the tall picket fence on the side of the McSween house. They came into the east wing by a back door and Ezra left Billy to find Dr. Ealy who was staying in the house.

"It's only a flesh wound," the doctor assured Billy minutes later, wiping away the blood on Billy's left thigh.

Taking a white silk handkerchief and a metal probe, the doctor pushed the handkerchief into the bullet hole, Ezra swallowed hard as he watched him push until the handkerchief, covered with blood, emerged from the bullet's exit hole. He pulled the cloth all the way out, then bound up the wound.

"Clean through," Dr. Ealy said. "Ought to heal nicely. Though I don't think you're going to do much riding for a few days."

"I can't stay here," Billy said.

A McSween man, Sam Corbett, who'd watched the doctor treat Billy, spoke up.

"I got me an idee. You come on with me."

Ezra helped Billy along a corridor and into a bedroom, following Corbett who'd stopped to pick up a pry iron. In the room, he shoved the bed aside and pried at the floorboards, easing three of the wide planks up. He tossed Ezra a blanket.

"Put it underneath there," he said.

Ezra lay on his stomach and pushed the blanket into the hole. He smoothed it out onto the dirt not more than two feet below.

"There's your hidey-hole," Corbett told Billy.

Billy grinned at Ezra. "Guess I'm bound to fit into a hole today, one way or the other. At least Brady ain't shoving me in this one." He eased down and stretched out on the blanket.

Corbett reached for the boards and began to fit them back across the opening. Ezra peered at Billy and saw he held his Colt in his hand.

"Anybody finds me, they're going to be sorry," Billy said, his words muffled as Corbett laid the last board in place.

Chapter 6

Peppin and Mathews searched the McSween house but overlooked Billy's hiding place. Two days later he rode south to join his friends in the hills near San Patricio. Ezra, asking permission from no one, went with him.

Dick Brewer was there to greet them.

"Ain't nothing I can do now about you killing Brady and Hindman," he told Billy. "They're dancing with the devil, I guess, and that's all right, but I don't want to see it happen again. We're going to serve these warrants I got and we're going to bring the rest of the bastards back alive. To hang."

Billy shrugged. "Suits me."

"I thought you were running things," Ezra whispered to him.

"Brewer's the constable, not me," Billy muttered.

"I got word that Roberts and Kitt are down the Tulerosa

by the Mescalero reservation," Brewer went on. "We're riding after them."

Ezra knew both Robets and Kitt had been in Brady's posse and he tingled with anticipation. This time he wouldn't freeze up like some greenhorn with buck fever. He'd killed an Apache, hadn't he?

The trouble with him back in Lincoln was that Brady and his deputies hadn't shot first. Hadn't even pulled their guns. The truth of it was, they'd been ambushed. Of course, ambush was all right in war. Even Tessa called it a war. Anyway, hadn't the posse done worse to Tunstall?

"Wish you were leading the Regulators," Ezra told Billy as they saddled up.

"I reckon Brewer's okay," Billy assured him.

Fifteen Regulators rode southwest under a warm sun. The grass had begun to shoot up green, transforming the brown hills. The cottonwoods unfolded new leaves and birds called everywhere. It was April sixth.

Words popped into Ezra's mind:

Oh, to be in England now that April's there
And whoever wakes in England sees some morning,
unaware,
That the lowest boughs and the brushwood sheaf
Round the elm-tree bole are in tiny leaf . . .

It was from some poem his father used to recite to him and Tess every spring.

"Robert Browning," he said aloud.

"What?" Billy asked.

"Nothing." Not for the world would Ezra admit he could remember lines of poetry and even the name of the man who wrote them.

He'd loved Papa, but it didn't take many brains to see that Texas and the New Mexico Territory were no place for men like Papa. No place for poetry either. Tunstall was

an Englishman, too. He probably would have known who
Robert Browning was, since Tunstall had been a lot like
Papa.

Good men. Law-abiding. Trusting in the good of other
men. Ezra shook his head. It hadn't worked for Papa in
Texas any more than it had worked for Tunstall in the New
Mexico Territory.

They were both dead.

Ezra glanced at Billy, who'd begun to whistle "Silver
Threads Among the Gold."

Billy sure didn't have to worry about growing old. Not
for a long time. He was eighteen, just a little less than
three years older than Ezra. He wasn't a tall man—about
five seven and a tad more, Ezra reckoned. He himself was
already two inches taller than Billy.

Age and height didn't mean much, though. When they
didn't have Brewer giving orders, The Regulators all looked
to Billy to find out what to do next. Billy didn't sit around
musing over lines of poetry, he was always practicing his
shooting even though he was the best shot in the Territory
already. He watched everything that was going on and
decided what ought to be done. Then did it. No sitting on
the fence debating which way to jump.

Ezra was bound and determined to be like Billy. Not
worry whether he was doing right. Not feel guily about
leaving Tess and Jules behind. Billy was the kind of man
who could call the Territory home. Who knew what a man
had to do to live here.

By noon the sun was actually hot. They were in sight of
Blazer's Mill on the Mescalero reservation.

"We'll get Mrs. Godfroy to fix us dinner," Brewer
said.

She was the Indian agent's wife and kept an eating place
for travelers. The Regulators left their horses in the corral,

carrying their rifles inside the building and stacking them against the wall near the dining room door before sitting down to eat.

Ezra had just put his spoon into the bean soup when Middleton leaped to his feet, pointing out the window.

"By God, here comes Buckshot Roberts, big as life!" he exclaimed.

"Let's get him!" Billy cried.

The Regulators shoved back chairs as they dived for their rifles.

"Hold it!" Brewer ordered. "I got a warrant for him and I intend to take him alive." He looked around the dining room until his eyes lit on Frank Coe.

"Frank," he said, "you know Roberts as well as any of us. You go on out and explain what we mean to do."

As Coe strode outside, Ezra stared at the approaching Roberts. The man got the name Buckshot because he carried so many bullets in his body from fighting—mostly against the Texas Rangers, Ezra'd heard. Buckshot wasn't a big man, he was getting old, and he limped, but he looked tough as old leather, not the kind who'd give up easily.

"You reckon Roberts'll surrender to us?" Ezra asked Billy.

Billy grinned and shook his head.

Roberts stopped when he saw Coe; then the two of them walked around the side of the building, talking to each other, and disappeared from sight.

"What if he takes Frank hostage?" Middleton asked. "Hell, he might even shoot him."

Brewer, pacing back and forth, didn't answer. Time passed. Frank Coe and Roberts didn't reappear.

"Buckshot ain't going to make it easy for us," Billy said.

Brewer nodded. He stopped pacing, pointed at George Coe, Frank's cousin. "You go out there, George. Take Middleton and Bowdre. Tell Roberts he's under arrest."

The three hurried out. Billy touched Ezra's arm and began to drift toward the door. Ezra followed.

"Bound to be trouble," Billy muttered. "Should have shot him to begin with."

Ezra and Billy were at the door when they heard Bowdre call, "Roberts, throw up your hands!"

A man shouted, "No!" A rifle cracked. Somebody yelped in pain.

Ezra ran outside with Billy, Winchester in his hand. More shots.

"Jesus, I'm hit," Middleton cried, staggering toward Ezra. Blood welled onto Middleton's shirt and dripped onto the dirt. There was no sign of Roberts. A bullet zinged past Ezra. Billy grabbed his arm and yanked him behind a wagon. They crouched by the wheels to peer underneath.

"Roberts is holed up in there." Billy pointed to an open doorway in a house some yards away. Ezra saw that a mattress had been shoved into the opening. When bullets from Roberts' rifle began spattering against the wagon, Ezra and Billy retreated around the corner of the building where the other Regulators had taken over.

"Your arm's bleeding," Ezra said to Billy.

"Grazed me, that's all. He's one hell of a mean old man."

George Coe had a blood-soaked bandana wrapped around his right hand and Bowdre was cursing the shot that had cut off his gunbelt. Middleton was breathing okay, so Ezra guessed he wasn't badly wounded.

Brewer turned to Bowdre. "You're sure you hit Roberts?"

"A gut shot," Bowdre told him. "Didn't you hear him

howl? Never figured he'd make it to that room. He oughta be dead."

"Just leave him there," Billy advised. "He ain't going to live long if he's gutshot."

Brewer shook his head. "I'm going to sneak up on him."

Billy shrugged.

Ezra watched Brewer cross the road and duck behind a small rollway of logs near the sawmill. Brewer crouched behind the logs as he eased along to get into position to see Roberts' doorway, disappearing from Ezra's sight.

"Damn, that's Brewer's hat sticking up over the logs," Billy said suddenly, pointing. "He ought to know . . ."

A sharp crack cut off Billy's words. Brewer's hat vanished behind the logs.

Billy took off across the road at a run. Ezra, racing behind him, stopped abruptly when he saw Brewer's body sprawled on its back, a dark and bloody hole between his eyes.

Billy shook his head. "Done for. Old Buckshot always had a good eye. Ain't no way we're going to flush him out, he'll pick us off one by one till he's dead." He jerked his head toward the rest of the Regulators, still waiting across the road. "Best thing to do is *vamos*."

As Ezra hurried to the corral with the others, he couldn't shake the feeling that it was wrong to leave Brewer where he'd fallen.

"Blazer'll bury him," Billy said. "Him and Buckshot, too, 'cause he's a goner."

Even the Apaches always tried to come back after their dead, Ezra thought. Still, Billy was right about needing to get away in a hurry. Fort Stanton was too close for comfort if Blazer decided to get soldiers down because of the shooting.

No one had argued with Billy; it was plain he'd be the leader of the Regulators now. If Brewer had listened to Billy, Ezra told himself, he'd still be alive instead of lying in the dirt with a bullet in his head.

That's where trying to go by the letter of the law got you.

Dead.

Billy had wanted to throw down on Roberts the minute the Regulators spotted him and that's the way it should've been handled.

Billy made the kind of leader a man could trust.

In the parlor of the McSween house, Tessa turned abruptly away from Calvin Rutledge.

"I didn't ask for a lecture," she said, "I asked for your help."

"I'm sorry, Tessa. God knows, I don't mean to offend you. But you'll have to learn sooner or later that no fifteen-year-old boy wants to be tied to his sister's apron strings. Let Ezra go his way."

She whirled to face him. "But the killings! And Sheriff Copeland claimes the Regulators have been rustling cattle. Ezra isn't the kind to be mixed up with thieves and murderers."

Calvin spread his hands. "There's nothing I can do, much as I'd like to."

Tessa tried to smile, but she was far too upset. "I don't mean to be cross with you, Calvin. Naturally I don't expect you to ride out alone to find Ezra."

The trouble was, that's exactly what she had half-expected he might offer to do. After all, Calvin was a friend of Alex's as much as any of the Regulators and certainly they wouldn't harm him.

She stared out the window into the courtyard where a

blue-green yucca thrust its candelabra of creamy white flowers skyward. May already. She hadn't seen Ezra since around the first of April, right after Sheriff Brady's murder. He'd sworn he hadn't fired at the sheriff or his men, but others had been shot since then and the Regulators blamed for it.

"I promised Alex I'd look in at the store," Calvin said, "but I'll stop by to see you again tomorrow, with your permission."

Jules came into the parlor and seated himself on the piano stool. He began to play "Home Sweet Home" with both hands.

The song always reminded Tessa of her father's death. She was fond of both Alex and Susie—they'd been wonderful to her and the boys despite their own troubles—but it wasn't the same as when Papa was alive. Would she ever have her own home again?

Calvin touched her arm. "Tessa?"

"Oh. Yes, of course, do come by," she said hastily.

When Calvin was gone, she stood beside Jules, watching his fingers on the keys. How determined he looked at the piano, earnest and frowning. Yet he loved to play. He was so different from Ezra. More like Papa, perhaps.

Calvin couldn't seem to understand her worry over Ezra. She mustn't be so upset because he wouldn't ride in search of her brother. Just the same, she was disappointed in Calvin.

Mark would have gone.

No, she wasn't going to think about Mark Halloran.

As if Jules had read her mind, he stopped playing and twirled the stool around to face her.

"Why doesn't Mr. Halloran come here any more?" Jules asked. "He plays the piano even better than Aunt Susie."

Tessa sighed. How could she explain? Jules loved Alex, calling him uncle, and grouped the townspeople into good men, if they were on Alex's side, and bad men if they weren't. Was Mark really bad?

In her first anger and grief after she'd heard of John's murder, Tessa had told herself Mark was no different from all the other terrible men who worked for Dolan.

But he certainly was no outlaw like Jesse Evans and his gang of cutthroats. Mark hadn't been in the posse who'd gunned down John. She couldn't imagine him joining such a posse.

If she asked him, would he find Ezra for her and bring him back to Lincoln?

Jules tugged at her hand. "Why, Tess? Doesn't Mr. Halloran like us any more?"

"I don't know," she told Jules.

"I wish he'd come back."

After the way I behaved when he tried to talk to me back in March, she thought, Mark will never come back, even if the hostility between Dolan and Alex eases. Would it ever? There were more grievances daily. Calvin wouldn't hear of her venturing away from the house without him.

The end of April there'd been some shootings in town, but since then things had been fairly quiet. Would it be safe for her to go out alone and look for Mark? He might not be in town, of course, but she'd never find him sitting here.

Ezra was more important than worrying about possible insults she might encounter on the streets of Lincoln.

Tessa changed into a calico gown, blue with a tiny yellow flower print. She'd made the dress from material salvaged from John's store after Dolan's men had finished looting it the day after they'd killed him. Now the building was back in Alex's hands and guards were on duty day and night to be certain it remained his.

Tessa tied on a Dolly Varden hat decorated with yellow silk roses. The hat had been brought from St. Louis by Susie as a present, and Tessa loved it. She'd never had such an elegant hat.

Rosalita assured her she'd keep an eye on Jules.

"*Señorita*, you look *muy bonita*," she said as Tessa went out the door.

The sun was decidedly warm, Tessa thought as she walked along the edge of the road, heading west toward Dolan's store. She passed loungers in front of the saloons, but though the men eyed her, no one said anything. A wagon rolled past and dust rose in its wake to choke her. She hurried on.

As she neared Dolan's store, her steps slowed. She'd never been inside. "House of Murphy," the sign said. Lawrence Murphy was no longer in Lincoln; he'd moved to Santa Fe because of illness before Tessa arrived in town. As his partner, Jim Dolan ran the store.

And tried to run Lincoln County as well.

A man stepped off the porch of the store and came toward her. She saw it was George Peppin. He was no longer a deputy since Sheriff Copeland had been appointed to replace Brady. Peppin stopped in front of her, forcing her either to halt or to go around him.

She decided to stop.

"Good afternoon, Mr. Peppin," she said. "Have you seen Mark Halloran?"

"McSween shouldn't be sending you on his errands," Peppin said. "My advice to you is to get home. Fast."

As he spoke, several other men drifted up to them. One man with dark red hair crowded so close to Tessa that she edged away. She didn't like the way the man's eyes lingered on her breasts.

"Mr. McSween has nothing to do with my asking for Mark Halloran," Tessa said.

"But McSween's got plenty to do with you, I hear," the redhead told her.

"Knock it off, Kilgore," Peppin said. "Miss Nesbitt, go home."

Kilgore paid no attention to Peppin. Grinning at Tessa, he said, "McSween was damn lucky to have a pretty little heifer like you to warm his bed all winter while Susie was in St. Louis."

Tessa was so shocked that she couldn't speak. Alex? She and Alex?

"How dare you!" she managed to say finally.

Kilgore caught her arm. "Any time you get tired of playing second fiddle to Susie, there's room in my bed."

Tessa tried to jerk her arm from his grasp. Two other men standing nearby laughed.

"Think you can brand that McSween heifer, Hank?" one of them asked.

"Let me go!" Tessa cried, angry and a little frightened at the way the men surrounded her.

Kilgore's fingers tightened, digging painfully into her arm. She stifled her gasp, knowing she mustn't show fear. The men's eyes, even Peppin's, had a hot, glazed look that made her stomach knot. What would happen if they forced her inside the store?

Tessa swallowed. She had to do something quickly. She straightened her shoulders. "Wait until Mark Halloran hears about this!" she exclaimed.

Puzzlement flickered across Kilgore's face.

"Mark asked me to meet him here," Tessa went on. "Is this how you treat a guest?"

Peppin frowned at Kilgore. "What's your business with Halloran?" he asked Tessa.

Color rose to her face. "I believe that's between Mark and me."

As Kilgore's fingers eased, she jerked her arm away but made no other move. This was no time to try to run.

"Mark!" she called loudly. "Mark Halloran, here I am!"

A man stepped from the hotel across the street to stare. A head thrust from a second-story window. Four men appeared on the porch of the store.

"It happens Halloran ain't in town," Peppin said.

"Well!" Tessa put all the indignation she could manage into her voice. "Then I'll thank you to tell him I don't appreciate being stood up."

"Won't I do?" Kilgore asked.

Ignoring him, Tessa turned on her heel and, heart beating so hard she was afraid its thumping could be heard a yard away, pushed past the men hemming her in. She was brought up short by a Mexican in a black sombrero who swept off his hat and bowed.

"Miss Nesbitt. May I escort you to your home? It would be my pleasure," he said, offering his arm.

She hesitated, heard Kilgore's voice behind her and quickly placed her hand on the Mexican's arm.

"Thank you," she said.

As they moved away from the group of men, she heard them muttering and expected any moment to have Kilgore confront her again. Then she noticed, for the first time, that five other Mexicans stood next to the cantina beside Dolan's store, all watching her.

"My friends," the man escorting her murmured. "Do not be afraid. I am Vincente Gabaldon and I will see you reach your home safely."

Her breath eased out in a sigh of relief. She glanced at Vincente Gabaldon, seeing him without a haze of fear. His dark hair was touched with silver at the temples, giving his dark handsomeness a distinguished flair.

"It's kind of you to rescue me," she said. "Brave."

He looked over his shoulder toward Dolan's. "They do not follow," he said. "*Ladrones*. Thieves. *Muy mal*. Very bad. It is not wise for the *señorita* to *promenade* alone. Such men as those do not know how to treat a lady. I only regret I did not see what was happening in time to save you embarrassment. It was not until you called out . . ."

Tessa, flushing, put a hand to her mouth and he paused. She'd truly made a spectacle of herself for half of Lincoln to see.

"Are you a friend of Mr. McSween's?" she asked Vincente.

"I am not his enemy, but I do not take sides in this *disputa*."

She wondered how anyone could manage to avoid being drawn into it and looked at him curiously, only to find him regarding her with open admiration.

Inside her a small glow began. There was something about Vincente Gabaldon that intrigued her. His eyes were so dark, like jet, strangely fascinating eyes . . .

She turned her head away from him. What was the matter with her, staring at a stranger like this?

"I can only thank you again for coming when you did," she said. "I assure you I won't venture out alone again."

"It has been my very great pleasure to be of assistance to the lovely *Señorita* Nesbitt."

Tess was glad to see they were approaching the McSween gate. She found his nearness unsettling.

"If I can ever be of service to you again, you have only to let me know."

"Thank you, *Señor* Gabaldon." Tessa lifted her hand from his arm, went through the gate and hurried to the house, her mind and emotions in an uproar.

If only Ezra would come home.

She was more than ever afraid there'd soon be open war between Dolan's men and Alex's. A shooting war that would last until Dolan or Alex died.

And Ezra was there somewhere with the man she'd begun to think was the most reckless and dangerous of them all.

Billy the Kid.

Chapter 7

Mark reined in the sorrel under the cottonwoods on the bank of the Rio Bonito opposite town. He sat in the darkness, listening. From somewhere upriver an owl hooted three times. Frogs, quieted by his coming, resumed their two-noted calling.

Across the river, muted by distance and the trees, he could hear men's voices. He was a little downriver from Lincoln; likely the voices came from the saloons.

Mark was almost certain no one had followed him, but he waited another few minutes before dismounting. He tied the sorrel to a sapling. He was leaving his horse a long way from where he meant to go, but it couldn't be helped—this was the only decent cover in quite a stretch.

The night was cool; summer hadn't set in completely, though it was already June. He'd deliberately waited for the dark of the moon.

That goddamned Peppin was sheriff now; he'd never

liked George Peppin. When the bastard had told him about Tessa coming to Dolan's store and being harrassed by Kilgore, it was all Mark could do to hold his temper. He'd had some respect for Brady, but he had none at all for George Peppin. It made him wonder, not for the first time, if it wasn't plain bullheadedness that kept him working for Dolan when he didn't cotton to Dolan's actions.

You might say Tunstall's death had been cancelled by the bushwhacking of Brady and Hindman, but that didn't excuse the way Dolan was harrassing McSween. Mark stuck with managing Dolan's ranch and didn't get involved in any gunplay, but there was such a thing as guilt by association.

Neither side was lily-white when it came to that.

Why had Tessa come after him? If only he'd been in town that day. As it was, he didn't get her message for over a week. And in that week, Copeland was ousted as Sheriff and Peppin put in.

There was no doubt at all that Peppin meant to get McSween by one means or another. The thought of him letting Kilgore put his hands on Tessa made Mark clench his fists. He forced himself to relax.

He'd be seeing Tessa soon if everything worked out. Excitement rose in him at the thought of holding her again. He pictured the two of them somewhere away from the Territory, lying together, Tessa's softness next to him, her golden hair like silk against his face . . .

Enough! Dreaming never got a man anywhere. Mark made his way through the cottonwoods, walking upriver. The trees thinned as he came to the ford where the spring runoff had lessened enough so that the crossing plank was back at the shallows.

Mark stood beside a clump of willow shoots, waiting to see if anyone was about, but there was no sign of it. He hurried across the stream, no more than wetting his boots where the plank sagged in the middle. He continued upriver, using what cover he could find. At the back of Wortley's Hotel a dog raced out to bark at him but didn't trail him as he went on.

He passed Schon's house without incident and approached the fence and wall surrounding the McSween house.

The north side of the adobe wall ran along the river and there was one gate in it. A high picket fence met the wall on either end and continued around to enclose the house. The fence had two gates, one to the east and one to the south, the southern gate directly in front of the house and almost on the street.

Mark stood at the northwest corner where fence met wall. He had to go in through the front gate because both the east and the north gates would get him no farther than the east wing of the house where the Shields lived with their children.

Jules and Ezra had their bedroom in the east wing, but Tessa did not. She slept in the McSween side of the house, the west wing, and all three of the Nesbitts spent their waking hours there.

Were the gates guarded? He'd heard McSween was hiding out again, in the hills near San Patricio, with most of his followers, but that didn't mean a guard wouldn't be left to protect the women and children still in the house.

Mark shrugged. He'd have to hope he spotted any guard before the man saw him. He hated to arrive like a thief in the night, but as things stood in Lincoln these days, a Dolan man couldn't go near the McSween house without being challenged. And turned back. Might even get shot if the challenger had a nervous trigger finger.

He eased along the outside of the fence and around the

corner to the front of the house. Headed for the gate. Slipped inside. Flattened himself against the fence.

Lights glowed from the windows. He could hear someone playing the piano—Jules, by the sound of it. Best not to try to get in by the front door. Someone might go by on the street and see him.

Had anyone along the street seen him enter the gate? He waited, finally pushing away from the fence and heading around the house to the back door. A metallic click froze him in his tracks.

"*Quien es?*" A man's voice demanded. "Who is it?"

Mark saw a dark shadow move in front of him. He knew the man held a gun cocked and ready.

A lie would be more dangerous than the truth.

"Halloran. Tessa Nesbitt sent for me," Mark said.

"I don't think so, *señor.*"

"She did. Ask her."

"Why you no come to front door?"

"I'm here secretly. Ask *Señorita* Nesbitt. She'll be very angry if you stop me from seeing her."

There was a silence. Finally the man ordered Mark to walk ahead of him. With the gun at his back, Mark opened the rear door and stepped into the kitchen.

Rosalita, grinding corn, jumped up, letting out a squeal when she saw the two men.

"He says Miss Tessa sent for him," the man told Rosalita in Spanish.

"She did send for me," Mark repeated in English. "I'm Mark Halloran."

Rosalita shook her head. "I know nothing, *señor.*"

The pistol muzzle jammed into Mark's back. "You tell me lies," the man snarled. "I know you now, Dolan *bastardo.*"

The kitchen door opened a little and Jules poked his head into the room.

"Leave!" Rosalita ordered. *"Vamos, pronto!"*

Jules didn't move, staring from Mark to the man holding the gun. Suddenly he flung the door wide open and rushed toward them.

"Don't shoot Mr. Halloran, Manuel," he cried. "Don't shoot my friend. *Mi amigo.*"

Manuel tried to fend off Jules and still keep his Colt trained on Mark.

"What on earth is going on?"

Everyone turned to look at Tessa who stood in the open doorway. Her eyes widened as she recognized Mark. He bowed slightly.

"I believe you wanted to see me," he said.

Mark rode south under the morning sun.

And just what the hell do you think you're doing? he asked himself. Being a hero? He snorted. A fool's more like it.

Heading into the hills around San Patricio looking for Billy the Kid and his *compañeros* was like heading into a duel blindfolded with your hands tied behind you.

"But Billy knows you," Tessa had said. "Surely he won't harm an old friend. And I'm positive if you talk to Ezra and tell him how frantic I am, he'll come back with you."

Mark sighed. That's all she'd wanted him for. To bring back Ezra who'd fallen in with the Regulators because he idolized Billy.

So much for dreaming of having Tessa in his arms once more. She hadn't even brought him into the parlor, telling him what she wanted right there in the kitchen, then urging him to leave the house.

She didn't get him out quick enough. Mark had heard that phony drawl of Rutledge's before Tessa closed the door. Rutledge was good enough to invite into the parlor, but Mark Halloran wasn't. He just did the dirty work.

Mark yanked his hat farther down on his head and scowled at an oriole that flashed across the trail in a blur of yellow.

What the hell was he doing this for?

For Ezra? He hardly knew the boy, not even as well as he knew Jules. While he wouldn't recommend Billy as a model for any youngster, he couldn't say he really cared about Ezra.

But he did care for Tessa. And she'd asked him for help.

Why hadn't she asked Rutledge? Mark grimaced. She probably had and Rutledge had bowed out gracefully, having better sense than to hunt for men who didn't want to be found.

Although it would have been a damn sight safer for Rutledge to come hunting Ezra than for a Dolan man like Mark.

He made a wide swing around the little town of San Patricio, not wanting his presence announced any sooner than it had to be. The hills west of town were pine-covered and riddled with long snaking canyons. On down a ways they rose to become mountains more than six thousand feet high. Lots of pinon pine and fir up there and maybe a few Mescaleros hunting until it was time to go back to the reservation for the government subsidy.

Somewhere in these hills Billy was camping with McSween and the Regulators. And Ezra.

Before he reached the higher hills, dust rising on the trail to the north caught Mark's eye. He was already off the trail but he climbed higher to reach the cover of a pine grove where he had a view of his back trail. He reined in and waited.

After a time a column of mounted men rode into sight. Men in uniform. Cavalry from Fort Stanton. What were they after? Apaches? The Regulators?

Mark urged his sorrel from the pines and hailed the officer leading the soldiers, then descended the hill to join them.

"Mark Halloran," he told the captain.

"Captain Carrol." The officer's voice was curt. "What's your business this way, sir?" he asked.

"I'm looking for someone who's with Alex McSween," Mark said. "Have you seen the McSween party?"

"Are you working with Sheriff Peppin?" Captain Carrol asked.

"Unofficially, yes." Mark thought the lie necessary.

"We left the sheriff and his posse near San Patricio," the captain said.

"Back at San Patricio?" Mark echoed, not wanting to admit he had no idea Peppin was anywhere about.

The captain nodded briefly. "I'm taking over the pursuit. I suggest you join Peppin."

"Which way were the McSween men headed?" Mark persisted.

"Toward the Pecos." Captain Carrol kicked his horse into a fast trot, pulling away from Mark. His men spurred after him.

So Peppin had managed to convince Colonel Dudley, the commander at Stanton, to go after McSween and the Regulators. Mark wondered how he'd managed it. Brady's killing?

What now? Was it any use to trail Carrol? If the cavalry caught up with the McSween party, Ezra would be brought back to Lincoln anyway.

Mark heard hooves pounding toward him, again from the north, and eased off the trail. A sergeant passed, riding hard after Captain Carrol.

A lagging trooper catching up? Mark shook his head. Sergeants weren't laggards as a rule. He looked after the soldiers, then kicked the sorrel into a gallop, following. He might be able to do something for Ezra if he was on hand when the Regulators were rounded up.

A half mile along the trail, Mark caught sight of blue uniforms. Dust rose as horses milled about. Mark reined in the sorrel. Damned if the troopers hadn't halted. He pulled off the trail again, not wanting the captain to spot him and wonder why he hadn't gone back to join Peppin.

To Mark's surprise, after a few minutes the entire company passed by, heading back along the trail toward Fort Stanton. Ordered back, by God, he told himself. That sergeant had carried a message from the colonel.

When they were out of sight, Mark climbed down onto the trail again and rode hard southeast, toward the Pecos. Toward the Regulators.

Ezra didn't care much for the new recruit Billy had added to their company. He was a lanky young drifter from Texas named Tom O'Folliard, who could almost outshoot Billy. McSween paid little attention to the men who guarded him, letting Billy choose whom he wanted.

O'Folliard rode alongside Billy, taking Ezra's place, cracking jokes and laughing, and Billy didn't even seem to notice Ezra wasn't there.

"You look kind of glum, Nesbitt," Charlie Bowdre said to Ezra. "Saddle sore?"

"I'm okay."

"We'll get some decent rest once we reach Chisum's,"

Bowdre went on. "Maybe get some decent grub, too. Old John's got a damn good cook."

Ezra nodded. He didn't seem to feel enthusiastic about anything since O'Folliard joined the Regulators.

"Reckon we've outrun them troopers; don't see no more dust back there," Bowdre said. He raised his voice to call to Billy. "Hey, Kid, you think they've given up?"

"Could be," Billy called back.

Ezra glanced around. There was a sharp rise to his left. If a man climbed that, he'd get a good view to the sides and the rear. He angled his horse to come up beside Billy.

"I'll go check," Ezra said. "See if anyone's tailing us."

He spurred away without waiting for an answer, his spirits on the upswing. Got to show what I can do, he thought. Got to let them know I'm as good as any man in the Regulators.

But as he began to climb the hill, he heard a horse behind him and looked over his shoulder. Saw O'Folliard.

"Billy says two scouts are better than one," O'Folliard announced as he caught up to Ezra.

Ezra scowled but said nothing, continuing to climb. Why had Billy sent O'Folliard? Didn't he trust him? Didn't Billy think he was capable of scouting a back trail without help?

To make matters worse, O'Folliard's horse, a tough little buckskin, scaled the hill quicker than Ezra's pinto and the Texan reached the summit first. He hunkered down behind an outcrop of rock and, when Ezra joined him, O'Folliard had already spotted someone.

"Looks to be alone," the Texan said.

Ezra peered along the back trail, saw a lone rider coming fast. As near as he could tell at this distance, it wasn't a trooper.

O'Folliard returned to his horse and yanked his carbine from the saddle scabbard. The gun was new, the brass shiny and the stock unscratched. O'Folliard winked at Ezra.

"Pretty, ain't it? Figured the Comanche I got this off lifted it from one of them green army recruits who can't spot an Indian till the redskin's scalping him."

"You don't mean to fire on him?" Ezra jerked his head toward the oncoming rider. "What if he's one of us?"

"I reckon you'll tell me if he is," O'Folliard said.

That's why Billy sent O'Folliard with me, Ezra told himself. He doesn't think I have the guts to shoot a man. Without warning, lines from another of Browning's poems flashed into Ezra's mind.

Our interest's on the dangerous edge of things

The honest thief, the tender murderer . . .

It came from a long poem, one that bored Ezra when his father had read it aloud during winter evenings, for he didn't quite understand what it meant. Something about a bishop explaining faith. What did church-going have to do with anything in Ezra's life?

What the hell made him remember some of the lines? A tender murderer? Didn't mean a thing as far as he was concerned. What use was poetry?

"He's getting in range," O'Folliard said, sighting on the man below.

Ezra focused his attention on the rider. Now that the man was closer, something about him seemed familiar. The horse was a sorrel, he knew that horse . . .

"Don't shoot!"

O'Folliard raised his head. "One of us?" he asked.

"I know him," Ezra temporized.

"That don't tell me nothing."

"Billy knows him, too. He's sort of a friend of Billy's."

O'Folliard eyed Ezra. "Seems like it'd be easy to say whether he's one of us or not. You been saying everything else."

"Jesus, he's only one man!" Ezra burst out. "He can't do us any harm, even if he does work for Dolan."

"So he ain't on our side." O'Folliard aimed the carbine.

"No!" Ezra flung himself at the Texan, knocking the gun from his hands, then scrambled to his feet, pulling his Colt as he faced O'Folliard.

"I'll see you dead before I let you kill Mark Halloran," Ezra snarled.

"Hey," O'Folliard protested. "You and me's working together, right?"

"Put the carbine away," Ezra ordered.

O'Folliard shrugged, eyeing the Colt. He shoved the carbine into the scabbard. "Okay, smart-ass, what now?"

Ezra took a deep breath. "We ride down and escort Halloran to Billy." He reholstered the Colt.

"And get shot for our pains."

"He won't shoot me," Ezra said, sounding more positive than he felt.

Mark did work for Dolan, after all, and no Dolan man was any damn good. Wasn't a one could be trusted.

"Then you go meet this old friend of yours," O'Folliard said. "I'll just mosey back to Billy and let him know what's coming. One more thing, boy. You don't pull a gun on me again and live to tell it."

They remounted and their horses scrambled down the hill. As O'Folliard galloped toward the Regulators, Ezra headed at a trot toward Mark, tense and nervous, but at the same time sort of pleased with himself for facing up to O'Folliard.

He hailed Mark, then stopped to wait for him, keeping his right hand hovering near the butt of his Colt.

"I've been looking for you," Mark said as he came up.

Ezra relaxed a little, seeing Mark was making no move to go for his gun.

"Here I am."

"Where you ought to be," Mark said, "is back in Lincoln."

Ezra shook his head. "I'm riding with Billy now. We're protecting McSween. I have to bring you on up to Billy so he can decide what to do about you following us."

"The only reason I'm here is to find you. I promised your sister I'd bring you back with me."

"Well, god damn it, you almost got shot, and all for nothing, cause I'm not about to desert the Regulators when they need me."

"Tessa needs you more than they do," Mark said. "Peppin and some of his friends had the nerve to insult her in the street last month. She isn't safe alone in Lincoln any more. She needs your protection."

"McSween wouldn't have left his wife in town if there was going to be trouble," Ezra said.

"There's going to be trouble."

"What's Dolan mean to do?"

"Dolan can't control those gunslingers he's hired any more than McSween controls the Regulators," Mark said. "Lincoln's got too many men on the prod—no man can control them. One of these days there'll be a hell of a shoot-out. You have a little brother in town as well as your sister. You're no good to either of them out here in the hills."

"If you don't like what Dolan's doing, how come you keep working for him?"

"I take care of his cows, not his other business."

Ezra sneered. "That's what you say."

Mark's expression didn't change. "You ready to ride back?" he asked.

As Ezra started to refuse, the sight and sound of horses coming up fast from the southeast made him pause.

It was Billy and O'Folliard.

Billy saluted Mark, grinning. "Come to join us?" he asked.

"Tessa asked me to ride after Ezra," Mark said.

Ezra flushed in anger and humiliation. Mark talked like he was still a little boy, for Christ's sake.

Billy glanced at him, then back at Mark. "Sounds like a good idea," he said. "Ain't no one protecting the women back at McSween's except Shield and he's no great hand with a gun. Ez is damn good."

"But the Regulators . . ." Ezra began.

"Old Texas Tom here can sit in for you, Ez," Billy said. "You get on back to Lincoln." He smiled and waved, then wheeled his gray and galloped away with O'Folliard.

As Ezra fell in beside Mark, headed the other way, he swallowed repeatedly, trying to get rid of a lump in his throat the size of a Mexican orange.

It was plain to see that Billy didn't want him around any more.

Just wait. He'd prove yet he was as good a man as O'Folliard. A better man.

Chapter 8

On the fourteenth of July Billy led McSween and the Regulators back to Lincoln. Ezra listened to the tales of Dolan's men attacking them while they were at Chisum's ranch near Roswell.

"Chisum's hacienda is a regular fort," Billy told Ezra. "Not a one of us got a scratch and after a couple of hours they gave up."

"You think they're on your trail now?"

Billy shrugged. "Most likely. McSween, he wanted to come home. Said he was tired of running and he was going to make a stand in his own house if it came to that."

"Men!" Alex shouted above the babble of voices. The talking died away as they all looked toward him.

"It's Sunday and I intend to lead us in prayer before we make our plans."

"Oh Lord," he intoned, "touch the hearts of our ene-

106

mies with Thy goodness and mercy that we may live to praise Thee another day."

Ezra listened, thinking it strange that Alex still persisted in hoping for peace while Dolan kept hounding him. He'd never seen a foxhunt, but Papa had described them often, and it seemed like what Dolan was doing with Alex, the fox he and his men harried from place to place.

Except Alex had Billy and the Regulators to protect him.

After the "amen" the men split up. Alex's Mexican supporters, twenty-five strong, took refuge in Montano's store next to the courthouse, across the street east of the McSween house.

Farther east, on the outskirts of town, another fifteen men holed up at Ellis' place. That left fifteen, handpicked by Billy to guard the McSween house.

"You know, Billy, there's fifty-six of us, counting me," Ezra said. "Why don't we get together and take over the town? I bet we could do it, 'cause there ain't many Dolan men back from the Pecos yet."

"I wanted to," Billy said. "McSween wouldn't hear of it. He's the boss. Come on, let's get at fortifying the place."

The house, like the rest of those in Lincoln, was of adobe thick enough to stop a bullet. Ezra organized Jules and the Shield children into a squad to fetch and carry supplies to the men. Rosalita, Tessa, Susie and Elizabeth Shield huddled together apprehensively as the men barricaded windows with adobe bricks, piled dirt-filled bags against outer doorways and drilled gunholes through walls.

"This is war," Ezra told Tessa. "We may have to withstand a siege."

She stared at him a moment, then straightened and turned to the other women. "We must help," she said.

"First of all, Rosalita, is there enough food to feed our army?"

"I don't think so," Rosalita said.

"We must bring extra food from Tunstall's store into the house," Tessa said. "We'll also need extra water stored inside. And more blankets."

By Monday morning the McSween house was well nigh impregnable.

In the early afternoon, Sheriff Peppin sent Deputy Long to the house with a demand that ten of the men, including McSween and Billy, surrender.

As Long stood by the gate, shouting out the names, Billy nudged Ezra.

"Watch this," he said. He sighted along his Winchester that was thrust through one of the gunholes.

The rifle cracked. Long's hat flew off, a bullet through its crown. Two other men fired, deliberately missing, kicking up dust at Long's feet. He turned and hurried out of range, disappearing from sight.

"I got to talk to McSween again," Billy said.

Ezra followed him to where Alex sat at his desk, Bible open in front of him.

"Like I told you before, we can take the bastards," Billy said to him. "O'Folliard slipped through town early this morning scouting, on account of they don't know him around here. He says there's only a few families in the houses—everyone else has skedaddled. And Dolan's maybe got ten men. Most of Peppin's posse's at San Patricio looking for us there.

"You can bet Peppin's sent for the posse. And those gunslingers from the Pecos'll be here sooner or later. What we ought to do is hit Dolan before their reinforcements get here or before he tries to call in the army again. We can wipe 'em out like a nest of rattlesnakes if we do it now."

Alex hesitated. "No, I think we ought to stay inside," he said finally. "Tom may be mistaken about the number of Dolan men in town. Besides, we're defenders, not attackers."

"I think we ought to take them on while we can," Billy persisted.

Alex touched the Bible. " 'Vengeance belongeth unto me . . . saith the Lord.' "

"Dolan thinks vengeance belongs to him," Billy said. "You got to fight fire with fire."

"We won't leave the house," Alex told him.

Billy shrugged and turned away, for once not smiling.

An hour or so later, a fusillade of rifle shots made all the men spring to their gunports, Winchesters ready.

"Some of the boys are trying to get over here from Montano's store," O'Folliard said, peering from the front of the house. "There's Dolan men hidden in that old Mexican tower the other side of Tunstall's store taking pot shots at them."

Everyone crowded around him to see.

"Back to your posts," Billy cried. "Peppin could walk right in the back with all of us gawping from the front like this."

Men on the east side of McSween's house poured a stream of lead at the old *torreon* where the Dolan men were holed-up. In return, bullets thudded into the adobe walls of the house. Some smashed windows and glass fragments flew between the protective bricks to scatter over the floor.

"Oh Lord, will You not put a stop to this hatred?" Alex prayed. "Will You not enlighten the sinful hearts of our foes before blood is spilled?"

"Not much chance of that," Billy muttered to Ezra.

The McSween men retreated back into Montano's store and the firing eased, finally stopping. Day passed into evening and then into night.

On Tuesday sharpshooters from both sides, stationed on rooftops, fired every time they saw someone make a move to leave a building.

By Wednesday the children, except for Jules, complained about being inside for yet another hot day. Jules sat listlessly on his bed, and when Tessa felt his forehead, she knew immediately why he was so quiet. He was running a fever.

As the day went on, Jules began to vomit repeatedly until at last he was bringing up only mucus flecked with blood. By late afternoon Tessa made up her mind Jules had to be seen by Dr. Ealy, who lived next door in Tunstall's store with his family and Susan Gates. Ezra offered to carry his brother over, but Tessa shook her head.

"Dolan's men aren't likely to shoot at a woman," she said. "They would at you. I'll take him."

"She's right," Billy told Ezra. "It's safer for her than for any of us men." He turned to Tessa. "Go out the front so they can see clear you're a woman."

Tessa picked up Jules who lay limp and semi-conscious in her arms. Ezra opened the front door and she stepped into the long shadows of early evening. The door thudded shut behind her. The town seemed eerily silent; not even a dog barked.

She hurried into the road and walked as fast as she could toward Tunstall's store. She knew there were still Dolan men in the old *torreon*, the stone tower, on the other side of the store. Were their rifles trained on her, following her? She half-expected to hear a shot, the zing of a bullet.

She breathed easier when she reached the store porch. A

moment later the door opened and Dr. Ealy took Jules from her arms.

"We saw you coming with him," the doctor said. "Has he been shot?"

"No, a fever and vomiting until blood came." Tessa bit her lip as she watched Dr. Ealy lay Jules atop a table. Her brother was so white and still that he almost looked dead.

Dr. Ealy finished examining him and turned to her. "He'll be all right after I get some fluid into him by clyster. You leave him here with us tonight and I'll keep an eye on him. Stay yourself, if you like."

"Thank you. Maybe it would be best."

Thursday morning Jules managed to eat a thin rice gruel prepared by Susan Gates and kept it down. Though still whey-faced and droopy, he was obviously improving.

"I'm so happy he's better," Susan told her.

"I'll take him back if the doctor agrees," Tessa said. "I haven't seen him or any of the Ealys this morning. Surely they didn't leave the building?"

"Oh, but they did. The doctor was asked to go and treat Ben Ellis yesterday for a neck wound. He just couldn't, because the men in the tower shot at him every time he tried to leave here. Then he saw that you weren't fired on, so this morning he took Mrs. Ealy and the children with him up to Ellis' place. My heart was in my mouth watching them, but it was all right. No one fired a single shot."

As Susan spoke, a rifle cracked. Both women sprang to their feet and raced to the window. There was no one in the road, but when Tessa hurried to look from a back window, she drew in her breath.

"Look, Susan!"

A man lay sprawled in the field between Tunstall's store and the tower.

"Oh, dear God, it's not the doctor, is it?" Susan cried.

"No, no, you can see it's not."

"Is he dead?"

"I think I saw one of his hands move."

The sun was rising higher, bright and hot. How long could a wounded man survive in July heat with no water, no medical attention? Tessa wondered.

"We have to go out and get him, Susan. Bring him into the store. Dr. Ealy will be back sooner or later."

Susan stared at her.

"We'll roll him in a blanket and each take an end. If he's too heavy, we can drag him."

Susan nodded, her face pale but determined.

As the two women eased the wounded man onto the blanket after removing his gunbelt, he groaned and opened his eyes briefly. Tessa, who'd thought at first he was a stranger, tensed, recognizing him as the man who'd humiliated her when Peppin halted her near Dolan's store. They were rescuing an enemy.

"What's the matter?" Susan asked as Tessa stopped helping her. She cast an uneasy glance at the stone *torreon* where Dolan sharpshooters waited.

"Nothing." There was no point in making Susan more upset than she already was. Tessa forced herself to pull the blanket ends nearest her together.

He was a stocky man, heavy, and hard to pull across the ground toward Tunstall's. Perspiration beaded Tessa's face and trickled between her breasts by the time they reached the nearest door which led to the part of the store where Susan and the Ealys lived.

Susan hurried to fetch cloths and a basin of water, then started to wash the blood from the man's head, but Tessa, after she'd hidden his Colt and gun belt in a hall cupboard, couldn't bring herself to help. She stood back watching Susan.

It was all very well to be a good Samaritan, but she didn't want to touch the red-haired man.

He opened his eyes and immediately reached a hand toward his head.

"Don't," Susan said mildly. "You've been wounded."

He paid no attention, pushing away her arm and probing his wound.

"Just a crease," he muttered, wincing. He tried to sit up.

"I think you ought to rest," Susan objected.

He seemed to really see her for the first time. "You're the Gates woman," he said, lying back. He glanced from side to side and spotted Tessa. His eyes widened.

"Yes, I'm Susan Gates."

He looked back at Susan. "Hank Kilgore," he muttered. "How'd I get in here?"

"We saw you lying in the field to the east. You'd been shot."

Frowning, Hank made another attempt to sit up. Susan helped him. He drew up his knees, put his arms about them and leaned forward, head down.

"Hurts something fierce."

"I'll see if I can find some opium," Susan said.

Tessa hurried after her as Susan left the room.

"Mr. Kilgore is one of Dolan's men," she whispered to Susan. "And not a very nice one."

"I can't see that it makes a difference. It's our duty to take care of the injured."

"I don't trust him. I don't trust any Dolan man." Tessa bit her lip as soon as she'd spoken, for Susan knew very well that Mark Halloran had brought back Ezra at Tessa's request.

"I especially can't trust Mr. Kilgore," she went on. "He . . ."

Jules called to Tessa from the room where he lay on a cot. She broke off to go to him."

"I want my own bed," he complained. "It's lonesome here."

Tessa could see for herself that Jules was much better but she didn't dare leave Susan alone in the store with Hank Kilgore.

"We'll wait for Dr. Ealy to return," she told him. "If he says it's all right, I'll take you back to Uncle Alex's."

Tessa stayed with Jules for a time, telling him the story he liked best, about how his great-great-grandfather Nesbitt, fighting for England in the war against Spain, had saved his company from death by a daring ruse.

Jules sighed when she finished. "When I grow up, I'm going to be a brave soldier, too."

"You don't have to be a soldier to be brave."

Jules nodded. "Ezra is brave," he said. "Like Billy."

Tessa frowned but said nothing. She hoped she wouldn't have to dissuade Jules from tagging after Billy as Ezra did. She was so tired of shooting and killing. Was there no place in the West where people lived in peace with one another?

Tessa sought out Susan, found her leaving the room where Hank Kilgore lay on the floor.

"I think the opium is putting him to sleep," Susan whispered.

Tessa peered in at him. He looked harmless enough, curled onto his side, eyes closed. And Susan was right. They couldn't have left him in the field, even if she'd known beforehand who he was.

The Ealys returned in the early afternoon and the doctor got Hank onto a chair to examine his head.

"Most likely a brain concussion from the bullet striking

against your skull," he told him. "That's what knocked you out. You'll have a headache for a day or two."

"Funny thing, Doc, I can't rightly recall getting shot, don't even remember why I was in that field."

"Don't worry about it. That often happens with head injuries. You'll be all right."

"I'm obliged to you," Hank said. "And to the ladies."

Tessa didn't like the way his eyes rested speculatively first on Susan, then on her.

"He works for Mr. Dolan," she told the doctor.

Hank nodded. "That's right, I do. But it ain't safe for me to go outside, what with McSween's boys in that warehouse in back of here and them others in Montano's store across the way. No, I reckon you're stuck with me, but I don't aim to cause no trouble."

Tessa mistrusted every word he said. She was glad she'd had sense enough to hide his pistol before he regained consciousness.

"You could leave after dark," she said. "The moon's not half-full."

Again he eyed her. She didn't care for his probing look.

"I'm a mite dizzy at the moment," Hank said, leaning his head against the back of the chair he sat in. He closed his eyes.

Dr. Ealy shook his head at Tessa and she turned away. After all, Hank Kilgore did have a concussion and could well be dizzy and in pain. Why did she feel so strongly he was faking?

Jules walked into the room.

"Can we go home now?" he asked.

Dr. Ealy put his hand on Jules' head. "You look fine to me, young man."

"I'll take him home then," Tessa said. "Thank you, Doctor, for helping Jules. I was so . . ."

In a whirlwind of motion, Hank Kilgore sprang from the chair, knocked Jules aside and grabbed Tessa from behind, hooking his arm about her neck. In his other hand he brandished a knife.

It was in his boot, Tessa thought confusedly. *He had a knife in a boot sheath. I never thought to look for one.* Jules sobbed, but Hank held her so tightly she couldn't turn her head to see if he was all right. She could hardly breathe.

"I'm taking her with me so they won't shoot," Hank growled. "You don't try to stop me and I won't hurt her."

He tightened his grip on Tessa's throat so that she gagged. Black specks danced before her eyes.

"Where's my gun?" he hissed into her ear.

"If you know, tell him," Dr. Ealy advised.

"Jules?" she managed to choke out, for she could still hear him crying.

"He's all right," the doctor said. "I'll take care of him."

"The gun," Hank said.

"Hall cupboard," she gasped.

Hank pulled her after him as he backed through the door. Without releasing her, he yanked open the cupboard. He bent to thrust the knife back into the boot sheath, then quickly pulled the Colt from his gunbelt, leaving the belt on the cupboard shelf.

He pushed her ahead of him through the front door of the store into the road. The sudden glare of the sun and his arm still tight around her neck made her stumble. Hank yanked her to her feet.

"Keep walking," he warned.

The fear he might pick her up in his arms and carry her made her try to stay on her feet as they made their way west toward Dolan's store.

She saw no one, but she knew men from both sides watched them walk along the road under the lowering sun and pulled unwillingly close to Hank Kilgore.

Someone will shoot, she told herself. Billy or one of the other expert marksmen. Can't they shoot and miss me?

Not a shot was fired as they passed by McSween's, then Stanley's and Mills'. They came even with the Wortley Hotel. Dolan's store was across the street, but Kilgore turned toward the hotel instead.

He lifted her off her feet and carried her the last few steps. Someone opened the door and he thrust her inside, setting her on her feet. She put her hand up to her neck, drawing in a deep breath.

The room was crowded with men.

Hank reached for her wrist, holding her firmly as everyone began to talk at once.

". . . can't keep a woman captive."

"Wish I'd of got myself one like her."

"McSween's filly . . ."

Tessa looked desperately from one bearded face to another, hoping against hope she'd see Mark.

He wasn't in the room.

"Hell, Hank, you're gonna have to let her go," a man with a drooping black mustache said. "She ain't no dance-hall floozie. It don't look good, one of us kidnapping a lady like her."

"She's McSween's whore," Hank said. "That don't make her a lady in my book."

Tessa swallowed, feeling herself flush under the hot and avid stares of the men nearest her. She straightened her shoulders, then turned to glare at Hank.

"Is this how you thank someone who saves your life?" she demanded.

He blinked. Before he could speak, she rushed on.

"I demand to be released this instant. I tried to help you, not harm you. You have no right to bring me here."

"Hush up!" Hank snapped.

"Jim Dolan ain't gonna like . . ." the man with the mustache began.

"You shut up, too," Hank told him. He pushed through the men, pulling Tessa after him.

When she saw he meant to take her up a flight of stairs, she began to struggle. Hank lifted her onto his shoulder and carried her up the steps. He threw open a door into a sour-smelling room where dirty covers trailed off a bed. He shut the door. Locked it. Threw her onto the bed.

Tessa scrambled to her feet. He shoved her backwards onto the bed again. She kicked at him. He grabbed her feet, thrust her skirts up and wrenched her legs apart, wedging his body in-between them.

She struck his face, her fingernails clawing, and he slapped her hard, twice.

"You gonna be nice or you gonna fight?" he asked. "You want to fight, the next time I'll use my fist."

"Let me go!" she cried.

"Afterwards," he said. "You can go afterwards."

He wrenched at the bodice of her gown and buttons popped off as it opened. He hooked two fingers in her camisole and ripped it from her breasts. His eyes glittered as he looked at her exposed body.

"No!" she screamed, trying to twist away from him. "No!"

Chapter 9

Mark came out of the back room of Dolan's store where he'd been closeted with Jim Dolan. Damn it, he'd ride the hell out of town this minute if it wasn't for those marksmen of McSween's.

He didn't want any part of what was going on and he'd just told Jim he didn't mean to use his gun on any man. He'd told Jim, too, he ought to get things quieted down, to stop the shooting.

"You tell McSween that," Jim had growled. "He started this."

Mark didn't believe him, had said so and had been called a stupid son-of-a-bitch.

To hell with both sides.

Mark stalked over to the barricaded window at the front of the store. Willis Jones turned from his gunhole.

"You missed all the excitement," he told Mark.

Mark shrugged.

119

"Kilgore took a woman into the hotel."

"I'm not interested in Kilgore's *putas*," Mark snapped, turning away.

"She wasn't no whore. She was a pretty little blonde. Looked like that girl who lives with McSween."

Mark whirled back, grabbed Willis' shirt front. "What the hell are you talking about?"

"Hey, let me loose," Willis protested.

"The woman," Mark demanded. "Who was she?"

"Don't know. She looked like the blonde from McSween's."

"Kilgore took her into the hotel?"

"Yeah."

Mark let go of Willis and strode to the front door.

"Wait!" Willis called. "You'll get shot, Halloran. They got men posted . . ."

Mark flung open the front door, slammed it shut behind him and ran zigzagging across the street toward Wortley's Hotel.

He heard a rifle crack. Another. Dust puffed ahead of him. More shots. Something stung his arm. Three more steps and he was inside the hotel.

"Jesus, man, you're bleeding," Mathews told him as he closed the door. "Your arm . . ."

Mark scarcely heard him, pushing past, looking from one side of the room to the other. He saw only men.

"Where is she?" he demanded.

"Who?"

"Tessa Nesbitt. Where is she?"

Mathews grinned. "Old Hank carried her upstairs a while ago. Reckon he's having hisself a bang-up good time." He nudged Mark, laughing.

Mark raced for the stairs, took them two at a time, reached the top, flung open the first door he came to.

A stubble-faced man snored drunkenly on a bed.

Not bothering to close the door, Mark strode to the next room, slammed the door open.

Empty.

The third door was locked.

"Kilgore!" Mark shouted.

No answer. He hesitated, was starting on when he heard a woman's muffled scream from behind the locked door.

Mark raised his foot and slammed it against the door. The heavy wood resisted his kick. The corridor was too narrow to give him room to run at it. He drew his Colt and blasted the lock.

The door swung open.

Kilgore stood beside the bed, gaping at Mark, a knife in his hand. Blood dripped from the blade.

Redness clouded Mark's vision. He thrust the Colt into the holster as he went for Kilgore, kicking the knife from his hand, knocking the man to the floor, fingers gripping his throat.

Kill. Kill the bastard.

A woman called his name over and over. He could barely hear her voice above the thrum of rage that blotted out sound.

"No, Mark, please. Mark!"

Someone was tugging at his arm. He came to partial awareness.

St. Louis. Brendon York's fat neck under his fingers. Kill Brendon. Kill him like the murdering sneak he was . . .

"Mark, he's dead! Stop!"

Tessa's voice. Tessa didn't belong in St. Louis. Mark blinked and his vision cleared. He let her pull his hands away from Brendon's throat.

No, not Brendon. Mark stared down at the mottled face. Hank Kilgore.

Tessa was on her knees next to Mark, clutching at his arm, still calling his name.

He rose to his feet, pulling her up with him.

"The knife," he said. "Are you hurt?"

"I stabbed him with that knife," she said, her eyes widening with remembered horror. "I pulled it out of his boot and shoved it into his side. Then he—he stood up and grabbed the knife and . . ." She put her hand to her mouth. "After that he meant to kill me."

Mark saw her disheveled hair, her torn dress. He clenched his fists.

"He tried to—to force me, Mark. That's why I grabbed his knife." She reached for him, burying her face against his chest. "Oh, Mark, it's so dreadful," she sobbed. "Take me home. Please take me home."

He held her close, stroking her hair. At his feet, Kilgore groaned.

Mark turned his head to look at him. Color had seeped back into Kilgore's face. Blood stained his shirt on the right side.

Mark felt both relieved and angry that he hadn't killed the man. Not that Kilgore deserved to live any more than Brendon York had. Still, Mark had made a vow seven years ago he'd never take another life except in self-defense.

The Wortley was no place for Tessa. Kilgore might be out of commission, but the hotel was filled with men Mark didn't trust.

Come to that, he didn't trust Jim Dolan any more either.

"You're arm's bleeding, Mark," Tessa said, pulling away to look at him.

"A scratch. We've got to get out of here, Tessa. I'll see you to McSween's."

The men downstairs stared at Mark and Tessa, but no

one tried to stop them when he pushed open the front door and they stepped into the street.

Someone shouted to him from Dolan's store as he headed east along the road, Tessa pressed close to him, her arm in his.

He ignored the shout, tried not to think of the Winchesters aimed at them.

When they neared McSween's house, Tessa said, ''Thank God you're on our side now.''

''I don't know if your side is in the right,'' he said, ''but I'm damn sure Dolan's in the wrong.''

Inside the house, Mark confronted McSween and the Kid.

''Dolan's convinced Peppin to send for the army,'' Mark told them. ''Colonel Dudley's been trying to find a reason to help Dolan and my bet is he'll come riding in with troopers by tomorrow.''

Billy and McSween eyed one another.

''Dudley hates your guts,'' Billy said to McSween. ''We can't fight the army.''

''I'd advise getting out of town tonight, under cover of darkness,'' Mark said.

''I'm through running,'' Alex said grimly. ''A man's house is his castle and I'll defend mine.''

Mark nodded. He understood how McSween felt. There was a time to run and a time to fort up and fight for what was yours.

O'Folliard, who'd come up to stand behind Billy, asked, ''How do you know this turncoat's telling you the truth?''

''Well now,'' Billy said, ''Mark and me rode the river together awhile back and he ain't never lied to me yet.''

O'Folliard shrugged and turned away.

''I expected to see Rutledge here,'' Mark said.

Billy grinned. "Seems like he's one sinner who gets religion when the shooting starts, except the church he picks is out of town. Seems he had important business in Santa Fe."

Ezra sauntered up and Mark resisted the impulse to raise his eyebrows. The boy had Billy's walk down pat and even tied his kerchief at the same rakish angle as Billy's. Only the fact that Ezra didn't have buckteeth made his smile different from Billy's.

"Glad to have you join the outfit," Ezra said. "Knew you'd change your mind some day."

"I'd feel better about it if you and Jules and Tessa were out of this house," Mark said.

Ezra's smile faded. "Jules is already over with the Ealys. Maybe Tess and the other women ought to leave, I won't argue that. But I aim to stay here as long as I'm needed. Right, Billy?"

"I can always count on Ez," Billy said.

Ezra beamed. "Always!" he said fervently.

Mark didn't see Tessa that evening, except briefly when she helped the other women serve the supper. He watched her, and when their eyes met, Mark felt his heart leap in his chest.

When the army gets this damn feud settled, he told himself, I have to do something about Tessa. Have to straighten out my past so I have a name to offer her. Lies aren't for Tessa.

If the army does settle anything. And if the past can ever be righted.

At ten-thirty the next morning, Colonel Dudley rode into Lincoln at the head of forty soldiers, both officers and men. He brought not only cavalry and infantry but a Gatling gun and a mountain howitzer.

He halted the troops in front of the Wortley Hotel and spoke to Sheriff Peppin, then proceeded east and set up camp in a field across from Montano's store, between Ellis' and McSween's.

Ezra, peering from a gunport, announced, "They've got the cannon pointed at Montano's. Reckon they're going to blast it?"

"Whatever happens, for God's sake don't shoot a soldier," McSween warned. "We've no quarrel with them and we'll really be in for it if one of them is even wounded, much less killed."

Men crowded to the ports to watch as the twenty-five pro-McSween Mexicans in the Montano house filed out the front door and trudged east down the road, past the army camp.

"Going for their horses at Ellis'." Billy said. "Hard to face a cannon."

"The men at Ellis' will leave next," Mark predicted.

"Not Bowdre," Billy said. "Middleton and Skurlock's there, too. They won't give up any more than I would."

During the night, some of the men at McSween's had slipped over to Ellis'. Manuel and Rosalita had gone with them. Ezra counted how many there were left in the house. Thirteen men, but Mark had no rifle with him, just a Colt, and Alex didn't shoot at all. Three women, five children.

The lookout on the roof was the first to spot the men riding from Ellis' to cross the Rio Bonito.

"More than just the Mexicans leaving," he reported to Billy. "They've all gone. Bowdre, too; I'd know that old hat of his anywhere."

"Here comes Peppin, bold as brass," O'Folliard said a few minutes later. "I reckon I could pop him off . . ."

"No!" McSween ordered. "Hold your fire. I can see soldiers behind him."

"Ain't gonna hit none of them black bastards," O'Folliard muttered. "Just Peppin."

"Don't shoot," McSween repeated.

Peppin halted some yards from the house, the soldiers stopping behind him. Deputy Turner, with five of Peppin's posse, came on, turned in the gate and walked to the door.

"I hold a warrant for the arrest of Alexander McSween," he called. "Come out, McSween."

"Yeah? Well, we got warrants for some of you," Billy shouted back."

"Damn it then, come out and serve them!" Turner called.

"A bullet's the only warrant I mean to serve," Billy replied.

McSween, who'd said nothing, sighed when he saw Turner turn away and walk back to where Peppin waited. The sheriff, his men and the soldiers all withdrew from the road.

"I'm not giving myself up to Peppin," McSween said. "It's certain death if I do."

"Then I think we ought to get the women and children to safety," Mark said. "The house is bound to be attacked."

"Wait," McSween said, sitting down at his desk. "I'll write an appeal to Colonel Dudley. Surely he won't let his men stand by while Dolan tries to force us out."

"Send the note if you want," Billy said. "Can't do any harm."

McSween handed his note to Minnie, one of the Shield children, and sent her to the army camp two houses away. She brought back a reply from the colonel's adjutant, informing McSween that Colonel Dudley refused to correspond with him in any way.

McSween sat at his desk chewing his lip. "I'll try once

more," he said. "I'll offer to give myself up to Dudley but to no other."

At noon, Minnie brought back an answer from the colonel's adjutant.

"Colonel Dudley wishes me to inform you he has no authority to accept your surrender to him, that he is here solely to protect the women and children."

"Dolan's men are surrounding the house," Billy reported as McSween sat staring at the reply. "They've holed up in Stanley's across the road and now they're slipping into Mills' and Chavez's houses west of us. We can't get a clear shot at them on account of those damn soldiers all over the place."

A child in the east wing screamed. Seconds later Elizabeth Shield cried, "Fire! Fire!"

As men rushed from the west wing to the east wing, shots cracked from the warehouse by Tunstall's store, were answered by rifle fire so close it sounded like it came from directly outside the house. Billy paused, then turned back to the west wing, followed by Ezra.

A fusillade of rifle fire popped as Billy and Ezra got their own Winchesters in position. Ezra knew Coe, Brown and Smith were in the warehouse, having gone over from Montano's two nights before. McSween men. But someone was shooting back at the three of them from the McSween stable to the northwest.

It had to be Dolan men. They must have slipped into the stable unseen by mingling with the soldiers patrolling the town.

The acrid smell of burning wood mixed with the sweet stink of kerosene hung heavy in the room.

"Seems like that east wing fire's pretty bad to make so much smoke," Ezra said.

"Wind's from the east," Billy reminded him. "Blowing smoke this way."

Ezra nodded. It was the wood in an adobe house that burned. Flooring, rafters, doors, windows. The fire would be spreading slowly, were it not for that damn east wind fanning the flames back against the house.

O'Folliard ran into the room. "That fire was set outside the east wing kitchen door," he told them. "We got it out, but we used up all the water."

Billy and Ezra looked at one another. Tendrils of smoke continued to drift into the parlor. With one accord they dashed for the west wing kitchen.

Flames licked through the charred wood of the kitchen's back door.

"Son-of-a-bitch!" Billy exclaimed.

"I'll tend to this fire," Ezra said. He yanked bricks away from a window, opened it and started to climb out. The fire was blazing against the back wall of ths house. A bullet whistled past his head and buried itself in the adobe. A second bullet clipped his pants leg. He ducked back inside.

"It's those Dolan bastards in the stable," he said. "We'll have one hell of a time getting past their bullets to put out the fire."

Billy stared at the flames. "Better here than in the east wing," he muttered. "The wind's in our favor. It'll take a long time for this fire to burn us out. Bound to be night before the house is gone. When it's dark, we can make a break for the river."

"Give up, you mean?" Ezra asked.

"Get away, I mean."

Ezra looked at Billy for a moment, then nodded. There'd be no choice but to flee or surrender if they were burned out.

"I'll tell Tess to get the women and children ready to leave," Ezra said. "They'll have to go over to the Ealys."

Susie McSween refused to go, clinging to her husband. "I won't leave you," she cried.

"Please go with your sister and the others," he said. "I want you safe."

Tessa put her arm around Susie. "Elizabeth needs you to help with the children," she said.

Tears in her eyes, Susie left Alex. As they gathered the Shield children, the tempo of shooting increased. Bullets thudded into the adobe walls.

"Down," Tessa ordered the children, dropping to her hands and knees.

They crawled to the front door where Susie stood up and opened it, exposing herself to the unseen Dolan gunmen. Ezra, watching, held his breath.

Susie stepped into the yard, walked quickly through the gate and into the street, followed by her sister and the children. Tessa brought up the rear. Rifles cracked but no bullets came near them as they hurried to Tunstall's store. When they were safe inside, Ezra let out his breath in relief.

Glass shattered as another window was hit. Ezra sprang back to his post. Sometime later he was startled to see Tessa and Susie back in the house.

"Alex, I'm going to appeal to Colonel Dudley," Susie said. "If he's here to protect women and children, he's certainly not doing so. I can't believe he won't listen to me. Why, this is murder, pure and simple! How can he allow such a thing?"

"You can try, Susie," McSween said. "I don't have much hope."

Susie left by the front door.

"Why did you come back?" Ezra asked Tessa. "It isn't safe.

"Susie's so brave. I couldn't let her come alone. Besides, you're here."

Ezra started to answer, then saw her glance at Mark who was frowning at her. She wasn't saying so, but she'd returned because Mark was here.

"How's Jules?" Ezra asked.

"He's fine," she said. "Colonel Dudley is having soldiers move the Ealys and the Shields out of the store to a safer place. Juan Patron's house, I think. Susan Gates is taking Jules along."

"You ought to go with them."

"Maybe it won't be necessary if the colonel listens to Susie."

Ezra shook his head. "He's against us."

Susie said the same thing a half-hour later when she returned to the burning house.

"He's a cruel and vindictive man!" she cried. "Heartless. I do believe he hates me as well as Alex."

The rattle of rifles was all but continuous as bullets thunked into the walls, penetrated through doors and smashed windows. The polished wood of the piano was splintered and gashed. Bullets plinked when they hit the strings.

The fire had eaten through the kitchen, and the parlor was buring before the men shifted their base of operations into the east wing. McSween sat with his head in his hands, seemingly oblivious to the bullets zinging past him.

"He's given up," Ezra told himself. He didn't realize he'd spoken out loud until Mark answered him.

"More likely, worn out," Mark said.

"You all heard what Mrs. McSween had to say about the colonel," Billy called out. "So we know where we stand, We got to stick it out till dark. If we run fast, we can make it across the yard and down the river bank without getting hit."

"No!"

Everyone turned to look at Ignacio Gonzalez. He'd been wounded in the arm early that morning. "I want to surrender," he muttered.

"You damn coward!" Billy cried. "I'll see you in hell before any of us surrender. We're going to stick here until dark. Brace up, damn you."

Billy turned to Susie. "Excuse me, ma'am," he said, "but a dress ain't very good to make a run in. You and Tess had best go now."

"I want to stay with Alex," Susie protested.

Billy shook his head. "It may cost some of us our lives to look after you when we make a run for the river. I can't risk that. You'll go now."

Susie embraced her husband. Tessa hurried over and hugged Ezra. She looked at Mark, hesitated, then Susie reached for her hand and Tessa went with her.

By sunset the men were crowded into the last two rooms. Smoke choked them.

"Going to be another hour before it's dark enough to make our move," Billy said. "Here's the plan. Me and three or four of the best shots'll run out and keep firing while we make for the gate in the plank fence to the east. While they're busy shooting at us, the rest of you run for the gate in the adobe wall to the north."

He looked from one face to the other, his blue eyes bright in his smoke-begrimed face. "Is that clear?"

Ezra thought he'd never seen any man with such courage and daring. He made up his mind he'd be with Billy on that first run, whether or not Billy chose him.

He'd be beside Billy, drawing the enemy's fire, risking his life to save the others. A thrill of fear shot through him as he thought of Dolan's men, hiding all around the burning house waiting for them to make a break. Waiting to kill them.

Ezra clenched his jaw. Damn it, he wouldn't be scared! If anyone could cheat death, that man was Billy Bonney.

Chapter 10

Thirteen men jammed together in the hot and smoky east wing kitchen, the only room of the McSween house left unburned. Outside, the darkness gradually deepened. Ezra figured it must be almost nine o'clock.

Billy pushed through the door and eased it open.

"French, O'Folliard, Morris, Nesbitt," he called out. "Follow me!"

He picked me! Ezra thought, tense with anticipation. His fear had passed. He watched Billy dart through the open kitchen door. Waited impatiently while French, O'Folliard and Morris followed. Dashed through himself, firing as he ran. Raced across the yard as bullets zipped by him.

Someone ahead of him, Morris, he thought, grunted and fell heavily. Ezra ran on, knowing it was sure death to stop. Rifles cracked. Flashes of flame from the darkness to the east located the marksmen.

Through the east gate, across the field. Ezra plunged into the underbrush along the river bank, heard men running ahead of him across the nearly dry bed of the Rio Bonito. He crossed and climbed the far bank. Ducked behind the shelter of a half-ruined adobe.

The shooting quickened. He heard Billy curse and ran toward him.

O'Folliard was with Billy. Also French.

"Morris got it," Ezra said.

"If McSween and the others didn't make their break right on our heels," Billy said, "then they're getting it, too. We can't wait around to see. *Vamos!*"

Tessa, sitting on the ground outside the Patron house, held the sobbing Susie to her breast.

"Like a dog!" Susie gasped. "They shot Alex like a dog. Oh, I can't bear it . . ."

Tessa stroked Susie's hair and looked toward Tunstall's store where, despite the darkness, triumphant shouts and the sound of smashing wood left no doubt in her mind that Dolan's men had broken into the store and were looting it. Nothing was left of the McSween house but part of the adobe walls and glowing rubble.

The firing had stopped less than an hour ago and, shortly after, George Washington had come to Patron's with word that Alex had been killed. Susie, hysterical, had to be restrained by force from rushing to find her husband's body.

"Come back inside," Tessa murmured. "There's nothing you can do tonight. Come inside."

As she persuaded the grief-stricken Susie to her feet and into Patron's house, Tessa tried not to think that Mark or Ezra might be lying somewhere in the night, dead, like Alex.

In the morning one of the Shield boys came into the bedroom where Tessa sat beside Susie's bed.

"Aunt Susie, Sheriff Peppin wants to know—" he swallowed and went on—"how you want to bury Uncle Alex. And Mr. Morris. He's dead, too."

Susie sat up in bed. "You tell the sheriff not to lay one finger on either of them!"

Her nephew gulped, nodding, and retreated.

"I want to go to Alex, Tessa," Susie said.

"You can't. It isn't safe. Lincoln is controlled by Dolan now and Colonel Dudley said himself that he won't answer for our safety if we leave this house. Send George Washington. Nobody will bother him."

Susie lay back. "Maybe you're right. I mean to stay alive if for no other reason than to avenge Alex's death."

Alexander McSween and his law clerk, Harvey Morris, were buried that day beside John Tunstall in the field behind the store. Dr. Ealy said a few words over the grave, then hurried the women back to Patron's house.

In the evening, Ealy and his family, Susan Gates and Elizabeth Shield and her children went with the soldiers to Fort Stanton when Colonel Dudley withdrew from Lincoln. Susie McSween refused to go and Tessa hadn't the heart to leave her alone. Jules stayed behind, too, for Tessa couldn't bear to part with him.

She knew Mark and Ezra had escaped from the burning house since only three other bodies had been found—two McSween men, both Mexicans, and one Dolan man. But when would she see either her brother or Mark again? They were fugitives now; the town belonged to their enemies.

By September the situation was worse than ever. After an unknown assailant shot through a window at Susie one evening, Susie and her sister decided to move, with the children, to Las Vegas for safety.

"You must come with us," Susie said to Tessa.

Tessa shook her head.

"But what will you do?"

"Since the Ealys and Susan Gates have returned east," Tessa said, "no one's left to teach the town children their lessons. I've been thinking I might do that."

"I wish you'd go with me," Susie said.

"I'll miss you," Tessa told her, tears in her eyes. Susie was very dear to her. But she couldn't leave Lincoln not knowing what had become of Ezra. And of Mark. They'd expect to find her here when it was safe to come looking. And once Susie was gone, Tessa thought she'd be safe enough.

"I'm not abandoning the fight," Susie said. "I'll be back. Those murderers haven't heard the last of me!"

Rosalita's widowed sister, Maria Zamora, took Tessa and Jules into her home. Tessa cleaned the vacant one-room adobe that had been used for a school, nailed an announcement on the outside of the building saying she was accepting pupils for a negotiable tuition, and opened its doors.

For the first week she taught only Jules. Then the Ferris family, who'd left town during the fighting, sent their eight-year-old-son and ten-year-old daughter to her, asking for a reduced rate, since there were two. Tessa agreed.

By the end of October she had ten pupils. She made little money since most of the parents paid her with food, but she and Jules managed. Tessa avoided going out alone if possible. Nobody had threatened her, but she didn't like the way some of the men stared at her when she passed by.

At least Hank Kilgore didn't seem to be in town.

Mark will come soon, she told herself. He'll come,

bringing Ezra, and we'll leave this town with its bitter memories. We'll make a new start somewhere else.

The Regulators camped together in the mountains south of San Patricio after the siege of McSween's house. Many had lost their horses, so early in August Billy called twenty of the men together.

"You know there's a bunch of Tunstall horses down along the Tularosa," he told them. "Now they don't belong to those bastards who took them, and that's a fact. Reckon if we mosey down there quiet-like we can take back what we need."

"Let's go!" Ezra agreed.

No one argued.

A little past noon they rode out of the timber near the Mescalero reservation, coming on six Indians driving a small herd of ponies.

Ezra riding ahead, saw the Apaches grab their rifles. He wheeled, yelling to Billy. The Regulators yanked their Winchesters from saddle scabbards as the Indians began firing.

"We ain't after their ponies," Billy said, "but if they want a fight, damn it, we'll give 'em one." He aimed, pulled the trigger. An Indian dropped from his horse.

Ezra, caught up in loading and firing, didn't understand at first when he heard Billy's shout.

"Don't shoot at that rider! He might be a soldier."

Glancing around, Ezra saw a horseman coming over the crest of a hill from the direction of reservation headquarters. He also saw that the man next to him, Martinez, was aiming at the rider.

"Don't shoot!" he cried just as Martinez fired.

The horseman jerked to the side. As he tumbled off his horse, Mark saw he wasn't in uniform. Not a soldier then.

The body rolled part way down the hill and Martinez spurred toward it.

"That's going to bring trouble," Billy said. "I think he was Bernstein, the clerk at the office. Let's get the hell out of here." He put his hands to his mouth. "Martinez!" he yelled. "Come back!"

Martinez waved his hand. *"Un minuto."* He dismounted and bent over the body.

Ezra brought his horse up next to Billy and O'Folliard.

"Reckon we may as well take a few of them Indian ponies with us," O'Folliard said, winking at Ezra.

Billy nodded, smiling again. "Might as well, We're going to be blamed anyway and we sure can use them."

When they rode back into camp, Mark approached Ezra as he dismounted.

"Those are Indian ponies," he said.

"Yeah." Ezra loosened the saddle. "Didn't start out to get Indian ponies. It sort of happened."

Mark frowned but said nothing more as he watched Ezra unsaddle and rub down his horse.

"I'm heading for St. Louis," Mark said finally. "I'd like you to come with me."

Ezra turned to gape at him. "St. Louis? What would I do there?"

"For one thing, you wouldn't turn into a rustler."

"Hell, we didn't steal these ponies. Not exactly. The Apaches . . ."

Mark rasied his hand. "I don't want to hear. You coming with me?"

Martinez came pounding into camp. As he passed, Ezra saw he had an extra rifle and gun belt and knew he'd taken them from the man he'd killed.

Robbing a corpse. Ezra scowled after Martinez. He didn't cotton to that at all. But it wasn't Billy's fault.

Hadn't he told Martinez not to shoot? And to leave the body alone?

"I'm not going anywhere," Ezra said to Mark. "I mean to stay with Billy."

Mark looked at him for so long that Ezra shifted his feet.

"Tell your sister when you see her that . . ." Mark paused.

After a time Ezra asked, "Tell her what?"

Mark shook his head. "Tell her good-bye," he said.

On the thirteenth of November the newly appointed governor of the Territory, Lew Wallace, issued a proclamation that amounted to a general pardon of all those engaged in the "disorders" in Lincoln County:

"Persons having business and property interests therein and who are themselves peaceably disposed may go to and from that county without hindrance or molestation . . ."

Susie McSween immediately returned from Las Vegas and moved into a house she'd had built across the street from Ellis'. She invited Tessa and Jules to live with her again, but Tessa declined. Jules, who'd had screaming nightmares for weeks after the McSween house burned, had finally begun to sleep through the night. He was fond of Rosalita's sister, calling her *Tia Maria* and Tessa feared another move might undo all the good.

Surely Mark and Ezra would be coming back any day now with the governor's new proclamation in effect.

In early December Sheriff Peppin resigned. A few days later a tall young man walked into the schoolhouse as Tessa was dismissing her pupils for the afternoon.

She stared at him, for a moment not realizing who he was. Jules launched himself at the man.

"Ezra!" he cried.

Ezra picked up his brother, lifted him into the air and hugged him before setting him on his feet. Tessa ran to Ezra and threw her arms about him.

"You're so tall I almost didn't know you!" she exclaimed. "Oh, Ezra, it's so good to see you. So good to have you back."

"I didn't expect to find you a schoolmarm," he said. "I'm sorry I couldn't come here any sooner, but until the new governor pardoned everyone, Peppin had warrants out for most of us."

"You've all come back to Lincoln?"

Ezra hesitated. "Most of us have. Middleton and Brown went home to Kansas. Skurlock and Bowdre live over at Sumner now, so they went there. But Billy's here and lots of others you know."

Something in Ezra's voice made Tessa's heart sink. He hadn't mentioned Mark at all.

"Has something happened to Mark?" she asked. "Is he all right?"

"As far as I know, he's fine."

Ezra, standing before her with Jules clinging to his hand, seemed to waver and recede. Tessa felt weighted down with apprehension.

"Where is Mark?" Her words sounded odd in her ears. A stranger's voice.

"Well, the fact is, he left for St. Louis a month or so ago."

Tessa couldn't speak. Left. Mark had left her.

"He told me to say good-bye to you." Ezra blurted the words out.

She looked at the worn pine boards on the floor between Ezra and her and they blurred as tears burned in her eyes. She clenched her fists, trying to force the tears back. There'd been no promises. She'd expected too much.

Yet Mark's touch, his embrace had made its own promise . . .

"I'm sorry if I'm interrupting a family reunion," Calvin Rutledge drawled from the doorway, "but I just arrived from Santa Fe and couldn't wait to see you, Tessa."

The Nesbitts all turned to stare at him.

Ezra held out his hand. "Glad to see you, sir," he said, almost sounding as though he meant it.

"Why Calvin," she heard herself say in that same stranger's voice. "I'm delighted you're back in town."

As the days passed, Tessa soon found that Ezra hadn't really returned to her. He wouldn't stay in Maria's house, preferring to bed down with Billy and O'Folliard wherever they decided to sleep. He spent most of his time with Billy.

"I've tried to talk to Ezra about staying away from the—the *tendejons*," Tessa said to Calvin near Christmas when he came by to walk her home from school. "He's too young to be in the company of such—such women." She blushed scarlet as she spoke, afraid she was shocking Calvin. She knew ladies never mentioned women of the night—it wasn't proper—but if she didn't speak out, how could she enlist Calvin in her efforts to save Ezra?

"I fear you still see Ezra as a boy," Calvin said. "I believe he sees himself as a man. He wants to do what men do."

"What Billy does, you mean," Tessa said. "I can't utter one word against Billy to Ezra without angering him. I thought that perhaps you might speak to Ezra about—well, about women who . . ." She broke off, began again.

"I don't know if my father ever talked to Ezra on such matters. It's something that should come from a man, even if I could bring myself to . . ." She stopped once more.

"Ezra and I are not friendly," Calvin said. "He won't appreciate advice from me."

"Dance with Pablita," Billy called to Ezra as he swung his own pretty partner about the tiny cantina dance floor.

Ezra shook his head, easing himself into the crowd as soon as Billy's eyes were off him. He slipped out the back door and took a deep breath of the frosty air. There was several inches of crusted snow on the ground.

The girls in the cantina scared him; he might as well admit it. They excited him with their thrusting breasts and curving hips. But frightened him, too. He didn't want to put his arms around them for fear he wouldn't know how to act.

A noise to the left, in deep darkness, made Ezra flatten himself against the adobe wall and reach for his Colt.

"*Quien es?*" he asked. "Who is it?"

A girl's light voice answered him. "Only I, *señor*." She stepped into the light falling from a window and he relaxed. A child.

She moved closer to him and he saw she wasn't as young as he'd thought; her smallness had misled him. She gazed up at him from wide brown eyes.

"I know you," she said. "You ride with Billy."

"My name's Ezra Nesbitt. What's yours?"

"I am called Violet Gabaldon." Unlike most of the Mexican women, she spoke English with only a whisper of an accent. She smiled. "Why are you not dancing inside?"

He could see little of her figure since she clutched a voluminous shawl about her, but he could tell she was slight of build. Maybe about sixteen. She was very pretty, he decided, far prettier than the women inside with their big breasts and seductive glances.

"I wanted some fresh air," he said. "Are you going in?"

"Oh, no. Papa forbids me. But I—I came to look in the windows. Everyone seems so happy dancing." Her voice was wistful.

"Do you like to dance?"

"Very much. When Papa takes me to a *baile*, I dance all night if he allows me to."

The throb of the guitar and wail of a fiddle came faintly through the thick adobe. Ezra stared down at her parted lips. Looking at her made him breathless, and yet at the same time he felt as though he could leap over Capitan Peak.

"We could dance out here," he said, surprised by his own words.

"In the snow?" Her nose wrinkled as she laughed.

"Why not?"

"Oh, let's!" she cried, offering him her hand.

Her shawl fell back as he put an arm about her and he saw her curling hair was lighter than that of most Mexican girls.

Ezra didn't think of himself as much of a dancer, but with Violet in his arms he spun and circled effortlessly. How light she was! With his hand on her waist he could feel her ribs under his fingers, as delicate as bird bones. He had a sudden longing to bring her to Tess and ask his sister to take care of her.

He grinned at his foolishness. Violet had a father who seemed to look after her very well. Except for tonight. But she was safe enough with him. He'd see her home after . . .

The sound of clapping hands made him stumble. Stop dancing. Release Violet.

Billy stood on the back stoop, applauding.

"No wonder you sneaked out," Billy said as he approached Ezra. "You had the prettiest girl of all waiting for you." He smiled at Violet.

Ezra's heart was suddenly as heavy as lead as he saw how worshipfully Violet looked up into Billy's face.

"I know you are *el Chivato*," she half-whispered. "Billy the Kid. Everyone talks of your bravery, how you saved the men in the burning house."

"I don't know you," Billy said, putting an arm about her waist, "but I plan to change that. Let's go inside."

Violet drew back. "I can't. Papa wouldn't . . ."

"Forget about Papa," Billy said, urging her toward the door.

Violet pulled away from Billy. Clutching her shawl about her, she fled into the darkness without another word. Billy put his fists on his hips, staring after her.

"Didn't mean to scare her off," he said. "She's as cute as a baby chick. What's her name, Ez?"

"Violet Gabaldon," Ezra said reluctantly.

"She your girl?"

Ezra wanted to say yes, but it would be a lie and one Billy was bound to uncover and laugh at him over.

"She's not anyone's girl," he said. "Her father doesn't let her go out."

"But little Violet gets out anyway, eh?" Billy clapped Ezra on the back. "Well, I'm going to see her again; you can bet on that!"

Ezra said nothing, there was nothing he could say. Billy was his friend, the best friend he'd ever had, and it was plain Violet liked Billy. She'd be pleased if Billy came calling.

But she was different from the other women Billy knew. It was like Violet *was* a baby chick, newly hatched and not aware of the dangers in the world. Ezra clenched his fists.

Billy took whatever woman caught his fancy, as long as she was willing. Violet wouldn't know any better than to be willing.

There wasn't a thing Ezra could do about it.

Chapter 11

Soon after the first of the year George Kimbrell was appointed sheriff. Never aligned with either side, Kimbrell started serving all the outstanding warrants on both the Regulators and on Dolan's men.

"The way I see it," Billy told Ezra and O'Folliard, "we're going to have to sit down and talk peace with those bastards who work for Dolan. Can't be fighting them and the law, too. My plan is to send a note to Jesse Evans telling him we want to either make peace or fight it out once and for all; let him take his choice."

On February eighteenth Evans, Dolan and Bill Campbell rode into Lincoln for a peace parley. Billy picked O'Folliard and Jose Salazar to go with him to the meeting.

"Hell," Billy told Ezra, "if it was shooting we planned to do, you'd be with me, but I told you I mean to make peace if I can. Dolan knows Salazar, maybe even trusts him a little, and old Tom didn't really get mixed up in the war till the end, so they don't have much of a grudge against him."

Ezra nodded, trying not to show his hurt at not being included. "I understand. But don't trust Evans and Dolan too far."

Billy laughed. "You think you need to give me that advice?"

It was a bitterly cold night. Ezra, who'd planned to hang around outside the meeting house to wait for Billy, retreated after an hour, half-frozen. As he headed for Susie McSween's, where he knew Tessa was visiting, he saw Houston Chapman, Susie's one-armed lawyer from Las Vegas, coming out through the gate.

Ezra wasn't sure whether he liked the lawyer or not. Susie thought Chapman's feistiness and persistence would get Colonel Dudley removed from his command at Fort Stanton as well as recover the cattle from Tunstall's estate that she felt belonged to her husband.

Maybe. All Ezra could tell so far was that Chapman had managed to insult pretty much everyone in the county. He wondered if that was the best way for a lawyer to go about his business. Colonel Dudley hated Chapman and Dudley still had the army behind him. A bad enemy to make.

"Hello, Mr. Chapman," Ezra said as he passed.

"Ezra." Chapman nodded without breaking stride.

Ezra went on toward the house and had a foot on the step when he heard a whoop, then a burst of laughter. He turned.

The peace meeting was over. Ezra made out Billy, O'Folliard and Salazar in a crowd of Dolan men. Nine of them, including Dolan himself. He tensed, eased off the stoop and into the deeper darkness by a fence. What was happening?

Judging from the voices and the singing, it was a groundhog case the group was drunk. Ezra watched them converge on Chapman. He saw Billy move away from the others, saw Evans grab him from behind.

Damn!

Ezra dashed across the street and around the rear of two buildings, coming out at a lane that ran into the road where Billy and the others stood. Keeping next to a corral fence, he edged as close as he could without being seen, stopped and eased his Colt from its holster.

". . . just to show you're as peaceable as all of us, you got to dance," a man Ezra didn't know said, his voice slurred by drink. His pistol was out and pointed at Chapman, who, like McSween, never carried a gun of any kind. Ezra decided the man threatening Chapman must be Campbell because he recognized all the others.

"I've no intention of dancing or of doing anything else for a damn drunken crowd," Chapman retorted. "Am I speaking to Mr. Dolan?" he added.

Evans answered, "No, but you're talking to damn good friends of his."

"I take it then that Mr. Dolan prefers to hide behind the guns of his good friends." Chapman spoke tartly, seemingly not the least afraid.

He's sure got guts, Ezra thought, his gaze shifting from Chapman to Evans who still held Billy's arms pinned. There was no way Ezra could get a clear shot at Evans.

"I don't hide behind anyone!" Dolan cried. He sounded as drunk as Campbell. "I resent that remark, sir!"

"You ain't dancing yet," Campbell told Chapman. "I mean to see you dance." He prodded him with the muzzle of his Colt.

"You can't scare me, boys," Chapman said. "You've tried it before and it's no use. Get out of my way, I'm going on." He brushed aside Campbell's pistol.

Two Colts roared. Ezra couldn't be certain whether Dolan or Campbell fired first.

"My God, I'm killed!" Chapman cried, staggering back and falling onto his side.

Ezra saw Billy break away from Evans, giving him a clear shot at Evans now, but he hesitated, finger on the trigger. O'Folliard and Salazar joined Billy and the three of them darted up the lane toward Ezra. He lowered his pistol.

"It's Ezra," he said as they neared, careful not to move until he'd spoken.

The four of them hurried toward Patron's house, one of the Regulators' meeting places.

"Damn, there's nothing like a shooting to sober you up," O'Folliard said.

"We going to leave Chapman lying there?" Ezra asked.

"He's as dead as they come. Nothing we can do for him," Billy said.

Ezra knew Dolan's men might make trouble if they went back, but it seemed wrong to leave the dead man in the street. Like they'd had to leave Brewer at the mill. For a moment dread raised the hair on his nape as the thought came to him—how many more of their men would die and be left behind?

"So the peace treaty didn't work out?" he said finally.

"Oh, we made peace all right. Drank to being friends, which wasn't such a good idea. It might still have gone okay if we hadn't come on that one-armed lawyer. Poor bastard." Billy touched the handle of his Colt. "Ain't no peace anymore. One way or another, I'll get Evans."

In March, when Governor Wallace came to Lincoln, Billy had a secret meeting with him that only Ezra knew about. Billy didn't tell him the details, but Ezra heard enough to know the warrants outstanding against Billy for the Brady and Roberts shootings would be withdrawn if Billy appeared before the grand jury in April with his account, as an eyewitness, of the Chapman killing.

Billy and the governor plotted a fake arrest for Billy with the militia, under the captaincy of Billy's friend, Juan Patron, acting as the arresting officers. Something went wrong. Both Billy and O'Folliard were taken by Patron, but then the sheriff's deputy stepped in and threw them into the miserable cellar jail in Lincoln instead of putting them under house arrest.

Wallace himself came to town to see to Billy's release into the custody of Juan Patron. Ezra joined the welcoming crowd of Regulators waiting for Billy at Patron's store.

"I been in that jail twice now and that's enough," Billy announced. "It ain't fit for a dog."

"They still have you handcuffed," Ezra said.

Billy grinned, wriggled his right hand back and forth, and a moment later held up the hand, free of the cuff. He slid it back into the handcuff with equal ease.

"One reward for having big wrists and small hands," he said.

While Billy was waiting under house arrest at Patron's, Ezra decided to seek out Violet Gabaldon, who'd been on his mind since the night they met. He rode out to the Gabaldon ranch across the river from town.

Her father, Vincente, at first refused to let Ezra see his daughter.

"I'll bring my sister with me if that would help," Ezra told him. "My sister is the schoolteacher. She . . ."

"Ah, *Señorita* Nesbitt," Vincente said. "I know her. She lives now in Maria Zamora's house, no?"

"Yes."

Vincente eyed Ezra. "I hear you ride with *el Chivato*. With Billy the Kid."

"He's my friend, yes."

"I have nothing against the young man. I admire his boldness, his courage. But, you understand, the life he leads, and you with him, is not suitable. Not at all suitable."

"I understand, *señor*. But I only wish to speak to your daughter. Here, in your house, in the presence of my sister—what harm is there in that?"

Vincente half-smiled. "You do not believe such a request is the beginning of a courtship? I think it is. Still, I will permit one such visit, out of respect for your sister. Come tomorrow. It will be only the one time. No more."

Ezra left the Gabaldon *casa,* where he'd not had so much as a glimpse of Violet, and went straight to Tessa.

"Why Ezra," Tessa said, "I had no idea you were courting a girl."

He flushed. "All I want to do is see her again, talk to her for a while. It's you and her father that mention courting, not me. I don't aim to get married. A wife means a house and staying in one place. I don't intend to be tied down. Not ever."

"I'll go to Vincente Gabaldon's ranch with you, if you wish," Tessa said. "I think, though, if you're not serious about Violet, you had better tell her so right away."

"All this fuss over talking to a girl! What does Violet care if I'm serious or not? She'd probably rather Billy came to see her than me, anyway."

"Billy? What's he have to do with this girl?"

"Nothing. I mean, he thinks she's pretty and she is, but he doesn't know her any better than I do."

By the next day, when Ezra and Tessa set off for Gabaldon's, she was full of information about the family.

"Violet's mother died five years ago," Tessa said. "She wasn't Mexican; she came from Kansas. Maria hints there was something peculiar about her death. She was shot, supposedly by a young cowboy she surprised trying to steal a horse from their corral. Violet's father killed the cowboy.''

"So?"

"Well, from the way Maria tells the story, it's plain there must have been talk about Violet's mother and the cowboy before the shooting. Vincente, I think, is suspected of killing the two of them when he caught them together. Now there may not be a word of truth in this; he's probably a perfectly innocent man. Since that time, though, he's kept his daughter practically a prisoner in the house."

Ezra said nothing. Poor Violet, without a mother to soften her father's strictness. Of course, he and Jules had lost their mother, too, but there'd always been Tessa.

He turned to his sister, leaned over and kissed her on the cheek. She stared at him, startled.

"You've been real good to me," he said gruffly.

He wasn't going to worry about whether Violet's mother had been a cheat or not—what difference did it make to him? Violet was her own person. His heartbeat speeded as he recalled the way her soft lips had parted when she looked up at him. He could hardly wait to see her again.

Vincente Gabaldon greeted Tessa with a smile and held onto her hand while he spoke to her. Ezra was a little surprised Tessa didn't draw away from him. Instead, she smiled, too. Of course, for an older man, Violet's father was good-looking enough.

"I am so happy to see you in my house," Vincente said to her. "It is my sorrow we haven't met since last summer."

She blushed. Tessa could look downright pretty sometimes.

"Thank you," she murmured. "It's my pleasure to be here."

Ezra glanced from one to the other. She hadn't said a

word about meeting him before and she was gazing at him, fascinated, like a bird at a snake. Ezra cleared his throat.

"Hello, *Señor* Gabaldon," he said.

Vincente's manner grew more formal as he greeted Ezra. He escorted them into the main room of the adobe ranch house and left them there with a final smile for Tessa.

Almost immediately Violet, accompanied by a maid, came into the room. Ezra caught his breath.

Violet wore all white, except for a pink ribbon threaded through the high neck of her gown, the pink exactly matching the color of her lips. The gown was modest but fitted well so that he couldn't miss the delicate curve of her breasts and the sweet flare of her small hips. She offered him her hand.

As he touched her fingers, a tingling fire traveled from his hand to shoot through the rest of him like fireworks on the Fourth of July.

"Violet," he stammered. "I mean, *Señorita* Gabaldon."

She took her hand from his and glanced at Tessa.

"Oh. I brought my sister. Tess, this is . . ."

Tessa held out her own hand to clasp Violet's. "I'm so pleased to meet you, *Señorita* Gabaldon. Ezra wasn't exaggerating; you're a very pretty young woman."

Violet's cheeks turned pinker than the ribbon as she smiled at Tessa. "Thank you. I am honored that you came to call, Miss Nesbitt."

Violet turned to the maid, giving orders in Spanish for little cakes to be brought with coffee and wine.

When everyone was seated, Violet leaned toward Ezra. "How is your friend, *Señor* Bonney?" she asked. "I heard he was arrested. It is a shame."

"Billy's all right. He's having a fine time at Patron's. Juan's really his friend, you know."

"So I've heard. I don't understand this arrest."

Ezra shrugged. "It won't be for long."

"I'm glad."

Ezra gazed at her, entranced. Her soft brown eyes had tiny speckles of gold; her brown hair was pulled back from her heart-shaped face, but wayward wisps escaped to curl enticingly on her temples.

The maid came in with a tray of food and drink, and Violet busied herself serving them. No one, Ezra thought, ever moved so gracefully. He could hardly believe he'd clasped that slender waist when he danced with her outside the cantina.

"You must come to Maria Zamora's house and visit me," Tessa said to Violet.

Violet touched the tip of her tongue to her lower lip for an instant and Ezra felt a flash of desire so acute he had to look away, lest he embarrass himself.

"I would like to," Violet said, "but I must ask Papa."

Ezra's heart thudded in his chest. If she came to Maria's, he might find the chance to be alone with her.

He couldn't wait that long. He took a deep breath. By God, he'd make a chance. Now, today. Somehow.

All too soon Tessa rose and began her farewells. He wanted to protest; it seemed they'd only been in the Gabaldon *casa* a few minutes, but he held his tongue, knowing Tess did what she thought proper.

"A lady or gentleman never outstays a welcome," his father used to say.

Whatever he might be, Tessa was a lady all right. And so was Violet.

Violet walked with them to the door. He held her hand for a moment, saying good-bye, then stepped aside to let Tessa repeat her invitation to visit at Maria's. Then, as

Tessa started away, Ezra moved back quickly before Violet could close the door.

"Meet me tonight under the cottonwood east of your house," he whispered almost in her ear, close enough so he could smell a delightful scent of roses.

Violet spoke so softly he hardly caught her words. "Tomorrow night." Louder, she said, "*Adios, Señor* Nesbitt," stepped back and shut the door.

He floated off the stoop and over the ground to join Tessa. Tomorrow. I'll see Violet tomorrow. Alone. Would it really happen? Would she come?

"You look as though you've been kicked in the head by a mule," Tessa told him.

The next day crawled along with all the speed of a land turtle. The sun shone warm; everywhere Ezra looked the hills showed green with spring, and the birds sang themselves hoarse, courting. Is that what he meant to do—court Violet?

The idea of marriage frightened him, but she wasn't like the cantina women Billy sought out. He knew those women could be had, sometimes for a few pesos, sometimes just because they took to a man. Billy wasn't shy about sleeping with them, but Ezra'd never had the nerve.

He wanted Violet in that way; it excited him almost beyond tolerance to even think of kissing her. But he wanted to protect her, too. Now that he'd seen her again, he couldn't imagine living the rest of his life without her.

"Violet is a lovely girl," Tessa told him, coming up to him as he stood by the Zamora corral, willing the sun to hurry down the sky. "I can see why you're so attracted to her." She laid her hand on his arm. "Promise me you'll not harm her in any way."

"Never!" he said fervently.

Tessa smiled and patted his arm.

"I reckon I'll have to find work," Ezra said.

She nodded. "*Señor* Gabaldon will certainly insist any man who courts Violet has something to offer besides himself."

At last the sun disappeared behind the western hills. Shadows deepened. Ezra ate Maria's chili con carne, afterwards telling her she was the best cook in the Territory. He wrestled with Jules, letting his little brother pin him to the floor. Lying on his back, he plucked Jules off his chest, lifted him into the air and held him at arms' length while Jules laughed as he struggled to free himself.

"You're in good spirits tonight," Tessa commented.

She couldn't suspect, he told himself. He set his brother down and rose to his feet. Jules immediately tackled him and Ezra swung him over one shoulder and, as an excuse not to talk to Tessa, carried Jules into the bedroom and tossed him on his cot.

"When I grow up, I'm gonna ride with Billy like you do," Jules told him.

Ezra tousled Jules' hair. "You'll have to learn to shoot some better if you want to do that."

"You can teach me." Jules looked up hopefully.

"Sure."

Yet, when Ezra stepped out into the night, he realized he didn't want Jules ever to ride with Billy. Jules reminded him of Papa in many ways. Jules ought to go east to a university like the one where Papa had always planned to send Ezra. His brother didn't belong in a hard-riding, fast-shooting crowd like Billy's.

I'll have to give it up myself, Ezra thought with a pang. If I mean to get a job. And I'll need a job if I intend to court Violet.

There was no one waiting in the deeper darkness under the big old cottonwood. It seemed to Ezra he could smell the new leaves; the spring night itself smelled fresh and cool.

Would Violet come? Had he mistaken what she'd whispered at the door? He leaned against the thick trunk, his eyes fixed on the lighted windows of the Gabaldon *casa.*

Off in the hills a coyote yipped. Another answered, and another, until their chorus started a ranch dog to barking. Early frogs croaked a love song from a nearby stream. He remembered lines from one of Browning's poems.

Never the time and place

And the loved one all together!

She must come to him tonight. He couldn't bear it if she didn't.

Something moved in the darkness. A stone scuffed under a footfall. Ezra held his breath, hoping, afraid to call her name for fear it wasn't Violet. He could picture Vincente's anger if her father caught him waiting under the cottonwood.

He breathed a faint scent of roses; his heart skipped a beat, then began to thud in his chest. He saw a slim figure approaching.

"Violet," he whispered.

She ducked under the low-hanging limbs and he caught her hand. She resisted when he tried to pull her closer.

"You must behave or I won't stay," she said softly, taking her hand from his.

He could see the white oval of her face like some night-blooming flower, smell her rose perfume mingled with the intoxicating scent that was her own.

"Violet," he murmured.

"I came to see you tonight for a reason," she said.

"Yes, I had to see you, too. Violet, you're the most . . ."

"Why I came is because I want you to do something for me."

"Anything, anything at all." He reached for her hand again, marveling at its tininess.

She let her hand rest in his. "I think of you as my friend and that is why I ask you."

"I am your friend. Always."

Her face was close to his. All he needed to do was bend his head and their lips would touch. Dizzy with anticipation, Ezra leaned forward.

"Good," Violet said. "Then you'll find a way to take me to see Billy without anyone knowing."

Ezra held.

"Billy?" he muttered.

"Yes, I want to go to him now, tonight. He promised me the last time we met that he'd come for me soon."

Ezra drew away from her, let go of her hand.

"Do you mean when you met him at the cantina?" he asked. His head buzzed with confusion.

"Billy and I have met four times since them," she said. "Secretly, of course. He is so brave, so wonderful. But now he's locked away and cannot come to me and I want to see him very badly. Oh, Ezra, I'm so glad you are going to help me!"

Chapter 12

Mark crested a hill and shaded his eyes against the afternoon sun to look at the adobe buildings of Lincoln spread out below along the Rio Bonito. His black snorted and tossed its head, as though to show contempt for the little town.

It didn't look like St. Louis, that's for sure, any more than the sparse high country looked like the lush river valleys of Missouri. Mark patted the black's neck. "You'll get used to it, Sombrio," he said.

He was glad to be back. St. Louis had stifled him with its burgeoning greenery, its thousands of people. He was traveling light, the two most important things he'd brought with him being Sombrio, born and raised in Kentucky and bought by the Judge two years ago, and his Deputy United States Marshal's papers.

The Judge was in poor health, though he claimed seeing Mark gave him a new lease on life.

"Hell, you could have come home any time these past seven years," the Judge had told him. "That warrant out for you was voided when Hiram York left office. He got caught with his sticky fingers full of bribes before the year was out. Everyone knew Brendon York was an even nastier chip off the same villainous block. No one mourned his passing. I tried to locate you. Where in the name of heaven were you?"

"In the New Mexico Territory," Mark said. "And I changed my name. Called myself Halloran."

The Judge grinned. "At least you stuck to an Irish monicker."

"I should have stayed here and faced up to what I'd done."

"You'd be seven years in your grave if you had, and you know it. Hiram was riding high when it happened. The warrant was for show—his boys were out to shoot you, not arrest you."

Mark sighed. "I never killed a man since. I won't, unless it's to save my own life, but I can't say I'm sorry Brendon York is dead."

He told the Judge about the mess in Lincoln County and about Tessa Nesbitt.

"If you're going back, and it sounds as though you are, you ought to carry some authority to get the place cleaned up," the Judge advised.

Mark nodded. "I'm going back. You ought to see that country. Rolling grasslands, mesas, mountains, canyons— it's got everything. Even the sky is different. Bigger. More stars. It gets into a man's blood."

"Sounds to me like something besides the country got into your blood," the Judge said. "Well, I'll tell you, you straighten things out and then I'll come for a visit and see for myself. It shouldn't be hard to get you appointed as a

Deputy United States Marshal. Later on, maybe you'll feel like settling down and practicing a little law."

Trust the Judge to try to arrange his life, just as he'd always done. But this time Mark didn't fight him. Coming into Lincoln County as a lawman made a lot of sense. As for ever going back to being a lawyer, time would tell.

So now he was Mark Dempsey once again; he had his name back, free and clear. He'd never suspected it would be so easy. In fact, he'd been afraid he faced a hangman's noose, once he returned to St. Louis.

What had Tessa thought about him leaving her without any more than a second-hand good-bye?

Somewhere down there she was waiting. But was it for him? Had that bastard Rutledge taken his place? Mark kneed the black ahead, anxious to get into town as soon as possible.

When he angled back onto the road, he saw a dust cloud that resolved into a rider galloping toward him, Winchester in hand, and Mark checked the impulse to reach for his own gun. There was something familiar about the way the man sat the horse, and besides, the rider was fleeing town, not coming after him. He pulled to the side of the road, so there'd be no question he meant to let the man pass unmolested.

Mark recognized the rider as the man hailed him.

"Halloran!"

Billy the Kid.

Billy slowed his horse; Mark halted and waited for Billy to stop beside him.

"Good to see you again, Billy," he said.

"Where you been?" Billy asked. "I heard you went to St. Louis."

"You heard right. I'm just back."

"Well, I'm just on my way out." Billy grinned.

"Things quieted down any?"

Billy shrugged. "You could say so. At least the new sheriff and the new governor ain't as bad as the old ones. I'd sure like to jaw with you, but I'm in sort of a hurry and I'd take it kindly if you didn't mention meeting up with me."

Mark nodded. "Good luck," he called as Billy spurred his horse.

The rest of the way into Lincoln, Mark wondered if he'd meet men riding after Billy, but no one came along until he was on the outskirts. Again he recognized the rider.

"Ezra!" he called.

Ezra pulled up his pinto. "Mark! I never expected to see you again."

"I rode down from Santa Fe. Your sister—is she still in town?"

"Tess is living with Maria Zamora. She and Jules. Look, I'm in a hurry right now; I'll see you when I get back."

"When will that be?"

Ezra hesitated. "I don't know. But I'll see you." He dug his heels into the pinto and galloped away.

So Ezra was still following Billy.

Mark stopped off at the sheriff's office. Tom Longworth, wearing a deputy's badge, was the only one there. He looked at Mark's papers and shook hands. Mark had always liked Longworth.

"Gonna need all the lawmen we can get," Longworth said. "Billy's on the loose again."

"On the loose?"

"Yeah, he's been under house arrest up to Juan Patron's and I guess he got tired of it—Patron sent a boy a few minutes ago to report Billy was gone. Hell, Juan probably saddled his horse for him."

"You going after him?"

"Naw, we got better things to do. You know yourself ain't no one gonna catch up to Billy if he don't want them to. Besides, he was supposed to get a pardon, courtesy of the governor. It may come through yet."

"Then why are you worried about him being on the loose?"

"He's bound to run off a few horses here, a few steers there, and get people to complaining. Been some grudge killings in the south county, but things have been quiet up this way. Except for the Indians. Some chief named Victorio has got the Mescaleros on the warpath again. Like I said, glad you're here; we need you."

Longworth told him of a place where he could get room and board. Mark brought his gear to the house, had something to eat, then set off for Zamora's.

"*Señorita* Tessa, she go off with *Señor* Rutledge," Maria told him. "I think to *Señora* McSween's *casa*."

Susie was back in Town? Mark was surprised. He'd have thought she'd want no part of Lincoln after last summer's horror. He asked Maria where Susie was living, started in that direction, then decided not to go there after all.

He was tired. Sombrio was tired, too; he'd pushed to get to Lincoln. And he sure as hell didn't want to meet that bastard Rutledge. Didn't want to see Tessa with him.

There was always tomorrow.

Mark hesitated as he passed Zamora's on the way back to his room. Blue shadows darkened the tiny yard as dusk settled in. He could wait here for Tessa. The door opened and Maria came out, her arm around a smaller woman. He could hear the woman sobbing. Before he could urge the black on, Maria caught sight of him.

"*Señor! Por favor.*"

He swung off the horse and walked toward her.

"What am I to do?" Maria asked. "This child, she is loco. She says she will run off."

Mark took a good look at the girl, not a child at all, but a very pretty young woman.

"What's wrong, *señorita?*" he asked.

"Oh," she sobbed, "oh, I don't know what to do. Billy is gone, and Ezra, too; they left without a word. Left me. Billy left me." She glanced wildly around. "I'll ride after him. I'll find him!"

Maria grasped her arm and pulled her toward Mark. "*Señor, por favor*, take Violet to her *padre*. He is Vincente Gabaldon."

"Do you want to go home?" Mark asked Violet.

"I want to go to Billy." She covered her face with her hands and sank to the ground weeping.

"Stop that!" Mark gripped Violet's elbow and jerked her to her feet.

She gasped and stared at him.

"You're behaving like a baby," he said sharply. "You're upsetting *Señora* Zamora."

"But he's gone." Her lower lip quivered.

"If you mean Billy, he'll be back; he always comes back to Lincoln. Now stop crying and I'll take you home."

Violet remained subdued as Mark guided the black toward the Gabaldon ranch. He wondered how a girl liks this had ever gotten mixed up with Billy, whose taste usually ran to an entirely different type of woman. What was Violet's father thinking of to let her even meet Billy?

A half-mile farther, three riders pounded from the cover of trees just off the road and spread out to block his way.

"*Alto!*" one of them ordered. "Halt!"

"Who are you?" Mark demanded.

"I am Vincente Gabaldon."

Mark reined in the black. "Good. You can take your daughter."

"What are you doing with her?" Vincente demanded. His two scowling associates kept their hands near their Colts.

"Maria Zamora asked me to bring the girl home."

"That is your story."

"Damn it," Mark said, "I don't even know your daughter. From the sound of things, you'd do well to keep an eye on her—she was trying to run off to join Billy the Kid."

"This I cannot believe. You lie!"

"Papa," Violet said, "this man has nothing to do with . . ."

"*Silencio!*" Vincente thundered. "*Hija de la puta!* You are no daughter of mine."

Violet flinched back against Mark. She began to cry.

"I think I recognize you, *señor*," Vincente said. "You are one of those who work for *Señor* Dolan. *Bastardo!*"

"I haven't worked for Jim Dolan since last July. I'm a Deputy U.S. Marshal now."

"Lie upon lie."

The two men with Vincente eased their mounts toward Mark and he saw they intended to flank him. He began to believe even his deputy marshal's badge wouldn't stop Vincente, who seemed driven beyond reason. Looked like the Mexican meant business.

Three against one. Bad odds.

Either act now or it would be too late.

Mark grabbed Violet tightly about the waist, at the same time whooping in imitation of an Apache war cry. He dug his heels into the black, yanking the horse's head to the right at the same time.

Sombrio swerved right and laid himself into a gallop as

Mark directed him off the road and across open ground toward the trees along the Rio Hondo. Hooves pounded behind him, and he hoped the Kentucky-bred Sombrio could hold to his reputation for speed, tired as he was and with a double load.

Would Vincente hold his fire because of Violet? Mark counted on it, but the Mexican had called Violet the daughter of a whore and maybe he didn't care whether the girl lived or died.

"I'll set you down under the trees," he told Violet. "Your father can pick you up there."

She clutched at him. "No, please, I'm afraid to go home. Papa will beat me, maybe even kill me. Take me with you. Anywhere, I don't care."

Mark had no time to argue. He slowed Sombrio at the cottonwoods, then plunged among the trees and headed downriver for the ford. A gun cracked and a bullet thudded into a tree trunk. Violet moaned in fear.

Hell. He couldn't dump her here and leave her for Vincente. The man must be mad.

Mark splashed through the water short of the ford and headed for the opposite bank. They wouldn't expect him to cross early—at least he hoped not. He had to buy time now that he was stuck with Violet.

The black struggled up the bank, coming out by the graveyard in back of Tunstall's store. Mark wished it were darker. He shoved Violet down against the horse's neck and crouched over her. A rifle spat from across the river.

Sombrio reached the street and Mark headed for the sheriff's office. As he neared, he jerked his Colt out and fired three times into the air, jammed it back and slowed the black.

Longworth dashed out the door, Colt in his hand, ready.

"Meet me at Maria Zamora's," Mark called to him, urging Sombrio on again.

Mark pulled the black up in front of Maria's just as Tessa and Rutledge turned into the path leading to the front door. They both stopped and stared at him.

He slid from the horse, pulled Violet down. "Run into the house," he ordered.

She picked up her skirts and did as she was told.

"Mark Halloran!" Tessa cried in disbelief. "What on earth . . . ?"

"Get inside!" he snapped. "Trouble's coming."

Hooves thudded, coming nearer. Tessa hurried after Violet.

"See here, Halloran . . ." Rutledge began.

Mark passed him, leading Sombrio around the house. "You want to get shot, stand there and argue," he called over his shoulder.

When the black was inside the corral, Mark sprinted for the back door. By the sound of it, more than one horseman was pulling up in front. He ducked inside. He could hear pounding on the front door and ran through the house.

"*Quien es?*" he called, motioning everyone away from the door and standing clear of it himself. "Who is it?"

"Longworth."

Mark opened the door.

"I've got three of the boys with me," Longworth said. "What's up?"

Mark told him.

Longworth scowled at Violet, who was crumpled on a settee with Tessa's arm around her.

"Leave it to that damn Kid to cause trouble one way or the other," he said finally. He glanced at Rutledge and Maria, then turned to Mark.

"I'll try to parley with Gabaldon," Longworth said, "but he ain't the most reasonable man in the world."

Violet sat up abruptly. "I won't go home," she cried. "Ever! No one can make me."

Longworth ignored her. He walked back outside, closing the door behind him.

Violet turned to Tessa. "You won't force me to go with my father, will you? I am afraid of him. He called me—" she bit her lip—"called my mother a terrible name. And my *abuela*, my grandmother, told me before she died that I must be careful never to anger Papa as my mother had done or something dreadful might happen." She grasped Tessa's hand. "Please help me."

Tessa pulled Violet close. "Of course I will. You can stay with me." She looked at her landlady. "You don't mind, Maria?"

Maria shrugged. "I don't like trouble, but I don't send a girl to die. She stays."

Mark listened to them uneasily. He didn't know much about Vincente Gabaldon. The man might be angry enough to beat his daughter, but would he kill her? Who could tell? It was plain the girl ought to stay away from her father until he cooled down. Mark didn't like to see Tessa mixed up in such a mess but there was no help for it.

A fine greeting this was. His first day back in Lincoln and he'd already brought Tessa trouble. He stepped to the window to look out. Longworth was gone. No sign of Gabaldon.

"I will make coffee," Maria announced, retreating into the kitchen.

Jules came into the living room, blinking as though he'd been asleep. He stared at Mark for a moment. A smile lit up his face and he ran across the room to Mark's side, stopped, and held out his hand.

Mark shook hands with him. "How are you, Jules?" he asked.

"Maria doesn't have a piano," Jules told him solemnly.

Mark remembered and reached into his shirt pocket. The reunion he'd planned to have with Tessa was so much snowmelt down the river, but he could still give Jules the present he'd brought from St. Louis.

"This is a harmonica," he told the boy, handing him the instrument. "Some call it a mouth organ. Have you ever seen one?"

Jules shook his head, turning the harmonica over and examining it on all sides.

"You put it to your lips and blow into those little holes," Mark said. "You can learn to play tunes on it, just like on the piano."

Jules blew into it and his eyes widened at the sound he made. "Is it mine to keep?" he asked.

"All yours. I'll teach you to play it, but not tonight. I want you to take the harmonica back to your room now and stay there. All right?"

Jules nodded, all his attention on the harmonica. He started to leave, turned at the archway and said, "Thank you. Thanks a lot."

Mark half-smiled. Jules had lost almost all of his English accent. He sounded like any other American boy.

Longworth rapped at the front door, calling to Mark. He hurried to open it.

"Gabaldon won't bother you," Longworth said to him. "I convinced him you'd just gotten into town and you really were an honest-to-goodness deputy marshal. He says to tell the girl she can either come home with him tonight or as far as he's concerned she's no longer his daughter."

"I won't go!" Violet cried.

"Well, I guess that answers that," Longworth said.

"I'll pass on the message." He eyed Violet. "Sure you ain't gonna change your mind?"

"Never!"

"Okay. See you around, Mark."

"Thanks, Tom. Any time I can return the favor, you let me know."

"Don't worry; I got a list." He grinned at Mark and went out.

"If there's an extra blanket around, I'll camp out by the corral tonight," Mark said to Tessa. "Just in case Violet's father has a change of heart."

"I'll take care of things here," Rutledge announced. "I think you've caused enough trouble already, Halloran."

Mark bristled. Tessa rose quickly. "I'd prefer you both went home," she said firmly, looking from one man to the other. "I've met Vincente Gabaldon and I believe he's a man of his word, whatever else may be bothering him. We're perfectly safe, but thank you both for the offer. Good night."

Mark tried to hold her gaze, but Tessa turned away from him to fuss over Violet. He suddenly felt very tired.

He was afraid he'd lost Tessa for good.

Chapter 13

Longworth woke Mark early the next morning. Sheriff Kimbrell was back from White Oaks, where he'd gone to check on counterfeit bills passed there. He wanted to see Mark as soon as possible.

It turned out that the sheriff had heard the men passing the bills were heading for Mesilla and he hoped Mark, as a deputy marshal, would go after them.

The lead sounded good and Mark could hardly refuse, since it was clearly part of his job.

He tried to see Tessa before he left, but she was in the schoolhouse, and when he rode there, she told him he'd have to wait until she was through teaching to talk to her.

"You haven't been in a hurry to visit me until now," she said tartly. "I believe it's been almost a year, hasn't it? A few more hours certainly won't matter."

"I have to leave town for a week or so."

She shrugged, turning away from him. He longed to

grab her, whirl her around and take her into his arms, but not with ten pairs of eyes staring intently at the two of them.

"I'll call on you when I get back to Lincoln," he said finally.

"I won't hold my breath waiting," she told him. She picked up a speller and asked one of the pupils to recite.

Mark thought about Tessa all the way to Mesilla. Somehow he had to redeem himself in her eyes. How the hell was he going to accomplish that?

Mark managed to catch up with one of the counterfeit bill passers; the other had fled across the border into Mexico. When he headed north again, he encountered cavalry attacking Victorio's Apaches and wound up fighting Indians with the army. He arrived back in Lincoln in the middle of July.

School was out, but Tessa wasn't in town. She'd gone to Santa Fe with Susie McSween, Maria told him.

"*Señora* McSween, she look for new *abogado*, how you say—lawyer?"

"When will she be back?"

Maria shrugged. "Who's to say?"

Mark started to turn away, paused to ask. "Whatever happened to Violet Gabaldon?"

Maria's face darkened. "She run off two, three days after I take her in."

"Did she go home?"

"No. Word comes she is at Fort Sumner with Billy. That one, he will not marry her. She is most foolish." Maria shook her head. "Violet's *padre*, he give up the *rancho*. They say he join up with Comancheros. *Muy mal.* Very bad."

Mark rasied his eyebrows. Violet's flight didn't surprise him, but the Comancheros were a wild and brutal bunch of outlaws—American, Mexican, and Indian—universally despised and feared. Vincente Gabaldon hadn't seemed the type of man who'd associate with such a desperate crew. Perhaps he *had* gone a little mad.

In the privacy of her bedroom, Tessa sighed in pleasure as she sloshed water over her bare shoulders. On the long ride back from Santa Fe, she'd thought at times she'd die from the August heat. At least she'd had the sense to leave Jules behind in Lincoln with the Banks. Their son, Bob, one of her students, was Jules' age and the boys had had a fine time together on the Banks' small ranch east of town.

In fact, Jules was still at the ranch as he'd been invited to stay there one more day to celebrate Bob's birthday. Maria was off visiting Rosalita, so Tessa had the unaccustomed luxury of being alone in the house.

She slid lower in the tin tub, savored the coolness of the water. Her breasts and thighs gleamed white, contrasting with her sun-browned arms.

She'd made the trip to Santa Fe out of duty, for it was increasingly difficult for her to enjoy being with Susie. All Susie could talk about were her plans for revenging herself on Colonel Dudley. Susie was certain it was at her instigation that he'd been removed from the command at Fort Stanton, but she wanted to see him cashiered from the army and ruined completely.

She was a vindictive woman.

Susie had reason to be, Tessa reminded herself, then shook her head. She couldn't imagine herself wishing to see a man destroyed. Terrified as she'd been when Hank Kilgore had tried to rape her, she'd been relieved to find that neither she nor Mark had killed him.

She'd never expected Mark to come back to Lincoln. While Calvin Rutledge didn't affect her emotions as Mark had, she'd hoped to come to feel more than a pallid affection for Calvin. Maybe in time she would have.

If Mark had stayed in St. Louis.

Tessa rested her head on the rim of the tub and closed her eyes. The moments she'd lain in Mark's arms in the ruined adobe were as clear in her mind as if she were still there. Her body, too, remembered his touch, making her restless during sleepless nights, making her dream he was with her again when she did sleep, his hands caressing her breasts, exploring in forbidden places . . .

No! Tessa sat up abruptly, splashing water onto the floor. That was over and done with. She must think of Calvin, who wanted to marry her, not some fly-by-night who didn't even have the courtesy to say good-bye when he left, then showed up almost a year later and expected her to behave as if he'd never been away.

She heard the kitchen door close. Maria must be back. It was time to get out of the bath and dress.

Tessa stood up and reached for the towel.

Through her closed bedroom door, she heard footsteps along the corridor.

"Maria?" she called, wrapping the towel about her. "I'm in the bedroom, taking a bath."

The footsteps ceased. After a moment they came on, closer, and Tessa frowned. Maria's shoes shouldn't make such a harsh sound on the floor.

The door latch pushed up and the door swung open. Tessa gasped and shrank back, clutching the towel tightly to her.

Mark stood in the doorway. Before she could cry out in protest, he kicked the door closed, strode to her and gathered her into his arms. His lips came down on hers, warm and demanding.

Her anger and outrage withered and died. Passionate

desire sprouted in their place, thrusting through her until she was consumed with need.

She reached to hold him closer, and when he eased away to lift her into his arms, the towel fell to the floor. She heard him draw in his breath.

"My God, you're beautiful," he said gruffly, carrying her to the bed.

Tessa lay on her side, watching him take off his clothes. His body was strong and lean. Like hers, it was whiter where the sun didn't reach. His manhood pulsed with his desire for her and a thrill of anticipation shook her.

He lay beside her, stroking her breasts, running his fingers along her body, kissing her mouth, her throat.

"Mark . . . oh, Mark," she murmured as she smoothed his hair.

It was as she'd dreamed, only more exciting than any dream.

His lips, his tongue trailed over her breasts, then lower, lower, tasting the soft flesh of her thighs, her womanhood.

Tessa moaned, beyond thought, her body throbbing with delicious enjoyment. She wanted him to go on forever.

He shifted to kneel over her and she reached to touch his hardness, heard his groan and knew he felt the same unbearable yearning to be joined. She led him down to her and cried out with exquisite pleasure when he entered.

Mark drew back and she pulled him closer. "No," she cried, "Please don't stop, don't ever stop."

She arched to him as he thrust deeply, felt the strange and wonderful inner quivering begin that she knew would grow into a rapturous flower.

Mark ceased moving, staying inside her as he kissed her, their tongues entwined, for long, long moments until, unable to wait, she began a circular motion with her hips.

"Tessa!" he cried, thrusting again and again, faster and

faster until her flower bloomed in ecstasy. He shuddered
and lay still.

He turned onto his side and drew her against him.

"I always meant to come back if I could," he murmured.
"I didn't want to leave you but . . ."

A door closed.

"Maria!" Tessa exclaimed, sitting up. She jumped from
the bed and began to dress hurriedly.

Mark did the same. "It's all right, Tessa," he said. "I
mean to . . ."

"Ssh! I couldn't bear it if Maria finds you here."

She bit her lip as she looked from him to the closed
bedroom door. All her doubts crept back into her mind.
What had she been thinking of? All Mark had to do was
touch her and she became a wanton.

"I'll go and keep Maria in the kitchen," she said. "You
can leave by the front door and she won't . . ."

"But I don't want to leave. We haven't talked. I want to
tell you . . ."

"You can knock and pretend you've just arrived. Oh,
please don't argue, Mark. I don't want Maria to think
I'm—I'm . . ." she couldn't finish and began again. "You
don't know what it was like in this town after the fire.
Men stared at me on the streets and I knew they were
thinking terrible things about me and—and Alex. As if
either of us . . ." She stopped again. "I won't ever go
through that again."

"All right," he whispered. "I'll do whatever you say."

Mark waited until he was certain Tessa was in the
kitchen with Maria, then eased out of her room, walking
on his toes so his boot heels wouldn't click on the floor.
He passed through the main room and out the front door,

feeling like a fool. Annoyance flickered in him. This wasn't how he'd palnned to do his courting, clandestinely.

He was careful to shut the front door without noise. He hesitated a moment before knocking on it, angry at himself as well as at Tessa.

He shouldn't have listened to her pleas, should have marched with her into the kitchen and told Maria they were to be married and that best wishes were in order.

He raised the iron knocker and slammed it against the metal plate with unnecessary force.

"Where the hell did you spring from?" Rutledge's voice said from behind him.

Mark whirled. Rutledge was advancing up the path from the street.

"I didn't see you turn in here." Rutledge eyed him suspiciously.

Try to hide something and you wound up with one lie on top of another. Damn it, he didn't owe Rutledge an explanation.

The door opened and Tessa's eyes widened as she saw Rutledge with him.

"Won't you come in?" she said rather breathlessly.

Tessa perched on the edge of a straight-backed chair. "Please sit down," she told them.

Rutledge sat on the settee, but Mark shook his head, moving to stand beside the empty fireplace. He leaned on the mantel, eyeing Tessa sardonically. Now what did she intend to do? She glanced nervously from one man to the other.

"Did you find out about Ezra, Calvin?" she asked finally.

"I'm afraid Ezra *has* been with Billy on those cattle raids," Rutledge said. "He was recognized by two different men."

She turned to Mark. "Have you heard anything?" she asked.

"Not much more than what Rutledge just told you. Ezra seems bent on making an outlaw out of himself."

Tessa clenched her fists. "He isn't a thief! He only goes along because Billy's leading him into it."

"You make him sound stupid," Mark said. "Ezra's got a good mind. He knows what he's doing."

Tessa tightened her lips. "It's Billy's fault," she insisted. "Look at poor little Violet, the way Billy lured her from her home. God only knows what will become of the child."

"Violet rode to Sumner of her own free will," Mark said. "Or so I understand. She wasn't fleeing her father; she could have stayed here. Wrong or right, Ezra and Violet both made a choice, Tessa."

"Someone ought to stop Billy," she went on as though he hadn't spoken. "It isn't right to let him corrupt others."

Rutledge, who hadn't put in a word since answering Tessa's question, nodded.

"I know Ezra's a good boy," he said. "A fine young man. Billy Bonney's influence is nothing short of pernicious."

Mark shrugged. He'd come to know Ezra quite well in the weeks they'd spent with Billy and the others in the hills south of San Patricio. While it was true Ezra idolized Billy and seemed blind to his faults, at the same time the boy had clearly been enjoying himself. It wasn't as though he was drawn to Billy against his will.

"Something should be done," Tessa said, looking at neither of them.

"My dear, I'll do all I can," Rutledge said solemnly.

Which will be nothing, Mark said to himself. He knew Tessa wasn't going to like what he meant to tell her, but it was the truth.

"I went after your brother for you once," he reminded her. "Ezra didn't want to come back with me, but I shamed him into it because you and Jules were in the McSween house, virtually unprotected. There's no such reason for him to leave Billy now."

"But you're a deputy marshal. Couldn't you force Ezra to come home?"

"Arrest him, you mean?" Mark demanded.

Her hands flew to her mouth. "Oh no!"

"Perhaps our deputy marshal's afraid to tangle with Billy's gang," Rutledge said. "You shouldn't blame him. It's well known Billy tends to shoot first and ask questions later."

Mark gritted his teeth. His impulse was to lift Rutledge by his shirt collar and toss him out the front door. He took a step toward the settee.

Rutledge rose to face him.

Tessa got up hurriedly and stepped between them, looking at Mark. "Maybe you'd better leave," she said.

"I came here to talk to you. We haven't had a chance."

"I beg your pardon," Rutledge said, staring at Mark over Tessa's head. "Tessa and I have a standing appointment to meet on Thursday afternoons."

Mark's fists clenched.

Tessa put a hand on his chest. "If you start a fight, I won't ever forgive you," she said to him. "It happens to be true, what Calvin says."

"Then perhaps it was he you were waiting for earlier," Mark growled.

He saw the shock in Tessa's eyes. Her face flamed. She reached up and slapped him across the face.

He turned away, picked up his hat and strode out of the house.

A week later, when the sheriff of Dona Ana County, on the Mexican border, sent an urgent appeal to Kimbrell for help in subduing Jesse Evans and his gang who were on a rampage down there, Mark joined Longworth and four other deputy sheriffs heading south.

Mark got shot in the leg in a skirmish with the bandits, and the wound festered, keeping him at Mesilla into the fall.

He'd long since realized his dislike of Rutledge had pushed him into insulting Tessa. It seemed as though everything he'd done since he'd come back to the Territory had been the wrong thing as far as she was concerned.

In November, when he could ride again, Mark didn't head straight for Lincoln, deciding to detour by way of Fort Sumner. He'd heard Billy and his boys had rustled some one hundred head of Chisum's cattle in the Texas panhandle, sold them to Colorado beef buyers, then hightailed it back to Sumner.

He didn't plan to nab Billy. The only one he wanted was Ezra. If he brought the boy back to Tessa, she was certain to forgive and forget.

At Roswell his plans went awry. As he came into town, a posse was forming to ride after the Comanches who'd just raided horses on a ranch near town, killing a man and his son. Mark joined the posse and, with a man named Pat Garrett and two others, stuck to the trail long after the rest of the posse returned to Roswell.

They finally caught up with eight Comanches driving the horses, surprised them at a night camp and killed them all. Garrett collected the Indians' moccasins in a sack and strapped it onto his horse.

"I keep count this way," he said to Mark. "A sight less messy than scalps."

As they drove the foot-sore string of horses back to

Roswell, the soft-spoken Garrett, who tended to be taciturn, began to talk to Mark when he heard Mark was heading for Sumner.

"Well, I live up Sumner way," he said. "I was down to Roswell looking at land when those damn Comanches raided."

"Mind if I travel up the Pecos with you?" Mark asked. He liked Garrett, a lean and very tall man with large dark eyes and a shaggy mustache.

"You'd be welcome. We've ridden through hell and high water together already." He gave Mark one of his crooked smiles.

Mark and Garrett arrived in Sumner just before Christmas. Mark had never been to the abandoned fort before and looked about with curiosity.

The Pecos made a wide turn to the southeast here and the town stood on its north bank. Stores and cantinas backed against the river. All the old adobe army buildings were in use as houses. Mark saw a Catholic church and a post office. Most of the residents seemed to be Mexican.

"*Hola, Juan Largo,*" they hailed Garrett. "Hello, Long John."

He waved back.

"Pete Maxwell lives over there in what once was the officers' quarters," Garrett said to Mark, pointing to a large building with a wide veranda across the front and along the north and south sides. "Pete gave me my first job when I came to Sumner. I'll ask him to put you up—he's got plenty of room."

Mark nodded his thanks, following Garrett past a rusted cannon outside the picket fence that ran in front of the house.

"I don't rightly know where Billy and his boys are staying at the moment," Garrett said, "but I'll spread the word you're bunking with Pete and want to see Ezra Nesbitt.''

Ezra didn't show. Mark did his best to find out where Ezra might be staying, but the townspeople didn't want to talk to a stranger about Billy and his *compañeros*.

Mark surveyed the country around the town as best he could, riding north between twin rows of winter-bare cottonwoods to the village of Punta de la Glorietta, then east to small ranches whose Mexican owners viewed him with suspicion.

On New Year's Day Mark rode through the leafless peach orchard on the northern outskirts. He looked at the frozen Pecos and the dusting of snow over the hills, feeling as cold inside as out. He might as well give up and head back to Lincoln.

''Halloran!''

Mark whirled around and saw Billy, Ezra and Tom O'Folliard riding toward him.

''Heard you were looking for us,'' Billy said.

''Looking for Ezra anyway,'' Mark admitted.

''I'm here,'' Ezra said.

Ezra looked thinner and far older than his sixteen years.

''Can we have a talk?'' Mark asked him.

Ezra shook his head. ''I can guess you're going to tell me to go back to Lincoln. No use jawing about it cause I ain't.''

Billy grinned. ''Come on, Ez, we'll all go; how about it? We ain't been into town in a coon's age.''

It wasn't what Mark had in mind, but once Ezra was in Lincoln, maybe Tessa could talk some sense into him. At least she'd have a chance.

''There's Violet . . .'' Ezra began.

''Well, she can come, too. Why not?'' Billy asked.

Ezra shrugged. ''It's okay with me, if you want to go.''

Mark rode into Lincoln with Billy on one side of him and Ezra on the other, the rest of the gang behind them. When he saw men on the street point and nudge one another, he shrugged.

He wouldn't be the first lawman to have rustlers for friends.

He tried not to think of the possibility that one day he might have to go after Billy and Ezra—and trail them to the death, as he had the Comanches.

Chapter 14

Ezra left the house whistling, his breath frosty in the chill evening air. He'd managed to persuade Violet to visit his sister, so he didn't have to worry about her tonight.

There wasn't anything wrong with saloons and cantinas—a man needed a place he could drink and gamble—but Violet didn't belong there. She wasn't his—she was Billy's—but he felt responsible for her just the same.

Tessa had been in a good humor, too, because he was home. He didn't spoil it by reminding her he wouldn't be staying long.

Ezra pushed open the door of Bob Hargove's saloon and went in. He didn't see Billy or the others, but he knew they'd be along. At the bar a red-faced man was toying with a pearl-handled pistol. Ezra held, tensing. The man saw him and grinned.

"Don't be afeared of Joe Grant, sonny; I don't shoot puppies."

A few men laughed nervously.

Ezra forced himself to unclench his fists. He'd heard of Grant. As fast as they came, sober. Right now he was half-crocked. A man learned early not to argue with drunks.

"I took this little baby from Finan Chisum," Grant boasted, his words slurring. "Yessir. Ain't no one owns a prettier one." He looked along the bar, then back at Ezra. "Ain't no one I can't beat to the draw neither, drunk or sober."

He peered at Ezra closely. "By God, if you ain't the pup that runs with that son-of-a-bitching Kid."

The man next to Grant at the bar edged away. The room quieted.

"Well, ain't you?" Grant demanded.

"I know Billy," Ezra said.

Grant lifted the muzzle of his gun, pointing it at Ezra's gut. "I mean to do for the Kid one of these days. This county ain't big enough for him and me both."

Ezra swallowed. If he went for his Colt, Grant would shoot. If he didn't, he'd have to stand here and listen to insults. Grant might shoot him even if he didn't try to draw; you never knew what a drunk would do.

"Course, I could start with you." Grant's finger touched the trigger.

Ezra made himself stare into Grant's eyes, unmoving. Bastard's trying to get me to go for my gun, he told himself. Then he'd have an excuse. His knees felt as mushy as refried beans. He took a deep breath.

"I sure do admire that pistol," he said, surprised that his voice didn't quiver. "I've never seen a pearl-handled one before."

Grant blinked and then glanced down at his gun. He smiled. "She's a beauty." The muzzle pointed away from

Ezra as Grant turned the pistol over in his hands again.
"Prettier than a ten-dollar whore."

Men began talking again, a little too loudly. Ezra looked
quickly around and saw that Billy had stepped in from a
back room. He didn't know how long Billy had been
standing there. Grant hadn't seen him yet.

Billy sauntered over.

"Evening, Joe," Billy said, grinning. "Nice little gun
you got there." He held out his hand. "Mind if I take a
look?"

Grant stared at Billy. Ezra could almost hear Grant's
thoughts: If I don't hand him the gun, I'm a coward. If I
do hand him the gun, he might shoot me. If I shoot him
instead of giving him the pistol, this other young pup'll
have a chance to get me.

"What the hell, take a look," Grant said. He put the
pearl-handled Colt into Billy's hands.

Billy examined the gun, twirled the cylinder and handed
it back to Grant. "Very nice," he said. "How about a
drink?"

"Don't mind if I do," Grant agreed, sliding the gun
into his holster.

"I know you ain't much of a drinker, Ez," Billy said.
"Why don't you play a little poker? I see there's an empty
chair."

Ezra knew Billy wanted him away from Grant. He
shrugged and said, "Sure. I feel sort of lucky tonight."

He eased into the seat, anted and picked up the cards
dealt him, watching Billy from the corner of his eye.

"Gonna be trouble," the cowboy next to Ezra muttered,
"as sure as my name's Gene Shelton."

"Stand or draw?" the dealer asked.

Ezra glanced briefly at his five cards. Two kings. He'd

keep those, discard three. A moment later, when the dealer threw him two cards, he realized he'd only tossed in two, keeping a jack with his two kings.

"I can draw faster than any man in the Territory," Grant said loudly.

Ezra turned his head toward the bar. Saw Grant pull the damn pearl-handled Colt as he spoke. Aim at Billy. Before Ezra was out of his chair, Grant pulled the trigger.

The gun clicked as the hammer fell on an empty chamber.

Almost leisurely, Billy's Colt came out of its holster. It roared just as Grant's clicked again.

Grant staggered against the bar, then fell headlong. He twitched once. Lay still.

Ezra jammed his half-drawn pistol back into the holster as he strode toward Billy.

Billy stepped over Grant's body. "Any luck?" he said.

It took Ezra a moment to understand what he meant, then realized he was still clutching the two kings and the jack in his left hand.

"I don't know," he said, striving to sound as casual as Billy. "I didn't look at my draw."

Billy strolled back to the poker table with him and watched while Ezra picked up the two cards he'd been dealt. Two jacks.

Ezra took the pot with his full house.

"Guess it's just your lucky night, Ez," Billy told him.

By the time they were outside, Ezra had figured out what happened. Billy must have seen there were only a few shells in the cylinder and twirled it to get the empties up front. Grant had been too drunk to understand what was going on.

Still, Grant would be alive if he hadn't pulled iron on Billy first.

Tessa cried when Ezra packed up to leave the next morning.

"Papa would roll over in his grave if he knew you were stealing cattle," she sobbed.

"You leave Papa out of this. He's dead. I'm not. I'm doing things my way. I like it. It's a free life—we live how we want and no one stops us. You got to understand, Tess, that you can't mother me forever. Why don't you get married and have yourself some babies to raise?"

For some reason this made her cry harder. He felt bad going off leaving her so unhappy, but it couldn't be helped.

"Your sister doesn't want to marry Mr. Rutledge," Violet pointed out to Ezra as they rode toward Sumner with the others.

"Well, Mark's back; she could marry him if she wanted to."

"I do not think he has asked her," Violet said.

Ezra didn't reply. Sometimes he didn't understand other people. He'd sure thought Mark and Tessa were in love. But maybe it was like Billy and Violet. Sort of one-sided. Billy was fond of Violet, true, but he didn't take care of her and he certainly didn't plan to marry her. In fact, Ezra didn't know what would become of Violet if he weren't around to look after her.

When they got to Sumner, John Chisum was there on business.

"No more of this chicken one day, feathers the next," Billy told his men. "Our worries are over. Chisum owes me at least five hundred for the work I did for him when we were riding as the Regulators."

Chisum thought otherwise.

"I never hired you," he said to Billy as they stood talking near the old army hospital, now a house. Ezra eyed the older man. He must be lying.

"There was no agreement you were working for me," Chisum went on.

"Damn you," Billy cried, pulling his Colt. "We didn't shake on it, but you know you asked me to clean out those Dolan bastards. Didn't I do it? I mean to have that money."

Chisum began to tamp tobacco into his pipe, paying no attention to the Colt. "I can talk better when I smoke," he said. "Now, Billy, you listen to me. You can go on jawing away until your hair is as white as mine, but you won't convince me I owe you a cent. Do you plan to shoot me over it? You've killed men, I know that, but they needed killing. I'm an honest man, or I try to be. Do you believe I need killing? Look at all the times I helped you out, letting the Regulators take anything they needed from my store at the ranch."

Billy reluctantly put away his Colt. "I reckon you don't need shooting," he said, "but if you won't agree to pay me that money, then I expect you're going to find yourself missing cattle until it's paid in full."

After they left Chisum, Billy called his entire gang together.

"No money from Chisum," he said. "We're going to add on a few more boys and go after the old bastard's cows. I'll make him damn sorry he ever said 'no' to Billy Bonney."

For the first time, Ezra not only mistrusted the men Billy added to their crew but downright disliked them. Dave Rudabaugh, for one, was, besides being mean, so God-awful dirty you tried hard to stay up-wind of him.

For a month or so they drove Chisum steers north from Texas, selling them to army beef suppliers. Then Billy decided they needed a little fun. A new town, White Oaks, had sprung up forty-some miles northwest of Lincoln. A rich town, what with the gold being mined in the nearby mountains. Billy took a notion to travel that way and try out the saloons.

They were in one of the White Oaks saloons having a drink when an old Regulator, digging for gold now instead of riding with Billy, hurried into the place and sidled up to Billy.

"Deputy Huggens is getting a posse ready," he said. "You better ride while you can, Billy. He aims to get you."

"Why we're here all peaceful-like!" Billy exclaimed.

"Huggens is out for your hide, is all I know. He claims White Oaks ain't a harbor for murderers and thieves. Just thought I'd pass the word."

Billy sighed. "Getting so a man can't have a quiet drink anymore. Well, you heard him, boys. We don't have a quarrel with this Huggens, so I guess we ride if we don't mean to fight."

It was late in the afternoon when they left, so they stopped at Greathouse and Kuck's stage station to spend the night. Near morning the sound of horses' hooves and men shouting roused them.

"You're surrounded," someone yelled. "Come out with your hands up."

Billy asked Greathouse to go out and see what was going on. Ezra, peering cautiously from a window, saw at least a dozen men on horseback milling about in front of the house.

There were only seven of them; the rest had gone to Sumner instead of White Oaks.

"Sheriff's posse," Greathouse reported. "They have the place surrounded, just like they said."

"I sure as hell ain't going to surrender to them," Billy said.

"There's this young fellow named Carlyle wants to come in and talk to you," Greathouse said. "Only thing is, they want one of you to go out and stay with them while Carlyle's in here."

"Don't like it," Billy said.

"I could go out there," Greathouse offered.

Billy shrugged. "That's okay with me."

Carlyle came in as Greathouse went out. Carlyle was a stocky young man, heavy in the arms and shoulders. He said he was a blacksmith at White Oaks, deputized for this posse.

"Don't cotton to blacksmiths, somehow," Billy said. "What're you after us for, Carlyle?"

"There's warrants out," Carlyle said. "You ought to know that. For shooting Brady and Roberts. And then there's the fact you been rustling stock."

"If you got warrants, let me see your papers," Billy said.

"We don't carry paper. But we know about you. We don't want your kind in White Oaks."

"You ain't arresting me," Billy told him. "I ain't going to jail for you or any man in that posse out there. What we're going to do, is keep you with us till dark; then you can lead us out so we can quit this damn place."

"I'm a hostage in good faith," Carlyle protested. "You sent a man out when I came in. You can't keep me here."

"We sure as hell can."

Someone banged on the door and a note was shoved underneath. Ezra ran to pick it up. He handed the note to Billy.

"Says that if I don't let you go in the next few minutes," Billy told Carlyle, "they mean to shoot Greathouse. Now what kind of good faith is that?"

Carlyle waved his fist. "Surrender!" he cried.

"You're loco. If they kill Greathouse, it sure puts your butt in a real deep crack. I told you what I mean . . ."

A Winchester cracked outside the house.

"Oh my God, they've killed him!" Carlyle yelled. He darted away from Billy and flung himself headlong at a window. Glass shattered as he leaped through it. Billy and O'Folliard, Colts drawn, ran toward the window, but before they could reach it, pistols barked outside. Billy shot back. So did O'Folliard.

Ezra stared from the window near him. Carlyle lay unmoving on the ground. He didn't know who'd shot him. Could have been the men outside or the shots Billy and O'Folliard fired. Bullets slammed into the wall and Ezra unholstered his Colt.

Ezra's window smashed as a bullet pierced the glass. He ducked back, edged to the opening to fire at a man racing past on his horse. He missed. Aimed again. Held. The posse was leaving.

A half-hour later Billy and the others rode away from the stage station.

"At least they didn't kill Greathouse," Billy said, "even if they did wind up shooting that loco blacksmith of theirs. He was down before me or Tom fired a shot." Billy shook his head. "I'm going to be blamed for that killing, sure as Pecos shad have gizzards."

It wasn't fair, Ezra thought. Billy had tried not to cause trouble and look what happened. It wasn't his fault.

All the other killings came out of the war between Dolan and McSween. Dolan was just as guilty as Billy of the deaths during the feuding, but they weren't organizing posses to chase Dolan.

You couldn't count shooting Joe Grant; that was Grant's fault.

Sure, they rustled a few steers here and there, but any time they took any large number of cows, it was from Chisum's herds and he owed Billy.

Ezra'd tried to make Tess understand, but she was a blind as anyone else when it came to seeing what was true and what wasn't.

Summer passed without any other run-ins with the law. In the fall Billy got word that Pat Garrett had been elected sheriff.

"Old Pat's not going to bother us none," Billy predicted. "He knows me, knows well enough it ain't no use coming after us." He grinned at Ezra. "We're lucky; maybe it's rubbed off from you.

"Supplies are getting low, though, so I think we'll take us a trip down to the panhandle and bring back some of those Texas cattle to sell."

The sun peeked over the rim of the world, tinting the sky pink as Maria stirred a pot of beans in her kitchen while Jules toyed with fried corn mush at the table. The November weather had been unseasonably mild, so Tessa turned away from the window, deciding to wear only a light shawl to school.

"Hurry and finish, Jules," she said.

"Don't want to go to school," he mumbled.

"Are you sick?" Tessa felt his forehead. "No, you're not hot. What's the matter?"

"Nothing."

"Jules, answer me."

"They said he was gonna get Billy."

"Who said?"

"The fellows at school."

"They say all kinds of things. Who do they mean?"

"The new deputy. The one who's gonna be sheriff next year."

"Mr. Garrett?"

"Yeah."

"Please don't say 'yeah'."

"Pat Garrett says he means to bring in Billy and see him hang. And the others in his gang, too." Jules jabbed at the fried mush with his knife. "They told me I'm gonna have to watch Ezra dance at the end of a rope. I hate all of them."

"Madre de Dios!" Maria exclaimed.

"No!" Tessa said at the same moment.

"They *said* so," Jules persisted.

"No such thing is going to happen!" Tessa cried. "Sheriff Garrett can say all he wants to, but no one's caught Billy yet."

Jules looked up at her. *"He* might."

"Even if he does arrest Billy, that has nothing to do with Ezra. Nothing's going to happen to Ezra. I won't let it."

As she tried to reassure Jules, Tessa felt her stomach knot. She, too, had heard that Pat Garrett was a man who got a job done, a man who never gave up.

"You can stay home from school," she said to Jules. "I don't feel well enough to teach today. I'll go and put a notice on the school door."

"I can take the notice," Maria offered. "You rest."

"No, thank you. I need the fresh air."

Tessa hurried along the road. She hadn't wanted Maria or Jules to know she was headed for Mark's rooming house because she was well nigh engaged to Calvin Rutledge. After all this time apart, what was she going to say to Mark?

She had money saved up, not much, but enough for Ezra to leave the Territory and get a start somewhere else. Maybe in California or Oregon. If Mark could locate Ezra and give him the money. Was that too much to ask of Mark?

She knew he was in town; she kept track of his comings and goings and he was gone oftener than not. That made it easier, since she couldn't help her pulse of excitement whenever he was in town and she caught sight of his lean figure riding past.

If Calvin's kisses didn't thrill her as Mark's had, neither would Calvin ever break her heart.

What made her think Mark would do any favors for her?

Not for me, she told herself. For Ezra. For Jules. Even though she didn't see Mark anymore, he'd kept his promise to teach Jules how to play the harmonica. She knew he was fond of the boy.

Tessa had never been to Mark's room, but she knew where it was. Jules had described how you went up the outside steps in the back of the building where he roomed. Though she met no one on the road, she felt terribly conspicuous as she ducked around to the rear of the place. Thank God it was so early that few people were stirring.

Rickety wooden steps led up to a second floor. Tessa climbed them.

"You go in through the door and there's a hall," Jules had told her. "Then there's three doors. His is the one in the middle. He leaves it open for me."

It wouldn't be open for her. She'd have to knock.

Tessa's heart beat faster as she opened the door at the top of the stairs and stepped into the hall.

She passed the first door. Here was the second. Ajar. Should she knock? Tessa bit her lip and touched the door with her fingertips. It swung farther open.

The first thing she saw was the metal footboard of a bed.

The second thing she saw was Susie McSween sitting on the bed kissing Mark.

Chapter 15

Tessa fled down the stairs, ran around the house and into the road. A drover shouted at her. Scarcely breaking stride, she swerved out of the way of his mule-drawn wagon and hurried on.

Lost him, lost him, I've lost him. The refrain played over and over in her head. Lost Mark. Lost Ezra.

She sobbed tearlessly. Her chest hurt. Images of Susie's red hair close to Mark's dark hair alternated with visions of Ezra dangling from the end of a rope.

Calvin. Calvin would help her. Not with Mark, Mark would never be hers; she knew that now. But Ezra could still be saved.

Calvin wore a short silk robe over his trousers; she hadn't seen a man in a dressing robe since her father had worn his out a year before his death.

"What's wrong, Tessa?" Calvin demanded, trying to put his arms about her.

She held herself stiffly away. "You must help me find Ezra. Right away. He's got to leave the Territory."

"Calm yourself, Tessa. Sit down. Tell me what's the matter."

She gripped the back of a straight chair. "There's no time for talking. This new sheriff, Pat Garrett, he's going after Billy and his gang. He boasts he'll see them all hang. I can't let that happen to Ezra!"

"Do you want me to speak to Mr. Garrett, is that it? Try to arrange a way out for Ezra?"

"No, no, I want you to find Ezra. I have some . . ."

"How do you expect me to locate your brother? Billy and his boys swarm over the entire Territory and into Texas and Mexico. We can leave word at some of the places they favor, here in town and at Sumner, saying you must see Ezra as soon as possible, but other than that . . ."

"Oh!" Tessa straightened and put her hands on her hips. "Are you afraid to ride after Ezra?"

A muscle twitched in Calvin's face. "You're being unreasonable. No one rides alone from Lincoln these days. It's only safe in groups of five or six, all well-armed. Billy's boys aren't the only cutthroats roaming the county. There are still stray Apaches as well as the Comancheros. You know that very well, Tessa. I'm not a coward, but I'm not an idiot either."

"Find others to go with you then."

He sighed. "That won't be easy. But I promise I'll try." Again he tried to embrace her, and though she didn't pull away, she remained rigid in his arms.

Was Susie still in Mark's arms? Tessa wondered. He hadn't seen her standing there, though Susie might have. Were they making love now?

She jerked back from Calvin's kiss. "Will you ride today?"

"For God's sake, Tessa. I gave you my promise. It'll take time to locate enough men. A week maybe. Then we'll have to make inquiries, find out where Billy was last seen and . . ."

"I can't wait!" She whirled and flung herself from his room and ran toward Maria's, only half-aware of the stares of others on the street.

There was no one she could count on. She'd have to do it herself.

Tessa rode east from Lincoln, on the Pecos road, heading for Sumner. The town had been Billy's headquarters for over a year and seemed the most likely place to start.

She wore some of Ezra's outgrown clothes she'd been saving for Jules—denim pants, a red flannel shirt, buckskin jacket—and she had her hair tucked up under an old wide-brimmed hat. Her father's Colt weighed down a jacket pocket.

It was nearly ninety miles to Sumner and so she'd fastened a bedroll behind the roan's saddle and carried a packet of food.

Maria had been aghast at what she intended to do and Jules had been angry because she wouldn't take him along. She'd swept their protests aside, hardly hearing them. Of course she could do it. Would do it.

Now, though, as the afternoon shadows lengthened and Tessa realized she'd have to find a spot to camp for the night, she almost wished she'd brought Jules so she wouldn't be alone. There were ranches along the way that took in night guests, but she was afraid to try one since she knew the men travelers shared a room and she wouldn't be able to conceal she was a woman.

She was counting on the fact that she looked like a boy, and a none-too-well-dressed one at that, to keep her from being bothered along the road.

When dusk lay hazy in the hollows between the hills, Tessa realized she must pick her campsite soon. There was a grove of leafless cottonwoods off the road ahead that might be a good spot. She urged the roan into a lope.

As she neared the trees, seven riders crested a hill on the opposite side of the road and saw her.

"Hey, kid!" one of them called.

Tessa resisted the impulse to kick her horse into a gallop. There were too many of them and, besides, they might shoot her if she tried to run.

She waved a hand in acknowledgement and kept on at her same pace. She had no intention of going into the trees now but would stay on the road, hoping they'd lose interest in a lone, poorly dressed boy.

Alarm tensed her muscles when she heard the pound of hooves behind her. She glanced back.

"Hold up there!" a black-bearded man shouted. He fired his Colt into the air.

Tessa reined in the roan. Don't panic, she told herself. It's getting dark and they can't see you clearly; you'll pass for a boy.

Seven riders clattered up and surrounded her. The one who'd fired the shot, a man with a full black beard, spoke first.

"Where ya headed so fast, sonny?"

Tessa kept her eyes on the bearded man and did her best to make her voice low-pitched. "Sumner."

"He's only carrying a bedroll," another of the riders said. "Not even a Winchester."

The bearded man ran an eye over the roan, which was not the better looking of the two horses Tessa owned. She'd chosen him today for that reason.

"Okay, kid, go on," the man said, easing his mount from her path.

Tessa swallowed. Not trusting her voice, she sketched a salute and kneed the roan into a trot. As she pulled away from the men, she sighed in relief.

She'd gone barely twenty paces when she heard hooves again and a rider pulled up alongside her. She glanced at him. He wasn't the bearded man but one of the others. A Mexican with silver conchos on his saddle.

"*Buenas tardes, Señorita* Nesbitt," he said.

Her eyes widened in shocked recognition. Vincente Gabaldon!

"It is an unexpected pleasure to meet you again." Vincente smiled as he spoke, a smile that thrust a dagger of fear along Tessa's spine.

She dropped her hand toward the pocket where her Colt nestled.

Vincente pushed his sorrel next to her roan. Dropped a lasso over her head. Grabbed the reins from her hands as he tightened the rope around her arms and chest.

She was helpless.

He lifted the Colt from her pocket, holding it in his hand. "A big *pistolo* for a *señorita*," he said mockingly.

Tessa stared at him fearfully, trying to gather her wits. "Let me go!" she cried.

The other six men rode up just as Vincente reached across and lifted the hat from her head. Insecurely pinned strands of hair fell to her shoulders.

"By God, it's a filly!" the bearded man exclaimed. "Old Vince has caught us a prize, after all."

"You are wrong, Ed." Vincente didn't actually point her Colt at the bearded man, but there was no mistaking the threat underlying his words.

"The *señorita* and I are old friends," Vincente went on. "I do not think you wish to interrupt our reunion, *no es verdad?*"

"If you mean you get to go first," Ed said, "I ain't got no objection."

Tessa, the import of his words suddenly clear to her, tried to conceal her involuntary shudder.

Vincente put the hat back on her head and kicked his sorrel into a trot, pulling her roan after him. Tessa swayed, balancing as best she could with her arms pinned by the rope tied to his saddle horn.

Dusk deepened into night. A sickle moon rode the sky. Tessa's fear of what would happen to her was gradually replaced by weariness as they traveled on and on. When they finally pulled up by an old wooden building, she almost fell off the roan.

Vincente eased her down, catching her in his arms and setting her on her feet. He didn't loosen the rope. Tessa stared at the dilapidated hut, probably an old line camp.

Were they all to sleep inside it? All of them forcing her, one at a time with the others looking on? Waiting for their turn? She bit her lip. No, she thought, no, oh, please, no.

She gagged, tasted the bitterness of bile.

Vincente pointed to a lean-to some yards behind the building. "The *señorita* and I will share that, I think. Alone."

"Okay, but don't take all night, Vince," Ed warned him.

Vince brought the two horses with them as he led Tessa to the lean-to.

"Why do you do this to me?" she asked, keeping her voice low. "I've never caused you any harm."

"You think not? Who was it, then, who encouraged my Violet to become a *puta*? Billy the Kid's whore. Was it not your brother and yourself?"

"No! Ezra was in love with Violet. He still is. He wouldn't hurt her. It was Violet who chose Billy instead. I

tried to tell her . . ." Tessa broke off. What was the use?
Vincente wouldn't believe a word she said.

"You will discover for yourself what it is to be every
man's woman," he said. "To be a whore."

Tessa straightened her back. "You're wrong. None of
this is my choice. You mean to rape me, but that doesn't
make me a—a whore. You're the one that's bad, *maloso*,
not me."

He said nothing. Clouds covered the thin moon and a
cold wind started to blow from the north.

"Snow comes, I think," Vincente said.

He gripped her arms and she stiffened. But he was only
loosening the rope. He jerked it over her head, knocking off
her hat.

"Pick up your hat," he ordered. "You'll need it."

I'll run, she thought. But where to? There was no
cover for miles except a few stands of bare cottonwoods
here and there. They'd find her easily.

"*Aqua Negra*," Vincente muttered.

Black water? It didn't make any sense.

He grasped both her wrists and drew her to him. "Listen
carefully," he whispered. "We will walk the horses. Stay
with me. If you try to get away, they will recapture you.
Do you understand?"

"Walk the horses," she whispered back in agreement,
her mind in a whirl. Was he helping her to escape? "I'll
stay with you."

They walked endlessly, her legs stiff from the long ride.
When he finally ordered her into the saddle, it was ex-
changing one discomfort for another, but she made no
protest, asked no questions. Wherever he was taking her it
was better than the line camp where six men waited to
violate her.

On and on they rode. Vincente looked back once in a

while, but they heard no pursuit. After a time Tessa went into a trance, half-asleep, half-awake. When Vincente spoke, she came to with a start.

"We are here. Stop, Dismount."

Tessa reined in the roan and slid to the ground, chilled to the bone by the icy wind. He took her horse as well as his, leading them. She hurried along beside him, suddenly aware, when the wind diminished, that rock walls rose on either side of them.

The walls narrowed until there was scarcely room for the horses to walk side by side. Then they were scrambling up, up, stones rattling and falling behind them. The rock underneath her feet leveled, but they didn't stop.

"Ah!" Vincente said at last. "I was not certain I could find it in the dark."

"Where are we?" she asked, the first time she'd spoken since he'd led her away from the other men.

"Behind Black Water Spring. It is a cave the Comanches showed me."

She'd heard of Black Water Spring. Remembered where she'd heard of it before.

A spring at the eastern foot of Capitan Mountain in uninhabited country where the trees shadowed the pool formed by the spring water.

Agua Negra, where the Regulators had murdered Morton, Baker and McCloskey.

Tessa shuddered.

"We will stay here," Vincente said. "Take care of your horse."

She did what she could for the roan, hampered by the pitch darkness and her fatigue. As she stood back from the horse, light flickered to her right and she turned to look.

Vincente had started a fire. She moved toward it eagerly, holding out her hands. As she warmed herself, Vincente laid out their bedrolls. It took her a moment to understand he was combining them into one.

She made an involuntary sound of protest and he glanced up at her, half-smiling. "I am far too tired to rape you at the moment, *señorita*. We bed together for warmth."

She was too exhausted to argue. They lay spoon-fashion, with the tiny fire giving off its slight warmth at their feet and the horses tethered to their left. Tessa held herself rigid for a few moments, relaxing only when she heard Vincente's breathing change to the slower, deeper pattern of sleep.

The next thing she knew it was morning. The light was dim, but she saw they were around a bend of rock from the cave's opening. She heard the wind whistling outside over the restless shifting of the horses. The fire was out.

She lay on her back with Vincente's arm flung across her breasts. As she carefully tried to shift position, he opened his eyes. His hand moved so that he cupped one of her breasts. Apprehension, tinged with something else she couldn't quite identify, shot through her.

He turned on his side, shifted her and pulled her closer. She felt his hardness against her. In horrified surprise she realized what the warmth in her loins meant. Her body was responding to his touch.

No!

Tessa twisted in his grasp, trying to pull away. His grip tightened.

"Do not fight me," he murmured. "*Mi linda*, my lovely one." He stroked her hair, "So fine, like golden silk; never have I seen such hair. And your eyes are as soft a gray as the breast of a dove. So beautiful."

His voice was soothing and pleasant in her ear; his words mesmerized her. She lay still as his fingers touched her face, tracing her lips, trailing under her chin to her throat where he loosened her neckerchief.

"Skin finer than any satin, lips as tempting as the honied sweetness of a mango." He unbuttoned her jacket, her shirt, bent his head to put his lips to her throat, then lower, lower. He pulled up her camisole to take her nipple into his mouth.

He was right, there was no point in fighting him—he was stronger, and she had no place to run to, there was nothing she could do . . .

The small glow in her loins spread, warming her. Upsetting her. How could she feel this way about Vincente? She had no love for him. What was happening to her?

He kissed her lips, her eyelids, her ears, while his hands deftly undressed her. "So lovely a woman, like a star, shining and beautiful," he murmured.

It was exciting to hear him saying such things. His hands touched her bare flesh, stroking, caressing. Her breathing came faster.

She closed her eyes as he raised himself above her.

"Ah, you welcome me to you, *flor de mi corazon*," Vincente said as he touched the liquid warmth between her thighs.

Flower of my heart, he'd called her. Unable to help herself, she opened to him, felt a stab of pleasure as he thrust deeply within her, moving first slowly, then faster.

She moved with him, her body apart from herself, her body needing what he was giving her, wanting it. Enjoying it.

At the same time, coiled in her brain, a part of her looked on, appalled. A wanton, as she'd feared she might be. A whore.

But his maleness inside her, his fingers stroking her taut nipples made her body rise to meet him, a wildness rising in her and growing out of her control. She heard the animal noises she made deep in her throat as though they came from a stranger.

Faster and faster he stroked.

"No!" she screamed as she felt herself dissolving in spasms of thrilling release. "No, no!"

She heard him give a growling laugh and then he, too, peaked and subsided.

"I think we will get along very well together," Vincente told her in a husky whisper.

Tessa turned away from him, tears in her eyes. How could she? With Vincente who'd cast off everything she believed in to become an outlaw. With Vincente whom she would never love.

With Mark there'd been the excitement, but there'd been more. As though they were giving themselves to one another to cherish. Her tears flowed faster.

Something prodded her in the back. She turned and saw Vincente's boot.

"Get up," he ordered.

He was fully dressed. He watched sardonically while she struggled to pull on her clothes under the cover of the blankets.

"Such modesty," he said mockingly.

She finished dressing, stood to pull on her boots, then knelt to straighten and roll up the blankets.

"No need to separate them so carefully," he said. "We're going to be traveling together for some time, *mi linda*."

She tightened her lips.

He handed her a strip of jerked beef. "We will eat better tonight. Now we must go to find food for the horses."

Tessa, hungry, chewed on the beef without comment.

He helped her saddle up, then, with her following on foot, led the horses to the mouth of the cave. Tessa gasped.

A white blanket covered the rocks. It had snowed during the night—a sight both awe-inspiring and depressing. The sky was gray with the promise of more snow to come. She'd been assuring herself she'd escape from Vincente at the earliest opportunity, but it was clear she'd have to wait until the weather improved.

She had no idea which way to head and it would be risking death to be lost in these mountains in bad weather. Her heart sank as she thought how long it might be before the weather changed. November was a month of storms.

"I was right to take you away from those others," Vincente said. "They would not appreciate your beauty. Now that you are mine, we will head for Mexico. I have a brother in Chihuahua. It is a good plan, no?"

Tessa, appalled at the idea, said nothing, but he went on without seeming to notice.

"You please me very much. Perhaps I will even marry you and allow you to bear my sons."

Chapter 16

Billy sold the Texas cattle, mostly Chisum's, to Pat Coughlin on the Tulerosa, but before he and his gang could head north to Sumner, a rider pounded into Coughlin's camp. He was a hard-faced *hombre* who spoke only Spanish.

"My name is Miguel," he said to Billy. "You don't know me, but when I heard *el Chivato* was here, I came. My cousin, Jose Chavez, an old friend of yours, is in jail."

"Where?" Billy asked.

"In Texas. At San Elizario."

Ezra, listening, nodded to himself. He knew the place, a small village on the Rio Grande near El Paso.

"Jose wants out, is that it?" Billy said.

Miguel smiled. "*No cabe duda.* There is no doubt."

"I think we might be able to arrange something."

"*Muchas gracias, el Chivato.*"

"Do you join us?"

209

Miguel shook his head. "Texas is not good for my health, you understand."

Billy grinned at him and nodded. "I'll give Jose your regards."

After Miguel rode out of camp, Billy talked over his plans with the others.

"No point in all of us heading for San Elizario. It won't take more than a couple of us to spring Jose." He looked around at the men and Ezra held his breath, hoping.

"Tom," Billy went on, "you keep an eye on things here till we get back."

O'Folliard nodded.

"How about it, Ez," Billy asked, "want to ride with me?"

Ezra nearly burst with pride. Billy had chosen him! He could hardly stammer out, "I'm ready!"

Billy and Ezra arrived in El Paso at dusk. San Elizario was about a three-hour ride down the river from here, Ezra knew. After they'd eaten, to his surprise Billy showed no sign of getting ready to travel.

"Used to be a pretty nice little *tendejon* in El Paso," Billy said. "Might as well see if it's still here."

"But I thought you meant to get to the jail tonight," Ezra protested.

Billy smiled. "After midnight, *compadre*. Haven't you noticed that along about two or three in the morning most men ain't got all their wits working? 'Specially if you wake them up."

Ezra nodded, knowing Billy spoke the truth. If he thought about it, it was something he knew but hadn't figured into what they meant to do. But Billy figured in everything. That's why no lawman could ever catch him.

The *tendejon* was still in business. Billy pushed into the

place with Ezra, following, careful not to look directly at any of women.

"Now, *mi amigo*," Billy said, "I'm going to see you get the prettiest *señorita* here."

Ezra glanced at Billy, who wore a teasing grin. Ezra thought he'd successfully concealed the fact he'd never taken a woman to bed, but it was plain Billy knew it.

"How about that one?" Billy nodded his head at a lushly curved woman in a low-cut red gown.

Ezra swallowed and shook his head. He couldn't deny she was attractive and even excited him, but her smile hinted of experience, of knowledge Ezra hadn't learned, and that unnerved him.

When I'm alone with her, she'll laugh at me, he told himself. Yet if he tried to back out completely, Billy would realize he was afraid. Ezra knew he couldn't bear that.

"Maybe you want to choose one for yourself," Billy said. "Which one?"

Ezra licked dry lips as he looked from one woman to the next. His heart hammered in his chest. He longed to be able to swagger up to one of them like Billy could and smile and slip an arm about her.

He couldn't.

It'd be far worse if Billy laughed at him than if one of these women did. He had to make a choice. Pick one of them.

He spotted a tiny woman, half-hidden behind a buxom *señorita* who was laughing up at a bearded man.

"That one," he said to Billy, gesturing with his head.

"The big one?" Billy sounded surprised.

"No. Behind her. See?"

"She's all yours, *amigo*. Go and get her." Billy gave Ezra a push that sent him stumbling toward her.

Ezra caught himself and walked on, his palms sweating, the blood roaring in his ears.

"*Buenas tardes, señorita,*" he managed to blurt out when he stood facing her.

She stared up at him with widened eyes. Fear lurked in their dark depths and Ezra blinked in surprise. There was nothing about him that ought to scare her.

She tried to smile.

Two guitar players put down their drinks and began strumming a spirited tune. Couples moved into a cleared space to dance.

Ezra hadn't danced with a girl since that time with Violet. He didn't know how well he'd do with so many people watching.

"What's your name?" he asked, speaking in Spanish.

"Juanita." The word was so soft he hardly heard it.

"Mine's Ezra."

"Ez-ra? That name is new to me."

"Do you want to dance?"

Juanita looked relieved. A genuine smile lighted her face, making her quite pretty for a moment. He thought she probably wasn't any older than he was.

"Oh, yes, let's dance," she agreed.

He put an arm about her waist and moved onto the tiny dance floor. Juanita was light on her feet so that he didn't do too badly as they whirled and dipped. The feel of her body against his began to arouse him.

He realized she was aware of this when she whispered, "May I have a drink before we go upstairs?"

God knows, he could use a drink!

They stood in a corner sipping *aguardiente*, sweet and fiery. He was in no more of a hurry than she to finish and finally they both had a second glass.

When that was gone, Ezra felt the liquor's warmth

spreading into his loins and suddenly he was eager to go upstairs with Juanita.

In a small room, barely big enough for the cot, a chair and a washstand, Juanita slid off her black dress, folding it neatly on the chair. She wore nothing underneath. He caught his breath, his hands fumbling with his belt.

Her small breasts were peaked with tan nipples that stood erect in the coolness of the upstairs. Her body curved in to a tiny waist, then out to the fullness of her hips. When he glanced at her face, he saw her eyes were cast down.

Ezra lifted her chin, forcing her to look at him. Her eyes had a glazed look, but he thought terror flickered beneath.

"What's the matter?" he asked.

"Nothing." Her voice was slightly slurred. "Do you not wish to undress?"

He was eager to feel her skin against his and hurried to get out of his clothes. He reached for Juanita, pulling her against him.

She was as cold as ice. He felt her shiver.

"We can get under the blanket," he offered, pulling her down onto the cot. She made no resistance.

Ezra lay on his side, holding her close to him, his throbbing sex thrust against the soft skin of her thighs. He caressed her back, ran his hand along the curve of her hip.

It wasn't as though he didn't know what came next. He did. And he wanted very much to do it. He was on fire with the need to thrust inside her. But he waited, stroking her. She yielded to every move he made, but he sensed her unwillingness. He wanted her to want him and he knew she not only didn't but wasn't even pretending she did.

"Is it me?" he asked hoarsely, pulling slightly away from her.

"What? I don't understand."

"Is there something about me you don't like?"

"No, Ez-ra, I like you very much. Better than most."

"Then why are you so afraid?"

"I'm not afraid of you. Not anymore."

He looked at her face in the flickering light of the candle on the wall. Her eyes were pools of shadow that told him nothing.

"But you were afraid at first."

She nodded. "Because you are a tall man."

Ezra tended to forget he'd shot up to six feet. Still, what did that have to do with anything?

"Big men sometimes choose me because I am so small. Because they like to hurt me." She seemed to sense his confusion. "Not when they take me, not that. It is not very much different, one man from another, doing that."

With her words, his desire lessened. She reached down and touched his sex lightly. He gasped as her fingers stroked him.

"I think we have talked enough," she said.

Her hands urged him to move over her, guided him inside her. Everything faded but the overwhelming excitement of her inner warmth and softness. He moved and thrust, his passion out of control, mounting, peaking. Exploding.

Yet when he was finished and lay resting on the cot, Ezra felt cheated of all he had wanted. He'd tried somehow to make more of this than Juanita was willing to grant him. He watched her wash herself, seeing for the first time a pattern of dark stripes across her bare back and buttocks.

He sat up. "What are those marks on your back?" he asked.

She glanced over her shoulder at him. "I told you. From a man who wanted to hurt me. He used his belt."

Her voice was matter-of-fact. "I can't tell which men will be like that until we come upstairs, and then it's too late."

He felt sick, the liquor sour in his stomach. He rose from the cot and dressed quickly. Juanita, her dress covering her once more, put her hand on his arm.

"With you it was very sweet," she said.

Her smile was also sweet, but Ezra thought her eyes were haunted. He realized with a shock he was seeing Violet's face instead of Juanita's, and he understood then that he'd chosen this girl because she reminded him of Violet.

Ezra leaned over and kissed Juanita gently on the lips. "I wish you didn't have to work here," he said.

She drew back. "It's not so bad. I'll soon have enough money so I can get married. Where else could I earn such money?" She smoothed her hair. "I don't think you understand, Ez-ra."

Hastily he reached into his pocket for his money, handed all he found to Juanita, thinking that, no, he didn't understand. Anymore than he understood why Violet let herself be hurt and humiliated by Billy's indifference.

"But I have given myself to Billy," Violet had told him when he'd tried to talk to her about it. "It's the same as being married. A wife must stay with her husband. Be true to him, no matter what."

"You're not married to him," he'd protested, but Violet had said he was a man and men didn't know how women felt about these things.

Ezra was sure Billy didn't care one way or the other whether Violet was with him or not. And Billy certainly didn't think of himself as Violet's husband.

Ezra trailed down the stairs after Juanita. He found Billy at monte table. Winning. Ezra sat down and managed to lose what little money he had left. He purposely didn't look around, not wanting to risk seeing Juanita with another man.

He and Billy left El Paso just after midnight, following a road that wound downstream along the Rio Grande. The country was desolate under a sickle moon. Barren.

"Enjoy yourself?" Billy asked.

"Lost all my money."

Billy laughed. "Maybe I got ahold of your luck tonight. How about the girl?"

Ezra shrugged. He didn't want to talk about it. About her.

"Well, *amigo*, you were the one who chose her. I have no complaints about my evening." He grinned at Ezra. "How'd you like to be a Texas Ranger?" he added after a moment.

Ezra stared at him.

"We're going to join up, Ez. Going to be full-fledged Rangers by the time we get to that San Elizario *calabozo*. First of all, though, we'll find a horse for old Jose. As I remember, he's partial to roans."

"You think we look like Rangers?" Ezra asked.

"Why not? It's all in the way you do the thing that counts."

Ezra's spirits lifted. It was plain Billy had one of his daredevil plans in mind. There'd be excitement and maybe fireworks. Nothing so dull as tying a rope to jail window bars and hoping your horse could pull them free from the adobe.

By the time they reached San Elizario it was past three o'clock. Ezra had gotten over feeling tired, his nerves were taut with expectation as he followed Billy along a narrow alleyway a block from the jail, leading a rangy roan Billy had separated from a *remuda* at an outlying ranch.

"We'll leave the horses here," Billy muttered.

They dismounted and tethered them to a gatepost at the end of the alley. No lights showed. The entire town seemed to be asleep.

Billy and Ezra stepped out of the alley. Up ahead a dim glow showed from a window in the jail. As they neared it, Ezra saw it was a dilapidated, small adobe.

Billy strode directly to the wooden plank door and thumped his fist against it.

"Open up!" he ordered, then repeated the command in Spanish, easing his Colt from his holster as he spoke.

Ezra pulled his own pistol.

After a moment a man's voice from inside called, *"Quien es?"*

"Texas Rangers," Billy said in Spanish. "Open up. It's cold as hell out here and we've got two American prisoners."

Ezra heard keys clank together. The door swung slowly open. Billy shoved in, thrusting the muzzle of his Colt into the fat belly of a sleepy-eyed jailer.

The Mexican raised his hands and Ezra, close behind Billy, disarmed the man, then grabbed his keys and handed them to Billy.

As Billy reached for the keys, a guard appeared in an inner doorway. His hand dropped toward his holster.

"I wouldn't," Ezra said, finger on the trigger.

"El Chivato!" the guard exclaimed, looking from Ezra to Billy. His hands rose into the air.

Ezra eased his finger off the trigger. After disarming the second man, Billy left Ezra guarding the two Mexicans and walked through the open door to the cells.

"Jose?" he called. *"Como le va, amigo?"*

"Nombre de Dios," a voice said, "it really is you, Billy!"

Ezra heard the key rattle in the cell lock and a moment later Billy appeared with Jose Chavez behind him.

"I spit on this miserable hole," Chavez said. "Give me one of those pistols, *compadre,* and I'll make certain these *bastardos* never lock me in it again."

"No shooting, Jose," Billy warned. "We been nice and quiet so far. Find yourself a saddle and let's *vamos.*"

Chavez didn't argue.

Ezra went for the horses, bringing them to the jail. Billy held the guards at gunpoint while Chavez threw a saddle on the roan. They mounted and galloped out of town, heading back toward El Paso.

As soon as San Elizario was behind them, Billy pulled up alongside Chavez and handed over a silver-handled Colt he'd taken from the fat jailer.

"Gracias," Chavez said. "How did you find me?"

"Your cousin Miguel. You planning to join up with me again, Jose?"

"I have a wife in Chihuahua now, Billy. You understand."

"Sure. If you happen to be around Fort Sumner sometime, look me up."

"I'll do that. Send for me if you're ever in jail, Billy."

"I don't expect to be behind bars again, old friend. Anyway, you don't look much like a Texas Ranger."

Jose laughed, waved, and turned off the El Paso road to be swallowed up in the dark.

Ezra tried to relax, his muscles still tense from the confrontation with the jailers. Would he have shot the guard if the man had grabbed for his gun?

He'd never yet shot a man face-to-face like that. He set his jaw. He could do it if he had to. Would have done it back at the jail if he'd had to.

"Well, now, Ez," Billy said. "We've got old Jose taken care of. I noticed some mighty nice looking horses at that ranch where I got the roan. I think we ought to bring a few of them back to the Territory with us. How about it?"

Ezra had almost gotten over his squeamishness about helping himself to other men's livestock. Still, it was hard to forget his father's teaching.

"A thief shall not inherit the Kingdom of God," Papa had warned. "Heed my words, Ezra, for of all the sins, it can be the most insidious."

He led a different life in a different land from Papa, Ezra told himself. What he'd learned from his father had no bearing on the here and now.

"Let's go find that *remuda*, Billy," Ezra said.

Chapter 17

By noon the sun had come out and Tessa's spirits lifted.

"I've no idea where we are," she said to Vincente. "I know I was headed for the Pecos when I started out, but now I'm all turned around.

He glanced at her and she managed a smile.

"The Pecos is that way." He waved to his left. "We will stay away from the road along the river since my former *compañeros* may seek me there. I think you would not care to meet up with them, no?"

Her grimace made him laugh.

She was determined not to let him know her true feelings. If he believed she wanted to be with him, he might relax his vigilance long enough for her to escape. But he'd reminded her that it was dangerous to be alone in this country. She might run from Vincente only to find herself a captive of another gang of roving desperados.

"You have not told me why you were traveling to Sumner," he said.

"I was looking for my brother. Pat Garrett has sworn to hunt down Billy and the rest of his men. He means to see Billy hang."

Vincente scowled. "I would like to be there when it happens."

"Perhaps Sheriff Garrett would arrest *you* for being an outlaw."

After a moment Vincente half smiled. "He might try. I will never be taken alive, I assure you."

That evening, Vincente stopped at a small rancho nestled in a mountain valley. The Mexican family greeted him with shouts of joy and heartfelt embraces. Tessa found, to her relief, that she was to sleep with the daughters.

They spent two days at the rancho, resting the horses and themselves. By cautious questions in her inadequate Spanish, Tessa discovered they weren't far from the Mescalero reservation.

"I have watched the Apache women prepare mescal," Concepcion, the eldest daughter, told Tessa.

"It's made from a kind of cactus, that's all I know," Tessa said.

"The women cut off all the thorny leaves and then chop out the heart of the mescal cactus. They dig a fire pit, put in the heart, cover it with the leaves and dirt, then let it cook slowly. It is like sweet mush when they finish. I have tasted it but it doesn't compare to tortillas and frijoles."

The tortillas and frijoles Concepcion's mother prepared tasted delicious to Tessa. What would it be like to live in Mexico and be part of a Mexican family? In this one, the parents, their two sons and three daughters all worked hard and seemed happy.

"Soon I, too, will be married." Concepcion smiled dreamily. "Diego is even now building our *casa*. He is very handsome. Of course Vincente is also a fine-looking man. I have no doubt he will make you a good husband."

Tessa couldn't respond to this. She looked across the room at Vincente. She wouldn't deny his good looks, slim, dark with a tinge of silver at his temples. He was even distinguished. But to marry him?

Tessa sighed. She longed for the warmth of a family, but she didn't want Vincente, wouldn't want him even if he hadn't turned outlaw. His ways were not hers.

She hadn't asked these friends of his for help, feeling they might refuse, and then Vincente would watch her more closely. If she ever did escape him, she decided, she'd marry Calvin and let him take her and Jules to Santa Fe where he preferred to live. They would have a settled life. She wouldn't ever be disturbed in mind or body by Calvin's demands. It was what she wanted.

Not Mark, fiddle-footing over the country, with, for all she knew, a Susie in every hamlet.

But she might not ever see either Calvin or Mark again.

Tessa and Vincente rode away from the rancho the next morning. After an hour on the trail, they crested a rise and saw a group of nine riders below leading a string of horses.

"Back," Vincente warned. "Best not to be seen."

Tessa, about to wheel her roan, held. She stared hard at one of the men.

"Ezra!" she cried, kicking her horse so he lunged ahead too fast, sliding and slipping downhill.

"Ezra!" she shouted again just as a shot rang out behind her.

The roan stumbled and fell, tumbling her over his head.

Dazed and short of breath, she struggled to get up. The horse didn't move.

Men shouted below her. Vincente's sorrel plunged toward her from the top of the hill; Vincente was coming for her, Colt in his hand. He'd shot her horse. Would she be next?

He didn't fire and Tessa realized he meant to scoop her up onto his horse. Recapture her. She tried to run downhill, but she knew she'd never make it; he was too close, reaching out for her.

She heard the clean crack of a Winchester. Vincente jerked back. A red flower blossomed over his heart; then he thudded to the ground and rolled past her to lie face up at her feet, unmoving.

Tessa stood frozen.

Finally she took a step. Another. Dropped to her knees beside Vincente. His brown eyes stared sightlessly at the sky. She covered her face with her hands, unable to bear the sight of his lifeless face. She'd wanted to escape from him, but not this way.

"Tessa."

Ezra's voice. His hand touched her shoulder.

She dropped her hands and allowed her brother to help her to her feet. Billy stood beside him, rifle in hand.

"Got him through the heart," Billy said.

Men climbed the hill toward them. One was much smaller than the others. Not a man. A woman. Tessa's hand flew to her mouth.

"No!" she cried. "Don't let her see . . ."

But Violet, ahead of the rest, was on them before either Billy or Ezra understood what Tessa meant.

Violet looked at the dead man. She fell on her knees, touched his face. Her mouth opened, but no words came. She swayed, then slumped across her father's body.

"Jesus, it's old Gabaldon," Billy said.

Ezra lifted Violet into his arms, carrying her down the hill. Billy offered Tessa his arm, saying, "Time to move on. One of the boys'll get your saddle."

"We just can't leave Vincente like this," she objected. "Think how Violet would feel."

"He threw her out, didn't he?" Billy said. "But I reckon we can bury him."

As Tessa watched the men pile rocks over Vincente's shallow grave, her throat ached with unshed tears. "Flower of my heart," he'd called her, this man she didn't love, could never have loved. And yet she mourned him. She sent up a prayer asking for his forgiveness.

It seemed there'd been nothing but deaths since she came to the New Mexico Territory. Her father. Her friends, John and Alex. And now Vincente.

He's the last, she vowed. I'll stick to Ezra like a burr until he agrees to leave this life.

They rode on, Tessa on a buckskin a good deal livelier than the roan had been. It took her a while to get used to him, and so it was some time before she could devote much attention to Violet, who rode between her and Ezra.

"I'm sorry about your father," Tessa told her.

Violet turned to her and Tessa was shocked at her thin, pale face. The girl must have some sickness besides the upset of her father's death.

"Even when he didn't want me, I still loved my father," Violet said.

"I think he loved you, too, despite everything."

Violet shook her head. "He could only love those who did what he wanted."

Tessa was silent. Violet might well be speaking the truth.

"You were traveling with him?" Violet asked.

"He rescued me from Comancheros," Tessa temporized. "He wasn't a bad man."

"My Billy shot him," Violet said. "Did you know that? He shot my father. It took only one bullet. My Billy is a very good marksman."

Tessa bit her lip. The girl spoke flatly with no emotion in her voice. She hadn't yet shed a tear for her father. The change in her from the vivacious, pretty Violet she'd first met made Tessa's heart ache.

Ezra leaned forward to look past Violet at his sister. "Do you mind telling me what you were doing that you had to be rescued from Comancheros in the first place?"

"I was on my way to find you."

"What for?" Alarm flared in Ezra's eyes. "There isn't anything wrong with Jules, is there?"

She shook her head. "He's fine."

"Now you've found me," Ezra said.

"Yes." This wasn't the time to go into her reasons.

Ezra shrugged. "I suppose you'll get around to telling me what it's all about sooner or later."

"You can be sure I will," she said tartly.

It took them three days to reach Sumner. On the way Billy sold the string of horses to a man near Roswell, but he refused to accept money from Tessa for the buckskin he'd given her.

"Hell, he didn't cost me anything," he said. "You're welcome to him."

Then she understood she was riding a stolen horse.

At Sumner she and Violet shared a room at Charlie Bowdre's house, which had been the fort hospital. Charlie's wife, Manuela, a plump and friendly woman, greeted Tessa warmly, then began to fuss over Violet.

"Ah, *poquita*, you must eat a little. You cannot get much tinier without disappearing altogether," she scolded.

Later, when Violet had been persuaded to go to bed, Manuela confided in Tessa.

"She is *encinte*, I think—how you say, with child? *Si*, I watch her throw up her food and she says she is dizzy and I think that is what is wrong. I ask her and she admits she missed her monthlies. Yet these men, they know nothing, they let her ride with them."

Tessa nodded. Yes, it would account for Violet's pallor, her look of illness. She made up her mind she would get Billy alone and talk to him about Violet. And about Ezra, too, for that matter.

Her chance came the next evening when Billy dropped by to see Violet. Manuela Bowdre was busy in the kitchen.

"Violet's sleeping and I don't want to wake her," Tessa told him. "She needs all the rest she can get. You really shouldn't expect her to ride all over creation with you now that she's carrying your child."

Billy blinked at her, then grinned. "She never let on."

"Well, what do you intend to do about it?"

He shrugged. "I reckon you're right. She can stay here with . . ."

"I mean, aren't you going to marry her? Give the child a name?"

"He can have my name; I don't care. I ain't planning to marry nobody. Didn't marry the other two, the ones who had my girls. I hope Violet's is a boy."

Tessa was taken aback by his casual mention of other children, but she tried not to show it.

"Billy, Violet can't take care of a child all by herself. She needs a home, a father for the baby."

"I'll see she's provided for."

"Why won't you marry the poor girl? God knows, she loves you."

Billy eyed Tessa for a time. "Your folks get along?" he asked finally.

"Why, yes. They got along fine. Until my mother died, when Jules was born."

"My pa left my ma with me and my brother Joe. She waited for my pa to come back, but he never did. After a while she got word he'd died, and we came down this way and my mother met Bill Antrim. They got married in Santa Fe.

"Antrim didn't cotton much to either Joe or me. As for Ma, she just sort of faded away and died the next year. I don't think much of marrying and that's a fact."

"Violet loves you."

"You know, Tess," he said, "I was taken with her looks. Violet's a pretty little thing. But I never asked her to come to me here in Sumner. She did that on her own. I didn't promise her anything. I ain't going to marry her just because you think I ought to, but I swear I'll take care of her."

She put her hands on her hips. "Do you take care of the women who bore you daughters?"

His eyes flicked away from hers. "I go see them when I can. They get along all right. Both of them live with their families."

"Violet has no family. Not any longer."

"Look. I was trying to do you a favor, shooting him. How the hell was I supposed to know it was Gabaldon?"

"I don't blame you for that," Tessa said hastily. "I'm sorry if I sounded ungrateful. But the fact remains, her father is dead and she has no one except you."

Billy sighed. "All right. I'll think about what you said. No promises."

"There's something else," Tessa said as he started to turn away.

"What?"

"I suppose you've heard Pat Garrett is after you and your gang?"

"I heard." Billy grinned. "I wish him luck finding us. Ain't nobody in this town would ever tell him where I was. They'd warn me if Garrett was anywhere near. They're my friends."

"But if he does catch you and you go to trial . . ."

"I ain't going to trial, Tess."

"It may surprise you, after I've taken you to task tonight, Billy, but I hope you don't. I wouldn't want to see you hang. But it's really Ezra I'm worried about. He's the reason I'm here."

"I didn't figure it was *my* skin you meant to save."

"I want him to leave the Territory. Make a new start somewhere else. I've raised Ezra since he was almost eight years old, Billy, and I won't stand back while he rides with you straight toward the hangman."

"What do you expect me to do about it?

"Tell him to leave! You know how he admires you."

"Tess, I ain't got Ez hogtied. He can do whatever he wants."

"He wasn't cut out to be a thief!" she cried.

"Maybe I wasn't either; did you ever think of that?" Billy asked.

"Well, you are thieves, the both of you!" To her dismay, she burst into tears.

"Jesus Christ!" Billy exclaimed. "Women!" He turned on his heel and slammed out of the house.

Tessa had barely dried her tears before Ezra came in.

"How's Violet?"

"Sleeping."

"She's been sort of sickly lately," Ezra said anxiously. "Do you think she'll be all right?"

"She's pregnant," Tessa said sourly.

Ezra stared at her.

"I want you to give this up," Tessa said. She reached up to touch his cheek. "Can't you understand? Billy doesn't care about anyone except himself—not you, not Violet, not any of the others. He isn't going to marry Violet. And what would he do if you were taken prisoner by Pat Garrett?"

"I expect he'd break into the jail and get me out," Ezra said. "Billy takes care of his friends. I'd do the same for him. But no one's going to jail. Garrett's just bragging."

"I don't think so. Those who know Sheriff Garrett say he follows through on his promises. Ezra, I've saved some money. I want you to take it and leave the Territory. Go somewhere else, where no one knows you. Start fresh."

He shook his head. "I ain't going nowhere."

Tessa stamped her foot, her face flushing with anger. "You even talk like an outlaw! Damn it, Ezra, I risked my life to come and find you. I didn't raise you to be a desperado and I won't stand aside and see you throw your life away. What on earth do you find worthwhile in consorting with thieves and murderers?"

"Billy never killed a man except in self-defense or to avenge someone. And Chisum owed him more than Billy's taken from him in cattle. Nobody understands Billy."

"Except you, I suppose," she said dryly.

"Sure I understand him. He's been wronged."

"I've been wronged, too, do you hear?" Tessa put her hand to her throat. "I don't see you worrying about me. Oh, Ezra, you must leave here. I couldn't bear it if you were sentenced to hang. And think about poor Jules."

"I got to do what I think is right," Ezra said stubbornly.

"Will you at least promise to think over what I've said?"

"I reckon I can promise you that much."

"You know, I've heard that in California a man . . ." Tessa broke off as the door burst open and Charlie Bowdre dashed in.

"We got word Garrett and Halloran's leading a posse that's coming this way," he said. "We gotta haul ass outa here."

Chapter 18

Tessa watched in dismay as Ezra mounted up with the rest of Billy's gang.

"Take care of Violet," he called to her as they pounded off. "We'll be back when it's safe."

I ought to have gone along, she thought, realizing at the same time that Ezra wouldn't have let her. She clutched at the shawl Charlie's wife had lent to her. It was bone-freezing cold outside and there was no use standing about getting chilled. She went back into the house.

Violet was sitting at the kitchen table, hands in her lap.

"They've gone," Tessa said.

Violet seemed not to hear her.

As the days passed and Christmas neared, Violet moved about as though she was in a daze. If not for Manuela's urging, Tessa doubted Violet would have eaten a bite of food.

"Do you want your baby to live?" Tessa asked her bluntly one morning.

Violet blinked at her.

"Well, do you? It's up to you whether the child will be born at all. The way you're acting now, he never will be."

Slight color came into the girl's face. "What are you saying?"

"If you don't start taking care of yourself, you'll die. So will the baby. Is that what you want?"

Slowly Violet shook her head. "I want my baby."

"Then take some responsibility for yourself. Eat. Help out around the house."

After that Violet became less of a ghost, but she spoke little and spent much of her time staring at nothing.

On the morning of the eighteenth, Tessa was outside fetching firewood for the kitchen when she saw a rider approaching. She recognized him and her heart leaped into her throat as the wood slipped from her arms.

What was Mark doing here?

She turned away and bent to gather the wood, hoping the Mexican shawl over her head and shoulders would disguise her sufficiently so Mark wouldn't give her a second look.

Mark was alone. Was he searching for Billy and the others? Rumors had been flying about town that Garrett was north of Sumner at Puerta de Luna, looking for more deputies for his posse. Was Mark scouting ahead for Garrett?

Juan Gallegos had brought word to Manuela last night that her husband and the others were about twelve miles east of town at the Wilcox ranch. Would anyone in Sumner reveal this to Mark?

Billy had been certain everyone here was his friend, but Tessa was skeptical. Someone always seemed willing to talk.

She stood up, the wood once more in her arms, slanting a glance toward the road. She started. Mark was heading directly toward her. Looking right at her.

"You scared the hell out of me," he said by way of greeting. "What do you mean tearing out of Lincoln all alone in the middle of the winter? Of all the idiotic . . ."

"How did you know I was here?" she demanded.

"Maria came and told me where you were headed. Only trouble was, she waited a week. You can be sure I'd have stopped you if . . ."

"If you had the time. If Susie wasn't keeping you too busy."

Damn. She hadn't meant to say such a thing.

He swung off his black, strode to her, took the wood from her arms, tossed it to the ground and pulled her to him. He glared down into her face. "You know who I want. If I can't have you, then what I do is my own business."

He kissed her fiercely, his lips at first cold against hers, then warming as they urged hers to respond. Her arms went around him, holding him tightly.

Moments later she was pushing him away. "No," she said. "I don't believe you're in Sumner just because of me. You really came with Pat Garrett, didn't you?"

"What in hell are you talking about?"

"Don't lie to me, Mark. You rode down from Puerta de Luna as a scout for Garrett."

"If you want to believe that, I can't stop you." His voice was as chilly as the north wind.

She took a deep breath. "It's no use prowling around here. Billy and the others aren't in town."

"And if you knew where they were, you wouldn't tell me. Right?"

She nodded curtly.

"Ezra didn't listen to you, did he? I could have told you he wouldn't, saved you the trip."

"I'll persuade him yet," she said stubbornly.

Mark shook his head. "Ezra's got one of the worst cases of hero-worship I've ever seen. I hope it won't prove to be fatal."

She wrapped her arms about herself, against the cold and against the inner chill his words brought.

"I want you to pack up and come back to Lincoln with me, Tessa," Mark said. "Jules needs you more than Ezra ever will."

"I can't," she said. "Not yet."

"*I* need you." he said softly.

She bit her lip. She wanted so terribly to believe him. Wanted to confess her own need for what he could bring her. She steeled herself. How could she trust him?

"I'd never forgive myself if I went away and something happened to Ezra," she said. "I mean to do everything I can to prevent Garrett from arresting him."

Mark's face hardened. "You won't come with me?"

She shook her head.

"I'll ask you again in the morning. For the last time." He turned away from her, remounted and rode off, heading into the plaza.

When he was out of sight, she knelt to pick up the wood again, her thoughts totally disorganized by her conflicting emotions.

What would she tell Mark in the morning?

That evening Mark took a stroll after finishing his meal of tamales. He tried to decide whether or not to walk past

the old army hospital where Tessa was staying with Manuela
Bowdre and Violet Gabaldon.

He shook his head. Not much point to it when he didn't
plan to go in. He spun on his heel and almost ran into a
tall, lean man with a long black mustache.

"Thought that was you, Mark," Pat Garrett said. "You
after the kid, too?"

"Not exactly," Mark said slowly. "He's not in town."

"I know that," Garrett said. "He's somewhere pretty
close, though. You going to help me corral him?"

Mark hesitated a moment. "Didn't think you wanted me
butting in after you rode out last month without me," he
said finally.

"You seemed kind of skittish about Billy's gang, about
maybe having to shoot at your girl's brother, young
Nesbitt."

"I'll try to help Ezra if I can; might as well admit it,
Pat."

"As long as it doesn't stop me from getting Billy.
That's who I'm after. Going to find the son-of-a-bitch
come hell or high water." Garrett looked around.

No one was in sight. They stood by themselves in the
road.

Garrett leaned close. "I got my men posted on the
outskirts of town. What I plan to do is get word to Billy
tomorrow that I've given up and taken the posse down the
Pecos toward Roswell. I think that'll bring him into Sumner to celebrate. We'll be waiting when he shows. How
does that strike you?"

"Ought to work. Do you know for certain where Billy
is?"

"I will by tomorrow. Billy knows damn well I'm here
and I figure he'll put a man to watching me. Going to nail

that one in the morning and sweat the Kid's location out of him.''

Mark nodded in approval. It was only after he'd left Garrett to turn in for the night that he realized he couldn't go to see Tessa in the morning. If she'd changed her mind about coming with him, she'd certainly be suspicious if he put her off about leaving Sumner.

Best not to see her at all until Garrett's scheme was played out.

By the next afternoon Garrett had captured Juan Gallegos and squeezed the information he needed out of him. Garrett sent the terrified Gallegos back to Billy at Wilcox's ranch with orders to tell the Kid it was safe to come into town. Mark had reservations about Gallegos doing as Garrett instructed—after all, he'd been a spy for the Kid—but Garrett brushed off his objections.

"Juan knows I meant business when I told him I'd get him if he didn't play this my way. Don't forget, Mark, I used to live in Sumner. They know what I'm like.''

"I hope you're right.''

"I am. Now, here's what we'll do as soon as it's dark. Wilcox's ranch is east of town, so the Kid and his boys will have to pass by that old adobe hospital where Charlie Bowdre lives.''

Mark felt his stomach knot, afraid he knew what was coming next.

"I'll have my men slip into that building and we'll wait there for the Kid to pass. He'll never suspect.''

Mark swallowed. He could do nothing. It was an excellent plan. At least he'd be with Garrett in the house and in that way could watch out for Tessa.

But he was damn sure she'd never forgive him.

* * *

Ezra rode to the left of Billy, as he usually did, O'Folliard to the right. The snow had stopped falling and the moon was up, its light silver-bright on the frozen crust that crunched under the horses' hooves. The breath of the men and animals steamed upward and hovered over the riders like icy halos.

He wondered how Violet was. It'd been a shock to find out that she was carrying Billy's child. He glanced sideways at Billy. Was he happy about it? He hadn't said a word.

Ezra hadn't liked Tess coming after him, but now that he knew about Violet, maybe it was for the best. Violet needed someone to care for her more than ever now. He tried to, but he wasn't around enough. You couldn't expect Billy to do it as he had so many other things on his mind.

Maybe Billy would marry her and they'd get a house in Sumner like the Bowdres. Somehow, though, he couldn't see Billy getting married.

At least they'd be back in Sumner for Christmas. Ezra had to admit he'd enjoy spending the holiday with Tess. Almost like old times, except Jules wouldn't be there.

Ezra smiled, recalling past Christmases—remembered teaching Jules the words to Christmas carols, showing him how to use the first small knife Papa had given Jules when he was seven, the year he'd shot the turkey on Christmas Eve and surprised Tess who'd been sure they'd have to have beef again for the holiday dinner.

Ezra sighed. Sometimes a man missed having a family.

The buildings of Sumner showed dark against the moonlit snow. It'd sure feel good to get in out of this cold.

Billy's gray snorted. Billy lifted his head and looked around. Nothing moved in the night except their group. It was damn chilly to be riding.

A dog began to bark at their approach.

Billy hunched his shoulders, twisted again in the saddle to peer about.

"Guess maybe I'll drop back and get me a chaw of tobacco off Wilson," he said. He slowed the gray, wheeled and rode back to where Wilson brought up the rear.

Ezra and O'Folliard edged closer together as they continued on. A light shone in Bowdre's house; they were almost there. O'Folliard pulled a little ahead, rode up to the porch. His horse stopped suddenly and Ezra started to rein in.

"Halt!" a man shouted from the porch.

Ezra saw O'Folliard grab for his holster as he reached for his own Colt. Before he touched it, two Winchesters cracked, almost in unison. Fire ripped along Ezra's side. He heard O'Folliard scream in pain, heard two more shots.

Ezra's mount bolted. Groaning with the agony in his side, he tried to wrestle the pinto under control, couldn't even hold on, slid off, slamming onto his back in the snow. The pinto raced off, following other riders fleeing back toward Wilcox's.

There were shouts behind Ezra. Shots. Hooves. Painfully, he rolled onto his stomach, pushed himself to his hands and knees and crawled into the shadows along an adobe wall. A dog jumped through a break in the wall and sniffed at him. With great effort he forced himself up and through the hole. The dog followed him.

Ezra tried to stand, bracing himself against the wall. Pain sliced through him; his head spun. As his knees sagged, darkness settled over him and he slipped into oblivion.

Tessa watched Mark help Pat Garrett ease the badly wounded Tom O'Folliard off his horse and carry him into the house where they laid him on a cot.

"I thought for certain it'd be Billy leading them." Garrett said to Mark. "He always leads them."

O'Falliard groaned. "Am I dying?" he gasped, blood trickling from his mouth.

Tessa looked at his chest wound where blood oozed in a steady stream from the bullet hole made by the sheriff's Winchester.

Garrett leaned closer to him. "Tom, your time is short," he said.

O'Folliard tried to sit up, gasped. Blood gushed from his mouth and he fell back, trembled all over and lay still.

Garrett shook his head and straightened. "The rest of the gang'll be making for Wilcox's," he said to Mark. "I don't reckon we'll head that way tonight. Wait and see what develops."

Tessa slipped away into the kitchen where she glanced toward the door, her hands clenched in apprehension. She hadn't dared leave the house, lest Mark suspect and come in search of her.

The minute she'd heard O'Folliard had been shot, she'd been in deadly fear. Tom, Billy, Ezra. Those three always led the gang.

What had happened to Ezra? Was he all right?

As soon as the shooting had stopped, she'd made Violet go out to reconnoiter.

"Make certain Ezra isn't lying someplace close by, wounded and helpless," she told the girl. "Look good." Then she'd thought of the incentive Violet might need. "Look for Billy, too. They both would have been riding with Tom O'Folliard."

Violet's eyes were wide and frightened. Tessa tried to assure herself it was better for the girl to feel some emotion than to drift around in a daze.

"You have to go," she said impatiently. "I can't."

"What if—" Violet spoke so low she could hardly hear her. "What if he's dead?"

"He's not," Tessa had said, now knowing which one the girl meant. She herself meant Ezra. He wasn't dead. He couldn't be. "Don't waste any more time. Go out there and look!"

That had been at least a half-hour ago and the girl hadn't returned. Where was she?

Mark came into the kitchen. "Tom O'Falliard's dead," he said. "We're going to have to leave his body here until morning."

"Why bother to tell me?" she said. "You didn't ask anyone's permission to take over the house and set up your ambush. I can't help thinking it might have been Ezra lying dead instead of poor Tom."

"I've been meaning to tell you I saw Ezra high-tailing it out of here on his pinto, following the others. He's all right."

Tessa clasped her hands together. "Did you really see him?"

Mark nodded. "Billy got away, too."

She closed her eyes momentarily. "Oh, I was so worried." She glanced at the door again and bit her lip. "I have to confess I sent Violet out to see if Ezra might have been hurt. I'd better go and find her."

Garrett called to Mark from the next room. He hesitated.

"Tessa, wait, I'll go with you," Mark said.

"No. I'll be right back."

Mark looked at her for a moment, then nodded. "Be careful. It's cold out there." He left the kitchen.

Tessa ran into the snow, calling Violet's name. Where had the girl gotten to?

"Violet! Where are you?" she cried over and over as

she hurried through yards and around buildings, heading eastward.

"Tessa!" the cry was faint.

Tessa called again, pinpointed the answering call. Violet was on the other side of a crumbling adobe wall.

"Come home; it's all right," she told the girl.

"No, I can't come. Please help me," Violet cried. "Hurry!"

What on earth could be wrong? Tessa wondered.

It took her a few minutes to find a way to get over the wall. She saw Violet huddled in the snow beside a dark figure and ran to her.

"What's the matter?" she demanded. "Who is it?"

"Oh, Tessa," Violet sobbed, "you told me he wouldn't be dead. Why did you lie to me? What will I do now that's he's gone? I can't bear it."

Billy? Tessa dropped to her knees and bent over the still figure whose head Violet cradled in her lap.

Not Billy's thin face, his wispy mustache.

"Oh, my God," she whispered.

Tessa touched Ezra's cold face with trembling hands. She felt along his temple to just above his ear where her father had taught her to find a pulse.

At first she couldn't believe what she felt, thought she was only willing herself to find the thready beat under her fingers. She moved her hand to his other temple and sighed in relief.

"He's not dead, Violet."

Tessa put her mouth to Ezra's ear, calling his name.

He moaned.

"Ezra, wake up," she said. "You have to wake up and help us."

His eyelids fluttered, opened. He looked directly into Violet's face. He whispered her name.

"Were you shot?" Tessa demanded.

His hand moved, reaching toward his right side. He winced. She saw the dark splotch of blood on his jacket. She glanced around, saw a dilapidated lean-to stable a few yards away.

"Can you move?" she asked.

"Can try," he muttered.

With their help, Ezra staggered into the shelter of the lean-to.

"Doesn't hurt so bad as it did at first," he said. "Don't think I'm bleeding much either."

Tessa thought quickly. "You can't stay in Sumner. They'll find you."

"If I had me a horse," he said, his voice sounding stronger, "I'd light out for Wilcox's ranch."

Tessa couldn't come up with an alternative. "Violet and I will go back to the house," she said. "I'll pretend to go to bed with Violet, then slip out and bring you a horse."

"Sounds good. Thanks, Tess."

"Thank Violet. She found you."

"I thought—I guess I was dreaming—that I was in heaven," he said, looking at Violet. He half laughed. "I reckon I don't have much of a chance of ever getting there."

Violet reached out her hand to him.

"I'll be back as soon as I can," Tessa said, taking Violet's ice-cold hand and pulling her away.

As she hurried the girl toward Bowdre's house, Tessa decided it was too dangerous to let Ezra try to ride to the ranch wounded and alone. She'd bring two horses when she returned to him. She'd ride with him.

If that made her an outlaw, so be it.

Chapter 19

As Tessa and Ezra rode toward Wilcox's ranch, snow began to fall. Tessa watched her brother sway in the saddle, hunched over against the bite of the north wind, and wondered if he could hang on until they got there.

When at last she saw the lights of the ranch house flickering fitfully through the veil of snow, she sent up a prayer of thankfulness.

She banged at the rear door of the house and was greeted by a Colt thrust into her face. It was held by Dave Rudabaugh, in her opinion the worst of the men who followed Billy. She detested him.

"I need help," she said. "Ezra's with me and hurt."

Dave thrust away his gun and called to Billy.

As soon as Tessa got Ezra inside, she took a look at his wound. The rifle bullet had gone through the flesh of his right side just below the waist, gone in and come out again. Ezra's pain was mostly in the hip now, and it was all he could do to move his right leg.

"Probably took a chip off the hip bone," Charlie Bowdre said. "I seen that happen before. Might take awhile to heal, but he'll be okay. Only thing is, he ain't gonna be riding a horse tomorrow or the next day."

"Can't we stay here, Ezra and I?" she asked, not understanding.

"You're gonna *have* to—leastways, Ez is," Charlie said.

Tessa put a pad of cotton against the wound and tied it on, realizing as she did so what Charlie had meant. They'd be left behind when the others moved on.

Billy knelt on the opposite side of the cot and grinned at Ezra. "You're still lucky, *compañero*." His smile faded. "Old Tom wasn't. How is he?"

"He's dead," Tessa said.

Billy's jaw clenched as he looked at her. "Garrett coming after us?" he asked after a minute.

In for a penny, in for a pound, she thought. "Not tonight. I heard him say so. But I think he means to follow you sooner or later."

Billy nodded. "We'll rest up and get out of here tomorrow," he said.

When the others left Ezra's side, Tessa rolled herself in a blanket and lay on the floor next to his cot. He woke later in the night, asking for water. She rose and made her way into the kitchen where a lamp burned low. She skirted the chopping block, where a slab of bacon lay with a knife thrust in it, and went to the water pail.

She'd lifted the tin dipper to scoop water out of the pail when an arm snaked around her throat from behind. Before she could cry out, her breath was choked off. The dipper fell from her hand and then darkness overwhelmed her.

She came to on the kitchen floor with her denim pants yanked down around her ankles, her legs shoved apart and Dave Rudabaugh's vile-smelling hulk above her, fumbling to open his trousers.

Tessa scooted backwards, sliding along the floor. She rolled over and staggered to her feet, aiming for the knife on the chopping block. Her fingers grasped the handle just as Dave's hands grabbed her legs.

Tessa twisted as she fell, raised the knife and slashed at Dave. Felt the blade slide through cloth. Into flesh. Heard his curse as he let go of her. She pulled the knife out. Scrambled to her feet and yanked at her pants with her free hand, pulling them up.

Dave advanced toward her, hands out, blood staining his right shirt sleeve. She leaped to the side and collided with someone else. She spun away and crouched, knife in hand, staring from Dave to the other man. It was Billy.

"What the hell's this all about, Dave?" Billy demanded.

"Fucking bitch sliced me," Dave muttered, holding his hand over his right shoulder.

"She had good reason, looks like. Leave her alone, you hear, Dave?"

"I don't take orders from you or any man." Dave glowered at Billy. But, after a moment, he lurched out of the kitchen, cursing under his breath.

Billy looked after him. "Trouble with this business is," he said to Tessa in a low tone, "it gets so you can't choose your company."

She didn't reply, still shaken by what had happened. Her hand trembled as she lay the knife on the chopping block and reached for the dipper on the floor by the water pail.

"I was bringing Ezra a drink," she said.

Billy took the dipper from her. "I'll do that."

When she was ready to curl into her blanket again, she saw that Billy, wrapped in his own blanket, was sitting in a chair on the other side of Ezra, his feet propped onto the metal frame of the cot. "Good night, Tess," he said.

But she couldn't sleep. Not that she feared Rudabaugh would return to attack her. Billy's presence guaranteed no one would bother her. It was as though she'd been defiled by Dave's dirty hands touching the bare flesh of her legs, by the lust she'd seen in his piggy eyes. And by the realization she'd meant to kill him.

The other time, in the hotel with Hank Kilgore, she'd been frightened when she used his boot knife, stabbing at him only in final desperation, with no intent to kill, only to get away from him.

She'd never thought of herself as someone who'd kill another person. She'd shot at Apaches, true, but that had been like a bad dream; she'd been scared out of her wits, with no conscious urge to kill.

Was she then no better than these outlaws?

Violet managed to conceal Tessa's absence from Mark until almost noon by simply looking so frail and ill that he couldn't bring himself to question what she said.

"Gone," she finally admitted when he forced the truth from her. "She took Ezra to Wilcox's ranch after I found him wounded in the snow. I thought he was dead."

Mark stood at the window staring out at the falling snow. He couldn't go after Tessa; it would upset Garrett's plans if he rode out ahead of the posse. Besides, likely he'd only get himself shot at. She ought to be safe enough at the ranch for the moment. Damn her for a conniving little minx. All for Ezra, of course. He wished she cared that much for him.

Garrett wouldn't ride until he knew Billy had left the ranch. No sense in attacking five, maybe six good marksmen all forted up in comfort while you froze in the snow. That was a losing game. But the waiting galled Mark.

Around midnight, one of Wilcox's hands brought word to Garrett that Billy and his gang had moved on. The man didn't know where they'd gone.

Garrett started out at first light with a seven-man posse and Mark. The sun came up before they reached the ranch. Its rays glittered from the snow covering ground and hills, the pinon branches thick and white and shining with diamond brilliance. The country was transformed into a land of eerie beauty.

"It'll make the tracking easy as shooting a treed coon," Garrett said to Mark, his Alabama drawl edged with satisfaction. "With any luck we'll bring them in before Christmas. Though, to tell you the truth, I'm aiming to just out-and-out shoot Billy and get it over with. The rest'll give up quick enough, once Billy's gone."

Mark couldn't fault Garrett's reasoning. If he caught Billy and had to keep him in jail for a couple of months waiting for the trial, there'd be the chance of a jailbreak and then he'd have to do it all over.

"What do you aim to do about Ezra?" Mark asked.

"Well, I reckon if he's shot up bad enough, he won't be with the others. If he ain't with the others, I guess I won't be after him."

When they reached the ranch, Mark was the first inside. Tessa sat beside Ezra's cot, staring defiantly up at him.

"It's no use asking where they went. I don't know. And don't you dare bother Ezra. He's feverish."

Ezra looked at Mark and Garrett without interest from glazed and dull eyes.

"Nothing for us here," Garrett decided.

Outside, the trail was plain, leading east toward Arroyo Taiban, the horses' tracks a straight line away from the ranch.

"There's a way station for herders at Stinking Springs," Garrett said. "As I recall, there's a rock house there to sleep in. That's where they'll be making for. I reckon Billy's just plain forgot I know this country as well as he does."

They were tracking five men, Mark knew. Charlie Bowdre, Billie Wilson, Dave Rudabaugh and a new recruit by the name of Tom Pickett. And the Kid himself. Billy the Kid.

"I heard you knew the Kid pretty well," Garrett said.

Mark nodded, thinking of riding line with Billy, the slight seventeen-year-old whistling his perennial "Silver Threads Among the Gold." He remembered them riding to rescue the Nesbitt wagon from the Mescaleros and fleeing from room to room in McSween's house as it burned— Billy leading the way out.

Damn it, he'd always liked Billy. How had it come to this, him tracking Billy down like an animal in the snow?

"I knew him when I lived in Sumner," Garrett said. "We used to play monte together. Likeable cuss, always smiling. I hear he keeps right on smiling when he guns down a man."

At dusk they were within a mile of the way station, still following the trail. Garrett stopped the posse.

"Billy and the boys are sure to be holed up for the night in that rock house," he told them. "We'll slip up and take a look-see before we decide what's best to do. When we get close, I want every man to be damn quiet; no sense in telegraphing we're here.''

When they were about four hundred yards away, Garrett split up the posse, half covering one side while he led the others into a dry arroyo running almost to the front of the rock house.

Mark saw it was a small hut, scarcely big enough for the five men and the two horses they must have brought in with them—only three were tethered outside. The building had no windows and only one entrance with no door on it. The opening gaped, dark and sinister. There was a chimney, but no smoke came from it. Must be cold as hell inside.

Garrett waved his men back and they returned to where they'd split up and waited for the others to rejoin them.

''Do we slip in and try to take them by surprise tonight? If they're asleep, we could go right into the hut. Or should we wait until morning when they'll know we're here?'' he asked.

''Wait,'' Stewart, the Texan who was second in command, said. ''I don't fancy our chances with those boys in the dark. They might be surprised and again they might not be.''

Garrett glanced at the others. One or two frowned, but none disagreed. Garrett nodded.

''Going to be a long, cold night,'' he said. ''Now most of you don't know Billy too well, so if any one of them comes out before it's good and light, I'll let you know if it's Billy by raising my rifle. Don't shoot otherwise. He's the one we want to kill.''

When they'd rolled themselves in their blankets in the snow, Mark said to Garrett, ''Does Billy still wear that wide-brimmed sombrero with the Irish-green hatband?''

''Still does. That's how I figure I'll know it's him if the light's not good.''

Mark lay shivering in the cold, unable to sleep. He was a deputy marshal, attached to a sheriff's posse. It was up to him to carry out Garrett's orders. But he knew he wasn't going to be able to pull the trigger of his Winchester if Billy came out that door the next morning and Garrett signalled to shoot. Not unless Billy was shooting at him.

Before dawn the posse was in position along the sides of the rock house and in front, huddled in their blankets with rifles ready. Sounds from inside the house made Mark tense in anticipation.

A gunman, his coat collar pulled up around his neck and face against the cold, stepped through the doorway, a horse's nosebag in his hand. He wore a wide-brimmed sombrero.

Mark glanced down the sights of his rifle. He couldn't be sure whether it was Billy or not. He looked sideways at Garrett.

Garrett raised his Winchester.

A volly of shots rang out, every man shooting except Mark.

The man screamed. Staggered backward. His hat rolled into the snow. Hands yanked him back through the doorway into the rock house, but not before Mark saw who he was.

Charlie Bowdre.

They'd shot the wrong man.

"Charlie's dying," a man shouted from inside a few seconds later. "He wants to surrender and he's coming out."

"Okay," Garrett shouted back. "We won't shoot."

Bowdre tottered out into the snow. His pistol was clutched in his hand but pointing down, unaimed. He staggered directly toward Garrett, blood running from his mouth, face sagging with pain.

"I wish," he gasped, "I wish . . ." He vomited blood into the snow. "I'm dying," he whispered and pitched forward.

Garrett caught him before he hit the ground and eased him down. "Sorry, Charlie," he muttered, "my mistake."

Mark turned from the dead man, his attention caught by the movement of one of the tethered horses. Someone from inside was trying to pull the animal into the house.

"No you don't," Garrett growled as the horse clopped into the doorway. He aimed. Fired. The horse dropped in its tracks, blocking the entrance.

Garrett aimed again and shot through the tethers of the two remaining horses. They bolted from the rock house.

"How're you doing?" he called to the men inside.

"Pretty well. Course we'd like some breakfast," someone answered. Mark recognized Billy's voice.

"Come out and be sociable," Garrett told him.

"Can't do it, Pat. Too busy."

Mark shook his head at the cheerfulness in Billy's voice. It didn't sound forced. My God, they were trapped inside the place and he must know it. They had two horses with them, but there was no chance now to make a break for freedom with the dead horse in the doorway.

The sun shone dully through high clouds as it climbed the sky. It shed no warmth and the icy wind blasted from the north. Garrett sent half the men back to Wilcox's ranch to eat and, when they returned, took the other half there and made arrangements for supplies to be sent to the site of the siege for the evening meal.

As Mark carried wood to their fire, he saw a riderless horse picking its way out of the hut over the dead animal. A second horse followed the first.

"They're sick of the stench," Stewart said. "Horses ain't good house guests."

Two of the deputies spitted a side of beef over the fire and soon its mouth-watering smell made the men smile in anticipation. Mark thought of the outlaws inside the house who hadn't eaten since they'd left Wilcox's, and he smiled, too. Garrett was as full of tricks as an Apache warrior.

A few minutes later a white rag waved vigorously from the hut's chimney.

"Parley!" someone inside called. "We want to discuss terms."

"Show yourself, hands in the air, and we'll talk," Garrett agreed.

Dave Rudabaugh stepped through the doorway and stood blinking in the light. "We'll toss you our guns if you promise you won't shoot," Dave yelled. "We want out of here alive. You agree?"

"I agree," Garrett said. "You have my promise."

Colts and Winchesters thudded into the snow. One by one the men emerged, hands in the air. Rudabaugh. Wilson. Pickett. Billy the Kid.

Garrett fed the prisoners a beef dinner before everyone mounted to make the long, cold ride back to Sumner. Mark rode ahead to the Wilcox ranch.

Tess was in the kitchen ladling stew into a bowl.

"Ezra's better," she said.

"That's good. Billy and the others finally gave up. Garrett's bringing them into town. He said he won't bother Ezra as long as you take him home to Lincoln when he can travel and he stays out of trouble from now on."

"I'll do my best to see that he does."

From the back room, Ezra called Mark's name. He went in to see him.

"Did you say Garrett got Billy?"

"Yes."

"Everybody all right except for poor old Charlie?"

"Well, they weren't shouting for joy. They're all headed for jail, you know that. You're just damn lucky you aren't with them."

"Billy always said I was lucky." Ezra looked up at Mark. "You think it's really the end of the line for him?"

"That's up to a judge and jury, but I'd guess it is."

"If it hadn't been for Billy, I wouldn't've stayed in the gang this long," Ezra said. "It was exciting at first, but after a while, when Rudabaugh and some of the others joined us, I got to feeling it was different. A dirty business. Except for Billy. He wasn't ever like that."

"Well, you're out now. After your wound heals, maybe I can get you some scout work. You must know every hangout in the Territory. Think about it while you're getting on your feet."

Ezra was silent for a few moments. "I guess I ought to be happy I'm going to be with my family for Christmas," he said finally. "With Tessa. But it's sort of like Billy got to be my family and I can't help thinking that he'll be spending Christmas behind bars, wondering what's going to happen."

"I'm afraid he'll hang," Mark said.

Ezra turned his face away.

Chapter 20

By the first of the year Ezra found he could sit a horse well enough to attempt the ninety-mile ride to Lincoln, but by the time Tessa helped him off his pinto at Maria's, he was feverish again and his right hip hurt so agonizingly he could hardly hobble into the house.

For a week or two he lay around, glad of Maria's good food and Tess's tender care. Jules often came to perch on the foot of Ezra's bed, to show off the latest tune he'd learned on his harmonica, and Ezra smiled and praised him, proud of his little brother's talent.

The coziness soon palled.

By the end of the month Ezra, still limping, was prowling restlessly around the house. His wound had not healed and now drained a yellow-green purulence that sickened him when Tessa changed his bandage.

"Do you think that doctor knows what he's doing?" he asked her.

"Dr. Greenway said you had to have patience," she reminded him. "The wound is healing from the inside out and that takes time. Besides, I think it looks better since he washed out those chips of bone."

"I was figuring on getting to Sumner before now to see how Violet's doing at Manuela's."

"You know you can't ride yet."

"Yes, but Violet needs someone to look after her."

"Manuela's very kind to Violet. I suspect she's more concerned about her than ever, now that Charlie's dead. Having Violet there gives her someone to fuss over."

Ezra couldn't explain his continuing worry to Tessa. Sure, Manuela would see that Violet ate and such, but there was more wrong with Violet than that. She'd started acting strange after Billy shot her father, and everything was bound to be worse now that Billy'd been captured and was in jail in Santa Fe, hundreds of miles from Sumner. She didn't have anyone at all now.

"I wish she'd have come to Lincoln with us," he muttered.

Tessa finished tying on the new bandage, straightened and looked at Ezra. "I asked her, even begged her. She refused. What more could we have done?"

"If I'd've felt better I could've made her come along."

"Kidnapping the poor girl wouldn't be any solution."

Tessa was probably right, but Violet's pale face haunted him. He'd had dreams where she was Juanita, alone and frightened in a *tendejon,* and he couldn't save her.

"Damn it, I'm fed up with being an invalid!" he shouted at Tessa.

"Well, don't take it out on me," she snapped, marching from the room and leaving him alone.

After a few minutes Jules bounced in with his harmonica.

"Mark taught me a new one," he said. "Do you wanta hear 'Camptown Races'?"

Without waiting for a yes or no, he put the instrument to his mouth and began to play.

Jules carried a tune well, but Ezra was heartily sick of listening to that damn harmonica. Mark ought to suffer being shut up in a house for a month with Jules playing it constantly—see how he liked it!

Mark didn't drop by much, though, even when he was in town. When he did visit, he and Tessa seemed more like enemies than friends, eyeing one another warily, once in a while skirmishing briefly. Yet, in her way, Tessa really paid more attention to Mark than she did to Calvin Rutledge when he came to call, which was too damn often to suit Ezra.

He plain didn't like the man; he guessed he never had. There was something too smooth about him that set his hackles on end.

Rutledge kept asking Tessa if she'd made up her mind.

"Calvin's willing to bring you with us, Ezra," Tessa had told him the week before. "That's if I marry him and move to Santa Fe. He says he can find you a job, maybe a clerk's position since you can write and cipher."

Ezra had grunted. Him, a clerk? Beholden to Rutledge for the job besides?

Never in a million years.

If his wound would ever heal, he might consider scouting for Mark; he wasn't sure yet.

"How did you like it, Ez?" Jules asked, breaking in on his thoughts.

"Huh? Oh, the song. Lively; I like that kind of a tune."

"You didn't look as if you liked the song. You looked kind of mad."

"I wasn't mad at you or your playing. You do fine."

"Was it because of Billy? Are you mad 'cause he's locked up in jail?"

Ezra sighed. "It doesn't seem right, him in jail, when there's worse walking the streets free as birds."

Jules' eyes widened. "Who?"

"Mathews, for one. I've never forgotten he was in that posse of Brady's when they shot Tunstall."

"You gonna go after Mathews?" Jules asked excitedly. "I'll help you!"

"Hey, wait a minute. I don't aim to go after anyone."

"When you get better, I mean."

Ezra shook his head. "Not then either. I promised Pat Garrett I'd stay out of trouble and I plan to keep that promise. There's been enough killing."

"What if Billy breaks out of jail? You told me there wasn't a jail that could hold him very long."

"I don't know, Jules. I reckon the jail in Santa Fe ain't the kind a man breaks out of easy."

"But what if he does?"

Ezra didn't answer and Jules poked at his arm.

"What if he does?"

Ezra grabbed Jules and tousled his hair. "Put all the what-if's in the world end-to-end and they'll take you nowhere, just like Papa used to say."

Jules squirmed away from Ezra. "Did Papa really used to say that? I don't remember. I remember the wagon and the Apaches and all, but not Papa."

"He was a good man. Better than I'll ever be."

"I think you're okay, Ez," Jules said earnestly.

"Play me another tune," Ezra said hastily, embarrassed by Jules' solemn approval.

The melancholy strains of "Danny Boy" filled the room. Ezra closed his eyes. When Jules finished, Ezra felt the prick of tears behind his lids and blinked, clearing his throat.

"That's a sad one. Mark teach it to you?"

Jules shook his head. "I listened to Buck McDaniels sing it so many times—you know he sings the same song everytime he gets to drinking; you can't help hearing him, he's so loud—it just sort of came to me what notes to play."

Ezra stared at him. His brother truly had a gift for music, he ought to go someplace where he could get schooling. St. Louis, maybe. I'll help him, Ezra decided. I'll get work as soon as I can, take that scout job Mark offered me, and I'll save money.

By the end of February, Ezra's wound was practically healed, with only a little drainage. He could ride pretty well, if he didn't go too far. Then his hip would start hurting so bad he could hardly get off the horse.

When Mark returned from Roswell, the first week in March, Ezra waited until he came to the house.

"I reckon I'm ready to scout for you, if you'll still have me," he told Mark.

Mark nodded. "I have to ride to Mesilla at the end of the month to be on hand when the court convenes. You could come with me. After the court session we'll go looking for Harry Yarrow; I heard he's thinking of leaving his hole-up in Mexico. He's wanted for robbing the U.S. Mail."

"I've heard of Yarrow," Ezra said. "Be glad to help you hunt him."

"One thing, Ezra. They're trying Billy at that session of the court."

"Figured as much." Ezra glanced at Mark and half smiled. "You looking for my word I don't aim to help him escape?"

"If I thought you'd do that, I wouldn't take you."

On April sixth Ezra walked into the Mesilla courthouse, an old adobe that doubled as a school when court wasn't in session. He took a seat on a wooden bench along with the other spectators.

A Mescalero squatted on one side of him; a pony soldier from Stanton slouched on the other. Billy, silent and handcuffed, sat near the side of an empty desk with armed guards watching him. Ezra tried to catch Billy's eye, but Billy was staring at the door.

It opened and Judge Bristol swept in, his black robes trailing the dusty floor. As he took his seat behind the desk, a soft warm breeze blew in the open window to his left, ruffling the papers on the desk. The day seemed made for being out in the open, enjoying life.

The judge listened to the lawyers read the federal charges against Billy, quickly dismissing the one that accused him of shooting Bernstein on the Indian reservation. Insufficient evidence.

Leonard, Billy's court-appointed lawyer, questioned the jurisdiction of the United States in the other indictment— Roberts' killing.

Judge Bristol readily agreed that Blazer's Mill, where the killing had occurred, was not the property of the government and so dismissed the second charge. Ezra's heart lifted. Was it possible Billy might walk out of here a free man?

"I order the United States Marshal to deliver William Bonney to the territorial authorities, since I understand they also have an indictment," the judge said. "Trial set for two days hence."

Two more days in jail for Billy, waiting to find out what would happen. Ezra had heard the Mesilla jail ranked among the worst in the Territory. But Billy'd been lucky so far, maybe the coming trial would go as well.

On the eighth the courtroom was so crowded with spectators that Ezra couldn't find a seat and had to stand just inside the door. The twelve jurymen were already in their places. All Mexicans, he saw. A good sign. Mexicans liked Billy.

This time Billy noticed him and smiled.

The charge was the murder of Sheriff Brady.

On the tenth a stunned and disbelieving Ezra heard Judge Bristol pass sentence on Billy; the jury had found him guilty.

"William Bonney, alias Billy the Kid, alias William Antrim, being found guilty of murder in the first degree, will, on Friday, May thirteenth, 1881, in the town of Lincoln, be hanged by the neck until his body be dead."

"It's not fair!" Ezra told Mark later. "There were five others shooting at Brady besides Billy. Anyway, he told me himself he was aiming at Mathews, not Brady, and was real put out 'cause he missed."

"They found him guilty, Ezra. The judged passed sentence. Nothing you can do or say will change it."

"But he's my friend. I thought they'd keep him in jail for maybe a couple of years, but I never believed what Garrett said about hanging Billy."

The man they were after, Yarrow, turned out to be still in Mexico, so Ezra and Mark rode back to Lincoln empty-handed.

Billy arrived under armed guard in Lincoln a few days afterward, on the twenty-second of April, and was incarcerated in the old "House of Murphy," Dolan's store, now serving as a courthouse and jail.

That night Ezra couldn't sleep. He pictured Billy handcuffed and in leg irons. Wouldn't he find it hard to sleep, a man sentenced to hang in less than a month's time?

It'd be more Billy's style, though, to be joking with his guards, saying something like, "Hanging ain't my idea of a fun Friday."

Ezra eased from his bed, hoping not to rouse Jules, and went out into the April night. He stood by Maria's corral, staring up at the Milky Way. He'd heard some of the Indians thought that warriors went there when they died.

He didn't know what he believed anymore. His father's God seemed to belong to another time and another country.

"Nesbitt." The whisper was as startling as a snake's hiss.

Ezra reached for his Colt, remembered he didn't have his gun belt on. He flattened himself against the corral rails.

"Who is it? *Quien es?*"

"Never mind." The man spoke in Spanish, his voice low and rapid. "I'm leaving a package by the back door. I tried to get it to Billy. Couldn't. Now it's up to you."

Ezra searched the darkness for the speaker, saw a dark figure slip from the yard and disappear. He hurried after the man, but there was no one to be seen in the street. Ezra returned to the back of the house to search for the package.

Someone sat on the back stoop and he held. "Who's there?" he demanded.

"It's me," Jules said. "Did you know someone left a Colt with a silver handle all wrapped up in a newspaper here?"

Only then did Ezra realize he'd been talking to Jose Chavez.

Early on the morning of the twenty-eighth Mark trotted up the stairs of the courthouse toward the rooms used as jail cells. Most of the prisoners were confined in the room at the head of the stairs that had once quartered the housekeeper. But Billy was locked up separately. You had to go through the sheriff's office to get to the northeast corner room, where Billy was shut away in solitary confinement, and then pass an armed guard sitting on a bench just inside the doorway.

The guard today was another deputy marshal, Bob Olinger. He looked up as Mark approached. Between his knees his shotgun was propped, breech broken open.

"Howdy, Mark," he said. "Just loading her up for the day." He dropped a slug with eighteen grains of buckshot into each barrel, winked at Mark and, looking toward Billy, who was chained to the floor some yards away, commented, "The man that gets one of these is going to feel it."

Billy grinned at Mark, ignoring Bob.

"I reckon it's too much to hope you brought a bottle," Billy said to Mark.

"Sorry."

Garrett had made a flat rule—nothing was to be given to Billy except by his guards. Mark was damn sure Olinger, who'd hated Billy since the McSween-Dolan feud, gave Billy nothing.

"Only fifteen more days to Friday the thirteenth," Olinger said. "Hanging day. That's the day I plan to celebrate."

"I came up to ask if you know where Garrett's got to," Mark asked Olinger. "The boys downstairs said something about him collecting taxes."

Olinger laughed. "Naw. He ain't advertising it, but what he's doing is buying the lumber over to White Oaks for the gallows. Ain't that so, Kid?"

Billy shrugged. "They never did like me in that town."

He looked small and defenseless, handcuffed and with

his leg irons chained to a bolt in the floor. Mark had no illusions; Billy had to be tightly corralled and closely watched, but he didn't enjoy seeing him this way. Nor did he care for the way Olinger taunted Billy.

Bell, the deputy sheriff who relieved Olinger as guard, was very different, a quiet, pleasant sort of fellow. Billy must look forward to the times Bell was with him.

"I'll see Garrett when he gets back then," Mark said. He waved to Billy and started to turn away.

"Mark."

He looked back at Billy, eyebrows raised.

"Could you arrange for Ez to come see me?"

"It can't be done. Sorry. Sheriff's order."

Garrett was taking no chances of some old *compañero* slipping anything to Billy. Surely the smart thing to do, but it was hard on Billy not to be able to say good-bye to his friends before he died.

"Jules, have you seen Ezra?" Tessa asked just before noon. "He didn't come home last night. Did he tell you where he was going?"

Jules looked away from her. "I don't know where he is."

"Are you sure?"

He nodded.

"I suppose I can't expect him to stay home now that he's feeling better, but . . ." She broke off, biting her lip. "Oh, I *wish* they hadn't brought Billy to Lincoln to hang."

"Yeah, well, I don't know where Ezra went," Jules said, picking up a bandanna-wrapped bundle and heading for the kitchen door.

"And where are *you* going?"

"Out to Banks'. Bob and me are gonna practice roping. I'm bringing my lunch."

"Be home for supper."

"I will."

Jules climbed onto his buckskin, shoving the bundle underneath his shirt. As the horse ambled along, Jules pulled his harmonica out and began to play.

Darling, I am growing old
Silver threads among the gold
Shine upon my brow today
Life is fading fast away . . .

Over and over he played the plaintive melody, stopping when he came by the courthouse. He reined in and dismounted. With his back to the building, he tethered the buckskin by Wortley's Hotel.

Sauntering across the street, he began to play the same song. He skirted the wall around the yard of the courthouse, moving slowly, heading for the rear, for the gate that led to the outhouse.

The privy was used by the public as well as the prisoners. Jules went inside the small shed and hooked the door shut.

When he came out of the privy, Jules moved faster but still didn't hurry. He got back in the saddle and walked the buckskin west, out of town, where he stopped and again tethered the horse in the cottonwoods along the Rio Bonito.

Quickly Jules made his way along the river bank as he headed back toward town. He wore the bandana around his neck.

At noon, in the jail, Bell relieved Olinger, who left his shotgun in the sheriff's office before going down the stairs and across the street to eat lunch at the hotel.

"How about taking me outside to the privy?" Billy asked Bell.

Chapter 21

Just after noon Tessa went out to help Maria take clean clothes off a line strung from the chinaberry tree to the back door. People riding past on the street called a greeting and she saw they were the Banks—mother, father, Bob and his older sister, Mabel. They were heading east and their horses all carried packrolls.

"Tell Jules I'll be back next Tuesday," young Bob called.

Tell Jules? Hadn't he been going to Bob's?

Tessa stared after them. She recalled how Jules hadn't met her eyes, how he'd slid out the kitchen door. She twisted her hands together. Jules seldom, if ever, lied to her.

What was going on?

It must be connected to Ezra's disappearance. Where was he? She'd assumed Ezra had finally gone to Sumner to look in on Violet. What if he hadn't? What if he was involved in something outside the law?

Like trying to arrange Billy's escape?

"Not with Jules!" she said aloud.

"Pardon?" Maria asked.

Tessa shook her head. She untied her apron and flung it atop the clean clothes in the basket. Without pausing to go inside for a bonnet, she hurried through the gate and ran down the street toward the jail.

, She heard two shots. She ran faster, saw a man stagger from the side door of the courthouse into the yard and fall to the ground.

Men ran from inside Wortley's onto the porch of the hotel. One hurried across the street toward the gate into the courthouse yard. Godfrey Gauss, the caretaker, appeared around the far corner of the building, yelling at the oncoming man.

"The Kid has killed Bell!"

Tessa stopped abruptly.

"Hello, Bob!" a familiar voice called.

Tessa knew then the man crossing the street was Bob Olinger. He halted, glanced up at the second story windows where the voice had come from. Tessa followed his gaze, saw shotgun barrels thrust from an upper window.

"He's killed me, too!" Olinger cried.

The shotgun blasted. Olinger dropped. Lay motionless on the ground. Tessa saw the barrels of the shotgun pulled back from the window. Moments later a figure appeared on the second-story porch.

Billy!

He carried a shotgun and was moving awkwardly to the railing. He looked down at the man he'd just shot, then fired the second barrel of the gun. The body on the ground jerked when the buckshot struck.

Billy broke the gun across the rail and flung it at the body.

"Take it, damn you!" he shouted. "You won't follow me around anymore with that gun."

Unable to collect her wits, Tessa stared as Billy yelled to the caretaker who was peering cautiously around the corner of the building.

"Gauss, throw me up something to get these leg irons off with. Hurry, damn it!"

Gauss tossed him what looked like a miner's pick. Billy disappeared into the building. At last Tessa was able to move. She stared all around, but didn't see either Ezra or Jules in the street. Or anyone else. She stood alone.

Men were sheltered behind barrels and wagons. They looked out from the hotel doorway. Tessa hurried toward the hotel porch, glancing from one face to another, searching for her brothers.

"The Kid's done for both Bell and Olinger," a man said.

"I sure as hell ain't going after him," another put in.

"How'd he get loose anyways?"

She ducked inside the hotel, but there was no sign of the boys, so she hurried back out, not knowing what to do next. Where to look. Could they be inside the courthouse with Billy?

She took a deep breath and started to step off the hotel porch. A man grasped her arm.

"Certain death out there, miss."

"Billy won't shoot me."

But she let him pull her back onto the porch, thinking that Ezra and Jules wouldn't be in the courthouse. They wouldn't have been allowed inside, for Ezra had tried more than once to visit Billy and had been turned away.

Likely they were waiting with horses and supplies somewhere outside of town. Waiting for Billy to join them. She might as well forget trying to find them.

She couldn't bring herself to leave and stared across at the courthouse with the others, waiting to see what would happen.

"Gauss is saddling a horse," a blond-bearded man said. "Look, there's Billy coming out!"

Tessa drew in her breath. Watched as Billy climbed clumsily onto the horse. He'd hacked through the chain connecting the leg irons, but the irons themselves were still around his ankles.

Colt in hand, he turned the horse to the west. As he urged the animal into a gallop, a small figure ran from between buildings into the street. A boy. At the same time men jumped out from shelter, pistols drawn. Billy looked back, Colt aimed.

Tessa heard three shots, not knowing who fired them. The boy fell. Billy galloped on. She ran, heart hammering in her chest, toward the small body lying in the street. Fell on her kneees beside him. Gathered him into her arms.

Blood trickled from a hole in his chest. His gray eyes stared at her.

"Jules!" she cried, closing her eyes and holding him to her breast and rocking back and forth. "Oh, Jules."

Hands touched her, tried to take him from her arms. She fought them, clutching him closer. She heard horse's hooves, heard a man call her name.

"Tessa," he said, over and over. "Tessa."

She finally recognized Mark's voice and opened her eyes. He crouched next to her.

"Tessa," he said gently, "let me have Jules. Let me see to him."

Reluctantly she relinquished her hold and Mark took

Jules from her. He stood up, carrying the boy. She rose to her feet.

The sun seemed too bright, the voices unnaturally loud, the rattle of wagon wheels too harsh to be borne.

"We'll take him to Maria's," Mark said.

Tessa trailed after him, refusing help from anyone. It took forever to walk the short distance to Maria's and yet they were there all too quickly. She followed Mark into the house. He strode into the boys' bedroom and laid Jules carefully on the bed.

When she started to bend to Jules, Mark put his arms around her, holding her away.

"Let me go!" she cried. "I must help him."

"He's beyond help, Tessa," Mark said into her ear. "Jules is dead."

She struck at him with her fists. "No! It isn't true. You're lying." She struggled to free herself, but he held her tightly against him.

All at once she went limp.

Jules was dead. Her baby was dead.

She'd known it as soon as she touched him there in the street.

Shot, like her father. Like John Tunstall. Like Alex McSween. And like Vincente Gabaldon.

Tessa leaned against Mark and began to weep.

After a time he disengaged her and led her to where Maria stood by the door, tears running down her cheeks.

"Take care of her," he said. "I'm going after Billy."

Calvin hurried in shortly after Mark left. It was Calvin who persuaded her to notify the undertaker and talk to the minister, Calvin who dealt with the people who came by to offer condolences.

It would always be like that, she thought dully. Calvin nearby, Mark off someplace.

By evening Tessa was moving in a daze of exhaustion.

"You must rest," Calvin told her. "I'll come by first thing in the morning."

She lay on her bed, more tired than she could ever remember, but sleep refused to come. After a time she thought she heard noises in back, by the corral.

Had Ezra returned?

Tessa rose and put a robe over her cotton nightdress. She slipped out the kitchen door and looked toward the corral.

"*Señorita,*" a man whispered from her left.

She jumped back.

"Do not fear. I bring a message."

Tessa saw he was holding a folded paper. She took it.

"I am to wait for your reply," he said.

Tessa hurried into the house, lit the kitchen lamp and read the note.

"Need money. Send with messenger." Ezra's name was scrawled at the bottom.

She stared at the words until they seemed to crawl like snakes across the paper.

She had no doubt at all that Ezra was with Billy. Send money to help Billy escape? Tessa tore the note into scraps and flung them away. She whirled to go and vent her rage on the messenger, but before she reached the door, she halted.

The messenger would be heading back to Billy and Ezra once he left Lincoln. He knew where they were. She nodded to herself.

Tessa slipped quietly into her bedroom and, with trembling fingers, picked at the threads holding her small hoard of money in the hem of a petticoat she never wore. After working out two silver coins, she laid them on the chest.

Tessa dressed quickly, throwing on the old shirt and

pants she'd worn on her ill-fated trip to Sumner. She thrust her feet into boots. In the drawer of her wardrobe was her father's old hunting knife from England, one she'd been saving to give to Jules on his twelfth birthday. She took the knife and sheath out and fastened them onto her belt.

Putting her robe back on to hide what she wore, Tessa picked up the money and tiptoed through the house to the back door. She eased the door open. The messenger crouched by the back steps.

"I'm sorry I took so long," she said. "I keep the money hidden." She handed him the two coins.

"*Gracias, señorita,*" he said, rising. His horse, she saw, was tethered to the chinaberry tree.

She hurried into the kitchen, flung off her robe and ran for the front door. Raced across the road and untied a horse hitched to the rail at Donaldo's cantina. Mounted him.

What difference did one more thief in the family make? It would take her too long to saddle her own horse.

She saw the rider lead his horse from Maria's yard, climb into the saddle and head west.

Tessa followed him.

She soon realized they were going toward Capitan Peak northeast of Lincoln. She tried to stay back so the messenger wouldn't spot her and once or twice she was shaken with the fear she'd lost sight of him.

After some time she began to suspect she knew where they were going. Ezra had told her about staying with Billy at a goat ranch once in the foothills of these mountains with a friend of Billy's. She was certain she was right when she finally smelled the unmistakable odor of goats.

The messenger was nowhere in sight when she reined in beside a corral, but somewhere ahead a dog barked furiously.

She dismounted, tethered the horse and headed for a glimmer of light.

She heard a man shouting in Spanish at the dog, telling him to be quiet. Tessa edged forward cautiously, and as she neared the light, she saw it was a lantern in a stable. Four men and a dog were inside, the dog showing its teeth and snarling, holding one of the men at bay.

"I'll take him to the house and tie him," another man said. He left, his hand grasping the dog's back fur to pull him along.

Tessa eased closer to the three who remained. The messenger. Ezra. And Billy.

Billy was squatting, working at filing off his remaining leg iron. The messenger handed Ezra the coins she'd given him.

"Did my sister give you a note?" Ezra asked.

"No, nothing except the money."

"Did she say anything?"

The messenger shook his head.

There was a silence. Tessa could hear the rasp of Billy's file and the calling of frogs from a nearby *ria*. A goat blatted somewhere in the spring night.

"*Muchas gracias, Pablo*," Ezra said.

The messenger shrugged, "*De nada*. I do it for Billy. *Adios*." He turned and Tessa drew back deeper into the shadows as he went past her and then disappeared into the darkness. She heard horse's hooves going away.

When she was certain he was gone, Tessa walked toward Billy and Ezra. Neither saw her until she was almost upon them. Billy dropped the file and sprang to his feet as Ezra yanked his Colt free, only to slide it back when he realized who she was. Both he and Billy gaped at her.

"I followed the messenger," she said.

"You shouldn't have done that," Ezra protested.

Billy smiled at her. "If you'll excuse me, I got pressing business." He dropped down to continue filing at the iron.

She stared at him for a long moment. Was it possible he didn't know what had happened as he fled from town?

"They shot at you," she said tentatively.

"Missed me," Billy said cheerfully.

"You killed those two deputies."

"Had to. Olinger got what was coming to him. Sorry about Bell, but it was me or him."

"How did you manage it?"

"Let's say a friend left me a pistol and I was lucky enough to find it."

Tessa glanced at Ezra. "You found a way to get a pistol in to Billy?" she asked.

Ezra shook his head. "I didn't dare go near the place. They'd have stopped me for sure."

"So you sent Jules."

"Now, Tess, I knew you'd be mad. I didn't exactly send him. Didn't want to, and that's a fact. But it was Jules who figured out how to do it. He thought up playing "Silver Threads Among the Gold" on his harmonica to attract Billy's attention. He said if Billy couldn't get to a window to see him, he could hear where Jules was headed if he listened and he'd know where to look. He's smart as a whip, that brother of mine."

"So you let Jules go. You encouraged him to head into danger."

"Come on, Tess," Ezra said, "he wasn't in any danger. Worst thing that could have happened, they'd have stopped him."

She swallowed. If Billy knew, he certainly hadn't told Ezra.

"Are the deputies the only ones you shot?" she asked

Billy. She heard her voice, thin and high, sounding like another person's.

"Far as I know. Oh, I fired once at those brave *hombres* who didn't show until I was on my way out of town. Don't tell me I hit one of them."

"I'm not telling you anything," she said.

Billy eyed her for a moment, then went back to filing. The iron was almost cut through. After a moment he snapped it in two with his hands and stood up.

"That's a relief. Mighty confining, leg irons. Hope you never find out about them firsthand."

"What do you intend to do now?" she asked.

He grinned. "Well, I figure if only I know that, then no one else will. No offense, Tess."

A nighthawk rushed through the darkness, swooping after insects attracted to the lantern, his wings swishing past so close that Tessa felt the movement of the air. Billy stretched and yawned.

"I suppose you'll be going with him," Tessa said to Ezra. "Again."

"Reckon so."

"So much for promises."

"But that was when Billy was in jail. When I thought it was all over. It's different with . . ."

"He'd still be in jail if it wasn't for you. Am I right, Ezra?"

"I realize you're upset, Tess. I know you don't have anything against Billy, that you're just mad at me. But I got to . . ."

"How can you say I don't have anything against Billy?" she demanded. "You have no idea how I feel."

"Look," Billy said, "I didn't mean to start a fight."

She turned on him. "You never mean to do anything,

do you? 'Just a friendly sort of fellow, trying to go his own way,' I think I heard you tell somebody once.''

She began to walk toward him. "How about the thieving? And the murders? How about those?''

He blinked at her, took a step backward.

Tessa flew at him, yanking the knife from its sheath. She raised it. Billy tried to knock her arm aside, but she dodged his thrust and lunged.

Ezra's hand caught her wrist. Twisting her arm behind her back, he squeezed until she was forced to drop the knife. He let her go and picked it up.

"What in God's name is the matter with you, Tess.'' Ezra demanded.

She held her right wrist, rubbing it. "You should have let me kill him!'' she cried. "You've talked to me for years about vengeance, but you wouldn't let me kill your brother's murderer.''

Ezra stared at her. "What in hell are you talking about?''

"Jules. He shot Jules.'' She covered her face with her hands and wept.

"Hey,'' Billy protested, "I wouldn't hurt Jules. I didn't even *see* Jules.''

Tessa dropped her hands and wiped at her eyes. "There were three shots. Yours was one of them.''

"Then it could have been those *hombres* who shot at me. Tess, I'm sorry . . .''

Anger dried her tears. "Jules wouldn't have been there if it wasn't for you, Billy Bonney, or whatever your name is. He'd be alive right this minute if it wasn't for you. If that's not killing him, I don't know what is.''

Billy sighed. "Ez,'' he said, "I'm getting out of here.''

Tessa stood, shoulders slumped, watching Billy lead out a horse and saddle him. Then she watched Ezra throw a saddle over the pinto's back.

"You ought to take Tess home," Billy said to him.

Ezra shook his head. His face held no expression at all. She'd told him his brother was dead and he hadn't even shed a tear.

"You monster!" she shrieked at Ezra. "I'm ashamed you're my brother. Go ahead—ride with thieves and murderers; that's where you belong!"

Ezra continued saddling up, not looking at her.

"Go with your brother's murderer," she half-sobbed. "I never want to see you again."

Turning, she fled into the darkness.

Chapter 22

It was as lovely a spring morning as Tessa had ever seen. A soft wind blew from the southwest, hinting of the summer to come but still pleasantly cool. A meadowlark trilled in the cottonwoods lining the Rio Bonito. The air smelled fresh, with a faint scent of blooming flowers.

The grass grew green on her father's resting place. The wooden marker was already weathered. Tessa shifted her gaze to the newly dug hole next to Papa's grave.

It seemed only yesterday that Jules had clutched her skirts, begging her not to let them "put Papa in a hole."

She closed her eyes. When she opened them, maybe it would turn out to be a terrible dream. Maybe Jules would be standing beside her, harmonica in hand, ready to play his newest song.

Calvin touched her arm and she sighed.

"Reverend Farnright is here," he said.

Tessa opened her eyes. The gaping hole still waited near

277

her feet. The pine coffin resting beside it held all that was left of her brother. He'd looked curiously peaceful, hands folded on his chest, the harmonica clasped in them as he would have wished.

"You must remember God reserves a special place for children," the minister said to her.

She nodded. A man striding toward them caught her attention and she looked away from the minister to watch him hopefully. She knew it was Mark before she saw his face. No one moved in quite the same purposeful way.

He'd come late to her father's funeral. She recalled how her heart had warmed to see him as she stood in the midst of strangers. The people with her now were no longer strangers and yet she felt the same thrill of recognition.

He walked straight to her and took her hand. She quelled the momentary weakness that would have had her in his arms and sobbing on his chest.

"I'm glad you came," she told him.

"Jules was my friend."

She knew it was true. Jules had felt the same. It would have broken Jules' heart if she'd married Calvin and they'd moved to Santa Fe, for Jules would have had to give up seeing Mark. Maybe that's what had kept her from the marriage.

A part of herself was in that coffin, would be buried with Jules. He'd been like her very own baby. Grief clawed at her. Tears filled her eyes. She couldn't bear to lose Jules. She couldn't bear it.

As she fumbled in her reticule for a handkerchief, Tessa realized that Mark and Calvin were glaring at one another over her head. You'd think they could put their differences aside for these few minutes.

Susie McSween smiled sadly at her from among the

other mourners and Tessa knew Susie must be remembering the hurried ceremony two years ago when Alex was laid to rest here. Tessa also noticed that George Barber, the lawyer who'd bought Alex's law library, stood attentively beside Susie.

I can never forgive Billy, Tessa thought, but I'm not sorry I didn't kill him. So many deaths. Why should I add to them?

"Dearly beloved," Reverend Farnright began, "we are gathered here because a lamb of God has been gathered into His fold . . ."

How Jules would hate being called a lamb. Tears spilled down Tessa's cheeks.

The minister's voice rolled over her, intoning familiar words. She closed her eyes again. Other sounds intermingled with his voice. A dog barking. The meadowlark, still singing. The rattle and clank of a wagon passing on the road. Hoofbeats in the distance, coming nearer and nearer.

Tessa's eyes flew open. She stared at the rider who pounded toward them. He reined in only a few feet from the grave and slid from the horse.

"Ezra!" she cried, running toward him. "Oh, Ezra, they're burying Jules." She flung herself into his arms.

Tessa felt the heave of Ezra's chest as he sobbed. "It should have been me," he said brokenly. "Me, not Jules."

She clung to him tighter.

After a moment Ezra eased her away. He strode to Mark, Tessa hurrying after him.

"After the funeral," Ezra said to Mark, "you can take me in. I'm ready to pay for what I've done."

Mark jerked his head, indicating that Ezra should stand next to him. Tessa slipped back into her place between Calvin and Mark. The minister, who'd gone on with the burial service through all the commotion, wound up his eulogy by asking the mourners to pray as the coffin was lowered into the grave.

Calvin offered his arm to Tessa. She took it, but stood unmoving, her eyes on Ezra and Mark.

"My notion is that the Nesbitts have paid enough," Mark told Ezra. "I'm not planning to take you in. How Sheriff Garrett will feel is another story."

Maria's house was soon crowded with those coming to express their sympathy. It seemed all of Lincoln had known and loved the boy with the harmonica.

In the early evening the sheriff paid his respects.

"Sorry to hear about your brother," he said to Tessa, his eyes shifting from one person to another as he spoke, then stopping on Ezra. He headed toward him. Tessa trailed behind.

"Ezra," Garrett said. "Too bad about Jules."

Ezra eyed him steadily, waiting.

"No use to beat about the bush. We both know you had something to do with Billy getting away. Now I'm a fair man and I'd be willing to forget about what I know if you'd be willing to help me."

"What kind of help?" Ezra asked.

"I reckon you could lead me straight to the Kid if you'd a mind to."

"No."

"No you couldn't or no you won't?"

"I won't."

Garrett shrugged. "I'll be taking you in with me then."

"I'm ready."

"Ezra!" Tessa protested.

"Don't interfere," Ezra warned her. "I don't want to hear what is or isn't right and proper. This is what I'm doing."

"But I thought . . ." Her voice trailed away. She'd

thought that when Ezra showed up at the funeral, it meant he'd repudiated Billy once and for all. She'd forgiven him on the spot.

Now she understood that wasn't what he'd intended at all. He'd left Billy, yes, but he wouldn't betray him. He still cared about Jules' murderer. How could he? She sent Ezra a scathing look and turned her back to him. Let Sheriff Garrett lock him up!

"I don't think there's anything I can do about it." Mark spoke almost into her ear, startling her. "Garrett has decided that Ezra's going to lead him to Billy or else."

"Never mind!" she cried, her anger at Ezra spilling over onto Mark. "You knew what would happen, didn't you? No wonder you could sound so noble at the grave. You knew the sheriff would do your dirty work for you."

Mark didn't reply. Susie, standing next to him, stared wide-eyed at Tessa.

"Oh, you poor dear," Susie murmured. "You're so upset you just don't know what you're saying."

"I know exactly what I'm saying! When men pin on a law badge, it seems to turn their hearts as hard as the badge."

"But Tessa . . ." Susie protested.

"Don't talk to me!" Tessa cried. "Naturally you'd be on Mark's side. He's a man."

Susie flushed, putting her hand to her cheek as though Tessa had slapped her. Before Susie turned away, Tessa saw her eyes fill with tears.

Tessa raised her chin. She wouldn't be sorry for what she'd said. It was true, every word.

Calvin touched her arm. "I thought you might feel the need for a bit of fresh air."

She turned to him gratefully. "Oh, yes, Calvin. This very minute."

The evening was cool. The sky, still deep rose to the west, showed the hills etched darkly against the fading light. Calvin led her through the gate and down the street.

"Surely you see there's nothing left for you in Lincoln," he said. "Santa Fe would be a new start."

"Yes," she said, sighing. "A new start."

"Does that include marrying me?" he asked.

Tessa tried to smile. "I wouldn't go with you to Santa Fe otherwise."

He took her into his arms, holding her close. "You've made me very happy. I've waited a long time for the right answer."

Had she really said yes? Tessa felt dazed and lightheaded. She leaned against Calvin's shoulder. He was the only one she could count on.

The sound of someone approaching made her draw back a little. Mark passed them, looking straight ahead. He said nothing. Calvin's hand was warm on her back, but it did nothing to ease the sudden chill inside her.

"I don't mean to tell you your business," Mark said to Garrett on May first, "but you could keep Ezra Nesbitt behind bars until he turned gray and it wouldn't change his mind about helping you find Billy."

"If you don't mean to tell me my business, then don't," Garrett snapped.

"What purpose does it serve? You haven't got a warrant on him. Suspicion isn't a valid reason."

"It's my reason."

"Can't you see he doesn't mind being in jail? He blames himself for his brother getting shot and so he feels he ought to be punished. He thinks it's fair. You can't expect him to change his mind and take you to Billy when he's got that attitude."

"Don't go talking fancy to me either."

Mark's eyes flashed. "I'll talk to you however I choose. If Ezra got himself a lawyer, he'd be out in no time. Legally, you can't hold him."

"So now you're a lawyer."

"As a matter of fact, I am. And I'm telling you what's legal and what isn't."

"The hell with what you're telling me. He stays in. That's final."

"What if I told you I needed him to help me with some unfinished business down near Mesilla?"

"I'd say you had as much chance of getting him as a snake has of hatching a chicken. Why don't you get the hell out of here and leave me be?"

Mark did just that. He took himself on up to Santa Fe, and when he came back, he had papers to show to Pat Garrett.

"Damn you, Halloran, what'd you go and do that for?" Garrett demanded.

"I told you I needed help. Now, will you get the new deputy marshal out of your goddamned jail or do I have to file suit? And my name's Dempsey."

Ezra kept shaking his head as he walked down the street with Mark. "Me, a deputy marshal?"

"Why not? I still haven't caught up with Yarrow, but I hear he's been spotted for sure around Mesilla. We'll ride down and round him up. Any objections?"

"No. But I sort of thought you'd be hunting Billy."

"That's the sheriff's job. He hasn't asked me for help. And somehow I don't think he will."

It was June when Ezra and Mark got back into Lincoln, Yarrow safely behind bars in Mesilla and no longer a threat to the U.S. Mail. Garrett wasn't in town and Billy was still at large. Most people believed Billy had fled to Mexico.

At Maria's the house was in turmoil as Tessa's wedding date approached. Mark, who'd thought himself resigned to the fact she'd soon be another man's wife, suddenly found he couldn't look at her without choking with rage.

He wanted to pick her up and shake her until her teeth rattled, tear off her clothes and fling her onto the floor and take her by force, make her admit she wanted him and not that phony Southerner.

He decided he'd better stay away from Maria's house altogether.

Ezra watched his sister darting here and there, sewing frenziedly, talking, talking, her voice high and shrill. She looked thinner and, despite her protestations of happiness, her eyes were shadowed. He didn't think it was only because she still grieved for Jules.

The wedding was set for the third week in June, only two weeks away. She claimed she could hardly wait, but Ezra kept seeing her pull back from Calvin's embraces and he knew something was very wrong in all this. But he couldn't just burst out and ask her if she really loved the man. He'd begin slow.

"What did you say Calvin did in Santa Fe?" he asked her, figuring that was a harmless question.

"Well, it's only me, I know, but I don't think I can explain it; I don't always understand what he tells me, he's such a brilliant man and I'm . . ."

"Whoa, Tess. Try to explain it to me."

"It has to do with investments."

"Does he work for a bank?"

"Not exactly. I believe he mentioned railroads once."

"It sounds like he hasn't tried very hard to tell you

exactly what it is he does. My God, Tess, didn't you ask any questions? You're usually full of them."

"I tried, but it seems I couldn't quite grasp the answers. Calvin says it's terribly complicated."

"But you're smart, Tess. Papa always said you were the brightest of us all. 'A real scholar' he called you. I should think you'd understand."

"The truth is, maybe I didn't listen as closely as I might have. It's such a relief not to worry anymore, to know someone will be taking care of everything, that I'll know what's coming next and there won't be any surprises . . ." Her voice trailed away and for a moment she looked wistful, as though she rather wanted to have a surprise to look forward to.

"So it boils down to the fact you don't really know what he does for a living."

"You make it sound sinister. I won't have you twisting things like that, Ezra. Calvin is a fine, upstanding man, a gentleman; anything he does is certainly honest and straightforward."

She sounded more like her old self and he grinned at her. "I guess that's more than you can say for me. You make him sound noble. But, Tess, are you certain you want to marry him?"

She nodded firmly. "I've made up my mind. I won't change it."

"I thought once that you and Mark might get married."

Desolation swept across her face making his heart contract. A moment later she'd put on her brittle new smile. "I can't imagine whatever gave you such a notion. Mark has no intention of ever settling down to one place or one woman."

The next day Ezra tried to sound out Mark.

"I thought you were pretty fond of Tess."

"I am."

"Then how come you're letting her marry Rutledge?"

"She accepted him; I didn't force her into it."

"Do you think she'll be happy with him?"

"Look, Ezra, I'm the wrong person to ask. I can't stand the man. Never could, from the first time I saw him. I can't help feeling he's a phony. But that's my prejudice. He probably is just what he seems to be—a respectable businessman, one who does well at whatever it is he does."

"What *does* he do?"

"Something to do with one of the Santa Fe banks, I understand."

"Then you're not sure?"

Mark shrugged. "What difference does it make?"

"I don't know. Maybe none."

Ezra pondered. He really hadn't worried about Calvin's line of work until he discovered no one seemed to know exactly what it was. Now he was determined to find out. By asking Calvin? He shook his head. If Calvin didn't give anyone a straight answer, he wouldn't give Ezra one either.

By heading up to Santa Fe and asking? Would anyone tell him? He was a deputy marshal now, so they might. And on the way he could stop at Sumner and see Violet. No word had come from Manuela about her since Billy had got out of jail. Had Violet gone to Mexico with Billy?

Billy hadn't told Ezra where he was heading, but Mexico was the only safe place to go and Billy was no fool. But would he take Violet?

It probably was a waste of time checking on Rutledge, but Ezra knew he wouldn't be satisfied until he did. Besides, he might get to see Violet . . .

"Mark, I've been thinking I'd like to travel to Santa

Fe,'' Ezra said. ''Got some business there. Could you spare me for a week?''

Mark eyed him for a few moments, then nodded. ''Reckon so.''

It wasn't until Ezra was riding alone on the ninety-mile stretch to Sumner that he began to think about Jules. He'd tried to keep from remembering, but with nothing to distract him, it was impossible.

Tessa blamed Billy. Ezra blamed himself. He should have taken Chavez's silver-handled pistol and thrown it into the river. He was older, wiser; he should never have gotten caught up in Jules' enthusiasm for helping, should never have let Jules be a part of Billy's escape.

It was his fault that his brother was dead.

How could he blame Billy? He hadn't even seen Jules when he fired the shot from that damn pistol. It might not even have been his shot that killed Jules, who could tell?

Jules had been more talented than either he or Tessa. And he'd been everyone's friend. Tears came to Ezra's eyes. He hadn't been able to stay with Billy after he'd heard, even though he didn't blame him.

Jules' death called everything he'd ever done, or believed, into question. It was no longer enough just to suit himself. There was more to being a man than that.

When the fight begins within himself

A man's worth something . . .

That was Browning, too. He thought he understood what the poet meant and for the first time understood why his father had so loved poetry. Those men with their fancy words weren't fools. They wrote of a man's life, of joys and sorrows. And of the struggle to find what was right. To try to do it.

He'd never betray Billy. Would he ever help him again? He wasn't quite sure.

Ezra rode into Sumner, his heart hammering at the thought of seeing Violet. He hoped she'd be there to welcome him.

"She's gone," Manuela said.

"I'm not asking where they went; I don't want to know," he said. "She did go with Billy, didn't she?"

Manuela shook her head.

Ezra stared at her. "Violet's not with him?"

"He come to Sumner, you know, after he escape the *calabozo*. He don't come here; he don't come to see Violet. No, Billy go to Maxwell's."

"I don't understand."

"He likes Paulita Maxwell, wants her to ride with him when he goes away. Paulita, she's too smart; she won't go."

"And he didn't even stop by here? Didn't see Violet at all?"

Manuela shook her head. "Violet, she find out. Everybody knows Billy wants Paulita instead of her. Paulita or Celsa Guiterrez." Manuela shrugged. "Men like girls better when they're not big, like this." She curved her hand out in front of her belly. "They like pretty little girls who will dance with them and tease them. It is their way. I tell Violet this, but she don't listen. The next day she is gone."

"But where? Where did she go?"

"Who can tell? I ask, but no one knows. She is not in Sumner or I would find out."

"You're certain she didn't go with Billy?".

"He rode off two, three days before Violet. Maybe she try to ride after him, I don't know."

"When is she—I mean, when is the baby coming?"

"Maybe this month, maybe next. I cannot be certain."

Ezra clenched his fists.

"I, too, worry," Manuela said. "Violet, she don't know how to take care of herself."

"I have to travel to Santa Fe," Ezra said. "I'll be stopping here on my way home. If you find out where she is, try to get her to come back here."

"If I can."

When Ezra arrived in Santa Fe, he'd lost his interest in Calvin Rutledge. All he could think of was Violet and what might be happening to her in God-knows-where.

He rode through narrow streets flanked by verandaed adobes into the plaza where the Palace of Governors fronted on a tree-shaded park with a bandstand in the center. The square towers of St. Francis Cathedral thrust up to the east.

Ezra crossed to the Exchange Hotel, more expensive than some in the city, but he meant to sleep clean and safe tonight. After he had a room, he made the rounds of the banks, asking about Rutledge.

Rutledge didn't work for any of them.

He talked to the sheriff who claimed he'd never heard of Rutledge. Finally, discouraged, but with a growing suspicion that Rutledge was at the very least a liar, Ezra returned to the Exchange. He wasn't much of a drinker, but he pushed through the batwing doors of the saloon, not wanting to be alone in his room. Anyway, the whiskey might help him to get to sleep.

He stood at the bar, his shot half-finished. It used to embarrass him when the others in the gang laughed at him because he couldn't down a whole shot at once. To tell the truth, he didn't like the taste of whiskey and that much at one time gagged him so badly he was afraid he'd vomit. Now he didn't care what anyone might think.

He finally downed the rest of his drink and left the bar, the whiskey warm and pleasant enough in his stomach. As he entered the corridor to his room, two men came toward him. A big redhead and a short, dark man. Strangers. He hadn't seen them come out of rooms.

He tensed, eyes flicking from one to the other. By the way Shorty held his right hand, he'd lay odds the man concealed a knife. And he'd seen Shorty someplace earlier today. Where?

Ezra reached for his Colt, jumped when he felt the sudden pressure of a muzzle thrust between his shoulders.

"I think we need to talk," a man's voice said from behind him.

Chapter 23

As Ezra took his hand from his Colt, he saw a door across from him start to open and caught a glimpse of an old man's startled face. The door began to close. At the same time, just as though Billy stood beside him, Ezra heard his voice in his mind.

"Coral snakes are deadlier than diamondbacks 'cause they don't hang around shaking their rattles."

Ezra whirled. His hand struck the Colt of the black-shirted man in back of him, knocking it to one side. He flung himself at the door he'd seen closing. Burst through it, knocking the room's occupant to the floor.

Ezra shot the bolt. Ducked aside and, stooping, yanked the white-haired old man with him, just as a bullet crashed through the wood of the door. He stood up. Grabbed a chair and flung it at the window. Glass shattered.

The man whose room he'd invaded huddled against the

bed, face as white as his hair. Ezra put his fingers to his lips, listening.

". . . outside, both of you!" he heard the man in the corridor order. Ezra nodded.

He reached the white-haired man in two strides, spoke into his ear. "What's your name?"

"Will Martin," the old man quavered.

"I'm a deputy marshal," Ezra said. "You won't get hurt if you do as I say. Start hollering when I tell you. Yell, 'Help a man's jumped through my window.' Understand?"

Will Martin swallowed. "Yes."

"Okay. We'll go to the door. Begin yelling as you start to unbolt it. Keep hollering as you open the door. Got it?"

Will nodded.

Ezra hurried him over to the door.

"Help!" Will cried weakly, hand on the bolt.

"Louder!" Ezra hissed. "Get the damn door open."

"A man's jumped through my window!" Will exclaimed, his voice stronger but quivering with fear. He slid the bolt back.

Ezra stood to one side of the door.

The door slammed open. Blackshirt pushed past Will as he ran toward the window. Ezra struck at Blackshirt's head with the butt of his Colt. Blackshirt fell heavily to the floor.

Ezra whirled quickly to face the open door, Colt ready, but the other two were nowhere in sight. He holstered the pistol and stuck his head into the hall where doors were cracked open.

"It's all over, folks," he called. "I'm a deputy marshal and I've collared the man responsible for the shooting."

He closed and bolted the door again, then knelt beside

Blackshirt and took his Colt, a derringer in an inside pocket and a boot knife.

"Why don't you sit in that chair over there?" he said to Will. "I won't be much longer."

Ezra threw back the coverlet on the bed, grinned when he saw sheets. Good thing he'd picked a nice place to stay. He ripped long strips from a sheet and tied Blackshirt's wrists and ankles behind him so the man lay curled in a backward arc.

Ezra crossed to the pitcher on the washstand, looked in. Smiled. Good service. He carried the pitcher to where Blackshirt lay on the floor, emptied the water over his head and waited for him to come around.

The man groaned and opened his eyes. Tried to move. Saw Ezra leaning against the wall watching him. "Son-of-a-bitch," Blackshirt muttered.

"You know who sent me?" Ezra asked.

Blackshirt said nothing

Ezra picked up the boot knife and tested the edge with his finger. "Seems like I asked you a question," he said.

"You're a marshal," the man said hoarsely.

"That's what I let out. The fact is, I ride with Billy the Kid."

Blackshirt's eyes widened. A spasm of fear flicked across his face. Ezra heard Will gasp and glanced at him. Still in the chair.

"Billy sent me to find out about Rutledge." Ezra began cleaning his fingernails with the knife. "You want to tell me now?" He pointed the knife at Blackshirt and did his best to grin like Billy. "Or later?"

"Railroads," Blackshirt muttered. "He buys land."

"You'll have to explain that."

"Buys land cheap. He knows where the railroad is

going, knows how it's been laid out ahead of time. Sells the land dear. Lots of money.''

Ezra frowned. "Why try to kill me over that?"

"They're all in on it. The politicians at the state house. The Santa Fe Ring. Rutledge is their front. They don't want questions asked. You came asking."

Ezra nodded. Made sense.

"Much obliged for your trouble," Ezra told Will Martin. He eased to the door, unbolted it quietly.

Colt in hand, he stepped aside as he threw the door open. There was no one in the corridor. He looked back at Blackshirt. The man's eyes were fastened on Ezra's Colt. Blackshirt thought he meant to shoot him. No point to that.

Ezra walked quickly down the corridor. Stopped where it turned into the lobby. Peered around the corner. Spotted Shorty near the door to the street. He remembered where he'd seen the man before.

At the sheriff's office.

Ezra swore under his breath. If the sheriff had sent these three after him, he was sure as hell on his own.

He'd seen a porch on the other side of the hotel when he left his horse in the corral. Ezra ran down the corridor of the opposite wing. Came to an open door leading onto the porch. Looked out. A couple of men lounged in chairs smoking. They glanced at him casually. Didn't seem to be after him.

He'd have to take a chance. He stepped out, jumped over the rail to the ground. Raced toward the corral.

Ezra stopped abruptly when he saw a hulking figure outside the tackroom where his gear was stored. Redhair.

He sure as hell didn't plan to ride home bareback, Ezra told himself. On the other hand, he didn't want to throw down on a deputy, easy though it would be.

Ezra bypassed the shed and climbed the corral fence. Located his pinto. Could he still ride Indian-style like he and Billy used to do for fun?

He yanked at the split logs on the corral fence, found a loose one, pulled at it until it came free, swished it through the air. Have to do.

Ezra opened the gate. Swung onto the pinto's bare back. Kneed him into a trot. Hung himself over the side of the horse away from the shed, leaving one foot hooked over the horse's back. He grasped the mane tightly with his left hand, holding the cudgel in his right.

When he could see Redhair's bulk under the neck of the horse, he slid up onto the pinto's back and, in the same motion, swiped at Redhair's head with the chunk of wood.

Ezra heard the thunk, saw Redhair stumble to his knees. He halted the pinto, leaped off and smashed the log over the man's head again. Redhair sprawled flat.

Ezra dashed into the tackroom and retrieved his gear from the startled hostler. When he saw Redhair trying to get up, he vaulted onto the pinto and pounded off, saddle in front of him. He didn't stop to saddle up until he was out of town.

Like the old days with Billy, he thought.

In Sumner he found that Manuela had heard no more of Violet. Ezra hadn't time to begin a search for her. Anyway, where would he start looking?

He arrived in Lincoln late in the evening, four days before the wedding. Guitars thrummed as he passed a cantina and he heard laughter from the open doors. It reminded him of dancing with Violet the night he'd first met her. She'd been so lovely, as delicate and sweet as a flower.

"Keep her safe," he whispered, not knowing if he meant to pray to a God he wasn't sure of.

Ezra stopped by Mark's room, found him sitting on the back stairs smoking.

"I want you to come by Maria's in about fifteen minutes," Ezra told him.

"Hell, it's almost midnight," Mark protested.

"It's for Tess's sake," Ezra said.

"All right. I'll be there. But don't blame me if she hollers at both of us."

Ezra rode on to Maria's. Tessa was in bed but not asleep. She put on her robe at Ezra's urging and came into the main room of the house. While he waited for Mark, he told his sister about Violet's disappearance.

"She's with Billy somewhere," Tessa said positively.

"He didn't want to take her."

"That wouldn't stop Violet."

"I don't know," Ezra said, hearing the click of Mark's boots on the steps.

Tessa turned her head. "Who's that at this hour?"

"Mark. I invited him."

She started to get up.

"You stay right here, Tess. I have something I want both of you to hear."

"But I'm not dressed."

"It doesn't matter. Stay here!"

She raised her eyebrows at his vehemence, but sat down as he went to the door to let Mark in.

After Mark was seated, Ezra, standing by the cold fireplace, looked from one to the other.

"Neither of you is happy," he said. "I'm going to tell you why and I don't want to be stopped. It's my business because Tess is my sister and Mark's my friend. So don't interrupt."

He took a deep breath. "I think Tess really wants to

marry you, Mark, not Calvin. And I know you want her. Why are you two so goddamn stubborn?''

As they both began to protest, he yelled, "Shut up!"

"I rode to Santa Fe and almost didn't come back on account of you being so foolish about this. I poked into things people didn't want me to know and damn near got shot for my pains.''

"Ezra!" Tessa exclaimed.

"I'm not through. Tess, you ain't going to marry Rutledge. You don't want to anyway, so it won't make you feel bad. Mark, now's the time to ask her." Ezra stared belligerently at Mark.

Mark looked at Tessa. "He's right, you know. I've wanted you ever since I came on you in the wagon shooting at Apaches with that Colt as big as you were."

"Then why didn't you ask me?" she demanded.

"I was going to, but it was always the wrong time."

"This is the last chance," Ezra put in.

Mark got up, pulled Tessa to her feet. "I'm asking you now. Marry me."

She stared at him. "But Calvin . . ."

"The hell with him. Will you or won't you?"

Her lips parted. "I—I—oh, yes, Mark, yes, yes!" She flung her arms around him.

Ezra cleared his throat. "Now that it's settled, I'll tell you what I found out about Rutledge in Santa Fe. Mark always thought he was a phony and he was right. Maybe Rutledge ain't a thief, but he ain't what he pretends to be either."

Sitting close together, Mark and Tessa listened to Ezra's account.

"Nothing you can send a man to jail for," Ezra finished, "but he must be ashamed of what he does not to tell even Tess."

"Why, I wouldn't have stood still for any such she-nanigans," she said tartly. She nestled closer to Mark, who stroked her hair.

"We'll be married as soon as my father can get here from St. Louis," Mark said to her. "You'll like the Judge."

"Of course I will," she murmured, gazing up at him.

"I got to see to my horse," Ezra said. He left them in the main room and walked through the kitchen to the back door, knowing they wanted to be alone together and that he was in the way.

He stayed with the pinto, rubbing him down, for a long time, tired, yet knowing he wouldn't sleep.

In a way, he was to blame for Violet getting mixed up with Billy just like he was to blame for Jules. There wasn't any way to bring Jules back to life. Maybe he couldn't do anything about Violet either.

But he sure as hell had to try.

"I hear you've sent your so-called assistant off again," Pat Garrett said to Mark around noon the next day.

"Ezra? No, he's back from Santa Fe."

"Ain't what I heard. Fellow dropped in from Sumner about an hour ago, said he passed Nesbitt at dawn, heading north. Got anything to tell me about that? You wouldn't be hankering to get your hands on Governor Wallace's five-hundred-dollar reward, would you?"

"I'm not hunting Billy. Neither is Ezra if he's headed north. Billy's in Mexico."

Garrett shook his head. "I got a message from a friend that says he ain't. Didn't know what to make of it, then figured you'd heard the same, seeing as how Nesbitt lit out for Sumner right after coming home from there."

"I haven't heard a word about Billy."

"Reckon you just lost yourself one assistant then. My guess is, Billy got a message to Nesbitt and he's off to join the Kid, just like the old days. Once they turn bad, you can't trust 'em.''

"Ezra wouldn't do that.''

Garrett smiled. "You willing to bet on it?''

Chapter 24

The July sun was still hot, though only a quarter of its red disk still showed above the western hills. The brown water of the Pecos was running low; there'd been no rain for a month. Tomorrow would be another sizzler. Cooler to travel at night. Pat Garrett tightened a strap on his saddle-bag and turned to Mark.

"I got to admit I'm glad you ain't coming with us any farther," he said.

"I didn't plan to go past Roswell," Mark said. "I told you that when we left Lincoln. I got business here, not in Sumner."

"I wasn't sure you wouldn't find more pressing business in Sumner."

Mark shook his head. "This is my last run as a deputy marshal. Once I'm finished here, that's it. Tessa and I are getting married next month; I'm opening a law office in Lincoln and settling down."

"Congratulations. We've had our differences, but I don't carry a grudge." Garrett thrust out a hand.

Mark shook it. "I wish you luck, Pat."

Garrett patted the wooden butt of the pistol in his holster. "I got a feeling this is my lucky gun." He slid the .44-40 Frontier Colt out and turned it over in his hands. "Got it off Billie Wilson at Stinking Springs, if you recall."

Mark nodded. "Only trouble is, the cartridge sometimes jams in the barrel in those."

"Haven't had that trouble." Garrett slid the Colt back into the holster and looked over to where his two deputies were mounting up.

"Looks like Poe and McKinney are about ready to hit the trail," he said. "I don't make any promises, but I ain't planning to cut down on young Nesbitt unless I have to. Course, I didn't plan to shoot Charlie Bowdre either. Ezra'll have to take his chances if I find him with Billy."

As Garrett and his two deputies rode north up the Pecos, he turned to wave to Mark, still standing by his black. "*Adios,*" he called.

By the thirteenth, when long evening shadows promised a night's relief from the July heat, the three men made camp in the sand hills five miles south of Sumner.

"You know," Garrett said as they laid down their bedrolls, "the Kid's a damn fool if he's really hanging around here. Hell, he speaks Spanish as good as any Mexican; he'd do fine in old Mexico."

"Pat, you know Pete Maxwell as well as I do," John Poe said. "What'd he be sending me word about Billy being in Sumner less'n it was true? From what I hear, he don't want Billy making up to his sister Paulita."

"Last I heard, Billy was sweet on somebody's wife up this way, only nobody'd tell me whose." Pat shook his head. "He has a way with the ladies, all right."

Poe nudged McKinney. "He ain't the only one, ain't that so, Tip? Some say the Lincoln County sheriff's doing all right with the fillies."

"Hell, you know I'm an old married man," Garrett protested.

Poe and McKinney both grinned.

"How about if you go into town in the morning," Garrett said to Poe. "Sort of mosey around, ask a few questions. They won't recognize you as quick as they will me or Tip."

Poe came back in the late afternoon.

"I think the Kid's somewhere around," he said. "No one'd tell me a damn thing, but they acted like they've got a reason not to."

"You didn't get a single lead?" Garrett asked.

"They're hiding something," Poe insisted. "It's more than them being Mexican and me not. Hell, they questioned me as much as I did them."

"We'll slip into town tonight without letting anyone see us," Garrett said. "Take a look at what's going on. I got doubts it'll do much good, but we're here and we'll check it out."

Ezra crouched in the dimness of the sheepherder's tiny adobe hut. Sweat beaded his face, sweat from the heat as well as from fear. On a blanket spread on the ground beside him, Violet moaned, her eyes closed.

She lay on her back, knees drawn up, her belly grotesquely huge. She looked exhausted.

Her eyes flew open and she reached for his hand, clutching at it and screaming as another spasm of pain began. She'd been having these pains since before noon and now it was evening, but still the baby hadn't come.

He knew she was in labor. He'd seen cows and horses give birth. They usually had an easy time, but every so often something went wrong. He didn't know much about human birthing, but his mother had died having Jules and so it was plain it could be a dangerous business for women.

He'd discovered Violet here this morning, after an old herder, who knew he was Billy's friend, stopped him as he rode near Sumner.

"The *señorita* is alone," the white-haired man had said, shaking his head. "No good to be alone with her time coming close."

Ezra had found Violet in this rude hut, lying curled on a filthy blanket. She sat up when she saw him.

"Where's Billy?" he asked.

She shook her head. "He didn't want me with him."

"He's right. It could be dangerous if Garrett comes hunting him. How could you get away?"

She shook her head again. "Billy doesn't want *me*. He's in town with Celsa Gutierrez. Or Paulita Maxwell."

Ezra looked at her, not knowing what to say. It was probably true.

"I thought he needed me," she said. "I was wrong."

"You can't stay here, Violet. I'll find a wagon and get you into town."

She grabbed his hand. "No! Don't leave me alone. It's too late for a wagon. Promise me you won't leave me, Ezra. You're the only one I can count on."

Then she'd grimaced with pain and he'd understood she was already beginning to deliver the baby.

If only Tessa were here. Or Manuela. Women knew about these things.

"Help me, Ezra," Violet cried, writhing on the blanket. Her hair was in tangles, her brown eyes sunken and pain-filled. There was no trace of the piquant beauty that had drawn him to her so long ago.

He had no idea what to do.

"Help me," she begged.

Blood stained her dress, rucked up above her knees by her twistings. He swallowed, trying to think.

Once he'd helped Papa when a mare couldn't birth her foal. Would such knowledge be of any use? He had to do something.

Ezra took a deep breath. "Violet, I'm going to take off your dress. I need to see what's going on."

"I don't care," she moaned. "Anything."

He left her clothed in a loose camisole top. Steeling himself, he knelt, pushed her legs apart, and looked at the birth opening. He saw a tiny hand thrusting from it.

Could that be right?"

Horses had foals hindquarters first. He'd heard babies came head first. When he thought about it, he didn't see how a baby could pass through the birth channel arm first.

Ezra chewed on his lip, remembering what Papa had to do with the mare. He couldn't do that to Violet.

She screamed as another pain wracked her.

Ezra took off his shirt. He looked at his hands, then at Violet. He didn't have a choice.

"Violet," he said, "try to trust me. I'm going to help you, going to do all I can for you. Take it easy; don't be frightened."

He kept talking in a soothing monotone, not really knowing what he said as he reached out and touched the tiny hand of the baby.

No good to pull, he could tell that. He'd have to push the hand back inside and somehow try to right the baby so it could come down properly. If he couldn't do it, then Violet might die.

The baby's hand and arm slid up inside Violet's body with surprising ease. She moaned as he tried to feel for the head. She was having another spasm of pain. The hand began to slide out again, but he held it back. When Violet's pain subsided, he groped again and this time he caught hold of what felt like the baby's feet.

In desperation, he pulled gently. As the feet slipped into the birth channel, Violet screamed and suddenly the baby was pushing against his hand, pushing down. He let go. Withdrew his hand.

The baby's feet appeared in the opening. The legs. Violet grunted with effort. So suddenly that he wasn't prepared, the entire baby slid through the opening, followed by a gush of blood.

Ezra grabbed the baby to get it away from the blood, being careful of the cord that was still attached inside. The baby was blue and looked to be dead. He used his shirt to clean the tiny face, felt the body shudder under his hands. Fluid oozed from its mouth.

Ezra, his hands sliding on the slippery baby, upended it so that the fluid could drain out. He realized for the first time that it was a boy. The baby choked and sneezed. Gave a gasping cry.

Violet tried to sit up. "My baby?" she whispered.

"He's okay. Lie still; you're not done yet."

Ezra wrapped the baby in his shirt and laid it atop Violet's belly. The baby wailed weakly. Ezra gazed with alarm at the clots of blood flowing from Violet. There was an afterbirth with horses and, he guessed, with women, too.

Would she keep bleeding until it came out? And what if it didn't?

*   *   *

The peaches were not quite ripe, but Pat Garrett could smell them as he and his deputies eased into the cover of the orchard behind the Garcia house where a *baile* was going on. If they were seen at all, it would be as shadows in the gathering darkness.

A fiddler played. Men swung their partners in a lively *cuadrilla*. The noise almost masked a murmuring ahead of Garrett. He stopped and held up his hand to warn the other two.

"*Querida*," a man said softly. A woman whispered something in reply.

Garrett groaned under his breath. He'd counted on the *baile* raising enough racket to cover any noise he and the deputies might make as they crept closer to see if the dance had attracted Billy. Garrett well remembered how Billy always enjoyed a *baile*.

Now they'd almost stepped on this courting couple. The sounds of lovemaking began and Garrett decided to wait, hoping the two would leave once they were satisfied.

After long minutes a man rose from the ground, clapped a sombrero on his head, sauntered toward a fence, vaulted over and disappeared. The girl walked slowly toward the dancers.

"The Kid?" Poe asked in Garrett's ear.

"Don't think so. Some *caballero*, more than likely."

"Well, you're gonna have to spot him—neither Tip or me know him from a red cow in a trail herd."

Could it have been Billy? Garrett wondered. He shrugged. Too late to do anything about it now.

Nothing Ezra tried slowed down the bleeding. He was afraid to pull any harder on the cord in case it broke off and left the afterbirth still attached inside. He asked Violet to try to push as she had when the baby came out, but she was too weak.

Suddenly something came into his mind. A conversation he'd overheard between Susie McSween and her sister when he'd lived at the McSween house. He'd come into the room without them seeing him.

"I've heard the Apache squaws stand up to have their babies," Susie was saying. "Some old wise woman uses an eagle feather to tickle their throats to make them gag. It's said to speed up the process."

"Heavens! I'm glad I'm not a . . ," Elizabeth Shield had begun, then caught sight of Ezra. Both women had reddened and quickly changed the subject.

He didn't have an eagle feather, but he had straw sticking out of the hut's adobe bricks. Ezra broke off a straw.

"Open your mouth," he told Violet.

It took three attempts to make her gag. He tried it again and again until she retched dryly.

Moments later a mass of purplish-blue slid from the birth opening. The afterbirth. A great gush of blood came with it, but then the bleeding lessened.

Ezra removed a lace from the bodice of Violet's dress and tied it tightly around the cord connecting the baby to the afterbirth. Taking his knife, he sliced through the cord. He picked up the baby and tried to lay him in Violet's arms, but she was too weak to hold him.

She lay still, eyes closed. A pulse fluttered thinly under his fingers when he felt her throat.

"Violet," he said. "Violet?"

"Ezra," she whispered. "I knew you'd come to me."

The baby whimpered and she sighed. "Vincente," she murmured. "Name him Vincente after my father."

Ezra crouched beside her with the baby, wrapped in his

shirt, held awkwardly in one arm. He grasped her hand with the other. Despite the July heat, her hand was cold. Outside, evening shadows deepened into night.

"I'm going over to talk to Pete Maxwell," Garrett said to his deputies. "He got us here to begin with, so maybe he'll give us some idea where to look next, because Billy sure as shooting wasn't at the *baile*. I got my mind made up, come hell or high water, I'm going to get the Kid if he's in Sumner."

"I promised Pete I wouldn't let anyone know he told me Billy was in Sumner," Poe said.

"We'll just slip over to his place easy-like and no one'll notice," Garrett said. "It's close to midnight."

They circled toward the Maxwell house from the peach orchard. Garrett spotted the room where Pete slept, off the south porch of the house. His door was open to let in the cool night air.

"No lights," Poe whispered. "Reckon he's asleep."

"I'll go in and wake him up," Garrett said. "You two wait out here."

Tip leaned against the picket fence and Poe followed Garrett onto the porch and sat beside a post. Garrett tiptoed across the splintered planks of the porch and eased inside the open door.

After a moment he saw the bed was to his right, against the wall. Someone was asleep on it. Garrett edged closer, finally sat on the edge. He made out Maxwell's round figure under the cover, leaned over and touched the sleeping man's shoulder.

"Pete," he whispered.

*   *   *

Billy headed his bay toward the sheepherder's hut where he'd been hiding off and on since he broke jail, but just past the outskirts of town he reined up. Violet would be there waiting.

He didn't want to go back to her. All his other girls had understood there was a time for fun and for loving and a time when it was all over. Violet couldn't seem to learn this.

Having her in that miserable hut with her swollen belly and accusing eyes wasn't something a man could take for long. She had a place to stay, a nice, comfortable room with Manuela. Why did she insist on being with him?

He'd thought of lighting out for Mexico, but all his friends, male and female, were at Sumner and he hated to leave them. Maybe he'd have to go anyway, if he couldn't get Violet to listen to reason. He sure as hell didn't plan to take her with him.

Trouble was, she made him feel guilty. Like he ought to be doing something for her when he didn't want to. He looked back toward town. Garcia's *baile* had broken up; the fiddler was gone and the men were climbing into bed with their wives or sweethearts.

What he had to look forward to was a girl too far gone with child to touch, one he didn't want to touch in any case. He recalled Celsa's slim waist and warm lips and the way she'd arched to him in the peach orchard earlier. If Celsa wasn't available, there'd be one of the girls from the cantina.

Billy wheeled his horse and headed back into town. He went directly to the long adobe where Celsa lived, but her husband Zaval had come home and so he bid her a quick *buenas noches*. On the way back to his horse, he saw a lamp burning in a friend's room and poked his head in through the open door.

"Up late, Bob," he said.

"*Hola*. Come in and set," Bob Campbell said.

Billy went in, took off his vest and boots and relaxed in a chair. "Got anything to eat?" he asked

Bob shook his head. "Pete's got a quarter of beef on his north porch. You could go get a slice or two of that. Here." He tossed Billy a knife.

Without bothering with his boots, Billy ambled out the door and across the yard toward Maxwell's.

He put one foot on the steps and froze. A man lounged against the post on the porch. He saw another by the fence. Billy jerked out his Colt.

"*Quien es?*" he demanded.

The man by the fence started to straighten, stumbled and nearly fell.

Billy relaxed slightly. Somebody from the *baile*, a little *borracho*, drunk. He tensed again when he saw the man had a Colt slung on his hip.

"*Quien es?*" he repeated.

Neither man answered but they made no attempt to draw. Who the hell were they? He'd never seen them before. Pete's friends?

Billy leaped up the steps and ducked inside Pete's bedroom. "Wake up, Pete," he said. "Who're those fellows outside?"

Someone on the bed moved and Billy saw a man sitting there. He made out Pete lying in the bed. Billy reached to touch the covers at the foot.

"Pete!" he said urgently. "*Quien es?*"

Pete stirred. Muttered something Billy couldn't hear. The man sitting on the bed shifted. Billy aimed his fully

cocked pistol at him. Hesitated. Wouldn't do to throw
down on a friend of Pete's.

"*Quien es?*" he asked, finger on the trigger.

A roar. A blow on his chest.

Billy tried to pull the trigger, but he was falling, falling . . .

Garrett fired a second time as the man fell to the floor.
He lay unmoving. Garrett jumped off the bed and raced for
the porch, bumping into Poe who stood with his Colt
drawn.

"That was the Kid in there!" Garrett shouted. "I think I
got him."

"Why would he come here?" Poe asked. "Pat, you
must have shot the wrong man."

Garrett stared back toward the room. Could he have
been mistaken? Maxwell had whispered to him it was
Billy. The voice had certainly sounded like Billy's.

Pete plunged from the room, dragging a blanket with
him. Garrett saw Poe aim and yelled, "No! Don't shoot
Maxwell."

Poe holstered his Colt. McKinney joined the three men,
all of them watching the open doorway to the bedroom but
standing well to the side of it.

"I think he was dead," Maxwell whispered. "Dying,
anyway," he amended.

Was Billy dead? Garrett wondered. It would be like the
Kid, even badly wounded, to be waiting until someone
stepped into the room to let fly.

He was damned if he was going in there.

Finally Maxwell got a candle from another room, lit it
and held it up to the open window farther along the porch.
Garrett, trying to stay back and look at the same time,
caught a glimpse of a man inside, lying face up on the
floor.

"It's him," Pete said.

Garrett took the candle from Maxwell and strode into the room.

Billy lay on his back, eyes open but unseeing. Blood trickled from a hole over his heart. A knife lay on the floor beside him. He still had a pistol gripped in one lifeless hand.

Billy the Kid was dead.

Chapter 25

After a half-dozen fumbling attempts to fold his bedroll blanket into a baby carrier that he could sling over his back as he'd seen Apache women do, Ezra managed to arrange the folds so that the baby was supported and yet not suffocated.

Walking gingerly, with the blanket in place over his shoulders, he lifted Violet's limp body and carried her to his horse. She roused as he started to lay her across the animal's back.

"It's all right," Ezra told her. "I'm taking you and the baby into Sumner."

He was certain she'd die if he didn't get her out of here before the sun rose to scorch the land, while at the same time he feared that moving her might make her worse.

He swung into the saddle and shifted Violet, lifting her so she sat across his lap with his arm supporting her.

"Can you hold on to me?" he asked.

"My baby?" she asked weakly.

"Little Vince is fine."

As if in response, the baby began to cry, the sound partly muffled by the blanket. Violet tried to reach for him, but Ezra stopped her.

"He'll have to wait until we get to Sumner."

He kneed the pinto into a smooth trot and soon the baby's wails subsided. Despite his worry over Violet and the awkward weight of the blanket, Ezra felt almost peaceful as they rode in the coolness of the night under the stars.

Just before dawn they approached the outskirts of town. Somewhere a dog barked. Lights showed in almost all the buildings. Ezra heard a faint sound of hammering. Sumner seemed unusually active for the early hour.

Violet stirred in his arms. She raised her head to look around. "What is happening?" she asked. Her voice sounded stronger, more alert.

"*Quien sabe?*" he said. "Who knows?"

He swung the pinto toward Manuela's.

"No!" Violet eased herself higher. "Something is wrong. Ezra, we must find out."

"First I'll take you to . . ."

"Please!" Her fingers tightened on his arm. "Take me with you; I have to know."

"You ought to rest," he said, a terrible suspicion of what might have happened tensing him.

"I couldn't rest. Not until I know."

Ezra realized she had the same fear and so he nodded. She had the right to come with him.

As they rode into the plaza, the sky was pink with dawn. Men stood in small groups in the street, eyeing them as they passed. No one called a greeting, but he saw them whisper to one another. The sound of hammering grew louder.

What made a man get up before dawn to use a hammer and nails? Ezra swallowed and headed for the sound.

He reined in the pinto when he caught sight of men fitting planks together beside what he knew was a carpenter's shop.

A coffin.

He looked at Violet. "Let me take you to Manuela's," he said.

She shook her head. "Find out," she whispered.

"Who's it for?" Ezra asked the men.

"The sheriff shot Billy," one of them said.

"Don't be so blunt," another man warned him in Spanish. "See who it is you speak to."

"Where is Billy?" Violet said. "I want to know."

The first man jerked his head toward the open door of the carpenter's shop.

"Take me there," Violet said to Ezra.

Reluctantly, he eased the horse toward the door. The dead man lay just inside, stretched out on a bench.

Billy wore a white shirt far too big for him. His face was unmarked and, eyes closed, he looked as young as Jules. Ezra's eyes stung.

"Yes, he is dead," Violet whispered. "I always knew it would happen." She turned her face into Ezra's chest and clung to him.

Ezra swung the pinto and rode away.

When Violet had been put to bed at Manuela's, the baby at her breast, Ezra headed back to the plaza.

Billy's body, in its rough coffin, had been hauled to the old military cemetery where, by the time Ezra arrived, a grave had been dug in the barren earth. He saw Billy would be laid to rest between Tom O'Folliard and Charlie Bowdre.

I could be lying six-feet-under right here myself, Ezra thought. It's only luck that kept me from it.

A man came up beside him. Pat Garrett.

"Word's around you helped deliver Billy's son," the sheriff said. "I suppose she named him after the Kid."

Ezra shook his head. He set his teeth and forced himself to answer. No good would come of making a ruckus at Billy's funeral.

"Vince is my son," he heard himself saying, the words coming out totally unplanned. "Violet and I will be married as soon as we can."

Garrett raised his eyebrows. "You could have fooled me."

"Things aren't always what they seem. I take care of my own."

Garrett eyed him a moment, clapped him on the shoulder, then walked away.

More and more of the townspeople, nearly all Mexicans, crowded around the grave as the coffin was lowered. They crossed themselves and bowed their heads in prayer.

Suddenly a woman burst through the mourners, her black hair wild, her cheeks wet with tears. She flung herself at Garrett.

"You son-of-a-bitch!" she screamed, clawing at his face.

Hands reached for her, dragged her away, still shrieking. Garrett hadn't moved or even changed expression.

Ezra knew her; she was Deluvina, a Navajo woman who worked for Pete Maxwell. She'd always had a soft spot for Billy.

Ezra stared at Garrett. No one stood between him and the sheriff. He could drop the hammer on him easy. Avenge Billy.

And be killed himself, shot on the spot. Or hanged later.

Then what would become of Violet and little Vince?

But that wasn't what stopped him when it came right down to it. He'd never liked Pat Garrett—he was a cold fish of a man—but Garrett had only been doing his job. What he was paid to do.

As the ugly caliche dirt thudded onto the lid of the coffin, Ezra raised his head so as not to see. Tears swimming in his eyes blurred the sun's morning light so it made a shimmering golden pathway across the far hills he and Billy had ridden over so many times.

A faint smile touched his lips as he remembered Browning's words:

And straight was a path of gold for him,
And the need of a world of men for me.

"*Adios, mi amigo,*" he murmured. "Good-bye, my friend, good-bye."